Library of the Soul

Library of the Soul

a Peter White mystery

SIMON BUCK

An Alnpete Book

Library of the Soul – A Peter White mystery
First published in Great Britain by Alnpete Press, 2006
An imprint of Alnpete Limited

The right of Simon Buck to be identified as the author of this work has been asserted in accordance with sections 77 and 78 of the Copyright, Designs and Patents Act 1988. Verse from the hymn *The God of liberation* by Patrick Lee and Stephen Dean, ©1993 Patrick Lee, reproduced with permission. No part of this publication may be reproduced, stored in a retrieval system or transmitted in any form, or by any means (electronic, mechanical, telepathic, or otherwise) without the prior written permission of the copyright owner. Apple, Macintosh, Mac, Xserve, iPod, iBook and PowerBook are trademarks of Apple Computer, Inc. Windows is a trademark of Microsoft Corporation. Use of trademarks has not been authorised, sponsored or otherwise approved by the trademark owners.

Alnpete Press, PO Box 757
Dartford, Kent
DA2 7TQ

www.alnpetepress.co.uk

A CIP catalogue record for this book
is available from the British Library

ISBN 0-9552206-0-2
EAN 978-0-9552206-0-9

This book is a work of fiction. All names, characters, places and events are either a product of the author's fertile imagination or are used fictitiously. Any resemblance to actual events, places, or people living, dead or undead, is purely coincidental.

Printed by Antony Rowe Ltd.

For Alison

Prologue

Think of a library. If you're from a small town you're probably thinking of a couple of rooms – one to read the newspapers and encyclopaedia and the other to look for the latest Catherine Cookson novel. If you're from a big city you're imagining something a bit grander – separate rooms for fiction, non-fiction and children's books. If you're a graduate you're probably remembering long days spent in your campus library trying to track down that obscure reference the professor included in your assignment. Bureaucrats will think of the British Library and Americans will think of the Library of Congress. Anyone under 18 is still struggling with that first sentence – "...isn't a library what they had in the old days before the Internet?" Classical scholars are dreamily imagining the Library of Alexandria, before the fire. Some of us are even lucky enough to be thinking of a particular room in our own house where we keep our favourite books. But all of these visions of libraries, past and present, real or imagined have one thing in common. They are limited in size and coverage, specialised (one way or another) and relatively recent collections (with the obvious exception of the defunct library of Alexandria!).

Imagine a library that doesn't have those limitations. That has been in place for some two thousand years and has vast resources behind it. A library that was started when many of our revered classical writers were contemporary upstarts. That began with papyri and scrolls and has lived through the introduction of new technologies many times over – vellum, paper, quill pens, hot lead, binding, impact printing, continuous feed, lasers, CD-Rom, memory sticks, PDF, eBooks. The medium changes; the language changes (once anything worth reading was written in Greek, then Latin, and now any and every language under the sun – natural or electronic); but the library remains intact. Now new technology is helping to keep the library safe – environmental control protects ancient parchments and fading inks, while digital imaging is preserving the contents in electronic form. Such a library, were it to exist, would need vast and secure storage space. The imaging technology would require sophisticated equipment, powerful processing and data storage and a reliable power supply and environment. Protecting such an invaluable collection would require an army. The dedication of the generations of staff needed to maintain such a library would require some higher motivation than money, politics or even academic pursuit.

Such a library does indeed exist. Although you're probably not imagining even one percent of the extent of it. It has a public face, which is itself huge and impressive. It even has publicly available 'secret archives' which attract researchers like bees to a flower. But what's really behind the façade is breathtaking in its breadth and depth. Everything ever published is contained here. Many items that were never 'published' are here also; original manuscripts, theses, treatises and revelations from the greatest philosophers and scientists throughout history – Pascal, Leonardo, Galileo, Augustine, Feynman, Einstein; public and private letters from writers and artists – Michelangelo, Raphael, Voltaire, Dante, Chaucer; documents written to or by the powerful men and women of the Western world – Constantine, Charlemagne, Napoleon, Catherine the Great. Many documents that have been lost to the rest of the world still reside quietly here, carefully protected and maintained, untouched by curious scholars, greedy dealers or unscrupulous collectors.

Along with this almost unimaginable history of

literature is an unrivalled installation of information technology that would leave most governments in awe. The use of this technology has enabled a step-change in the core activity of the staff at the heart of this library. While many governments have recently come to understand the need for cryptography to protect their secrets and crypto-analysis to steal other's secrets, here they have been employing the best cryptographers and steganographers for nearly two thousand years. Many of the 'traditional' cryptographic techniques used since Roman times have been developed here. The American National Security Agency claims to employ the best cryptographers in the world, but even they are unaware of the people or work that goes on in this library. The NSA, like other secret government agencies around the world, are only interested in the use of cryptography to further their masters' political and economic ends and employ those who are equally politically and financially motivated. This library has never been interested in such trivial concerns. It is interested in only one thing – the fight between good and evil. A staff motivated by the ultimate struggle with an infinite timeframe have a very different perspective on their life as well as their work.

However, sometimes the dirty world of politics and economics impinges and they use their resources for more prosaic purposes. On these occasions the cryptographic department becomes the single most effective (and oldest) secret service in the world.

On one such occasion I was drawn into their world...

SATURDAY

Rome

The phone beside the bed rang shrilly. I reached over and lifted it.

"Pronto."

"Signor."

"Si?"

"Your visitor. She 'as arrived and is on 'er way in the lift already."

"Grazie."

"She is not alone."

"Oh?"

"No. She 'as two Carabinieri with 'er."

"Okay. Grazie." I dropped the phone back down and sat up. Two Carabinieri. Why would she bring armed police with her? I thought we had parted company on good terms in Venice two years ago. Now I was a little confused. Costanza D'Andrea-Mancini was one of the smartest and funniest women I had ever met. She was also stunningly beautiful and seemed to enjoy my company. All in all she would have been the perfect choice for wife or partner; I had often considered it over the ten or so years we had known each other, since first working together in London. Two things stood in the way. The age difference of 12 years would have been embarrassing if not insurmountable – I had been taken for her father or uncle on occasion – but more of a barrier was Sandro, the love of her life and husband since her early twenties. When I had arranged this short trip to Rome I had emailed to let her know where I would be staying, hoping we might all get the chance to meet again. She had responded almost immediately to suggest we get together for a meal and a gossip. She hadn't mentioned police backup!

I combed my hair, put on my shoes and sat on the end of the bed waiting.

There was a gentle knock on the door. Barely loud enough to be heard when listening intently. She knew the receptionist would have phoned ahead. Which means she also knew I was expecting her companions. The gentleness of the knock was clearly meant to re-assure me.

I opened the door to see the familiar smiling angel. Her escort was nowhere to be seen. She saw my eyes flicking both ways along the corridor and said

"I left them by the lift. Hello Peter. Come stai?"

"I'm well thanks, and you're as radiant as ever. Are you coming in?"

"Briefly. There's something I must ask you and then I hope you'll come with us."

She entered the room as smoothly as a ghost. Wherever she went she seemed to glide rather than walk. Years ago I had concluded it was because no-one was ever watching her feet, they were always transfixed by that beautiful face. Yet she never played on her beauty – I'm not sure if she even realises how beautiful she is, she's always had that effect on people and so for her their reaction is normal. She would be the perfect interrogation tool for any secret organisation – five minutes with her and anyone (or at least most men and quite a few women) would willingly do anything, admit anything or agree to anything just to please her.

Before I knew it she was sitting in the suite's only armchair. She seemed to melt into the chair fluidly – the result of breeding, natural elegance and a year at a Swiss finishing school.

"Can I get you a drink? The mini-bar here is pretty well stocked. They even have your favourite Campari soda, although it's pre-mixed." My heart was beating faster than normal, not least because of the two machine guns waiting down the hall.

"Thank you, but not now. We'll have time later I

hope. Peter, sit down for a minute."

I sat back down on the bed and gazed at the vision in the armchair. Her hair, longer than I'd ever seen it, tumbled over her shoulders while at the same time still managing to look elegantly arranged.

"Are you alright? You look like you've seen a ghost" she said.

"I'm sorry, it's two years since I last saw you and, well, there's something about you. You're even more beautiful than ever. It's quite unsettling really."

"Oh," she half grinned and half frowned, "I've been called lots of things but never unsettling."

"Unsettling isn't really the right word. I don't think there is a right word. It's just that you redefine the concept of beauty every time I see you." I managed not to blush.

"Peter White. If I didn't know you better I'd think you were flirting with me. Or worse!"

"If I didn't know you better I might try. But, as you well know, I'm very bad at handling rejection. Besides I don't want to upset Sandro…" I grinned.

"Enough of this." She stood up again as smoothly as she had sat down. "Aren't you going to kiss me, or have you become an archetypal Englishman?"

I stood up and kissed her three times – left cheek, right cheek, left cheek. She took my hand.

"You do look well Peter. Although I'm sure you used to have more hair." Her eyes twinkled and a broad grin appeared on her face that was as infectious as any virus known to medical science.

"You, however, now seem to have more" I said.

She put her hand to her upper lip and sighed.

"Oh! Did I forget to shave again? I must have inherited my father's moustache."

We both laughed. She sank back into the chair and I

dropped onto the bed. The mandatory insults were out of the way, everything was normal (or at least as normal as it ever had been).

"So. Why the police escort?" I asked.

"If you agree to come and help me they'll get us through the traffic quicker."

"Help you? Do what? Now, I am intrigued."

"Good. I'm afraid I must talk shop for a bit."

"Okay." I sat up.

She looked me straight in the eyes and took a deep breath – this was the first time I'd ever seen any sign of nerves in this amazing woman.

"The people I work for have uncovered a … problem. I have been trying to solve it but I need some help. When you said you were coming to Rome I knew God had sent you to my aid. Peter, I'm a distressed damson and you're *damsel* my knight in shining armour." She smiled coyly.

"Flattery will get you everywhere! But what can you possibly need me for? I taught you everything I knew and then you went and got a doctorate on top."

"Now it's you who is the flatterer. Is that the right word in English? Yes?"

I nodded.

"Okay! I've been back in Rome so long my English is getting rusty." She took another deep breath, "Okay, it's a crypto problem of course. I haven't been able to solve it even with all the resources at my disposal. I need a fresh pair of eyes looking at the problem. But the right eyes."

"And you don't have anyone else working with you? Or for you?"

"Oh yes. But we don't want this problem too widely broadcast and I think you're the best chance I've got of solving it. But even talking to you required a lot of persuasion of my bosses."

"Who are your bosses anyway? You've never told me

15

where you work these day."

"I've told no-one. Well, one person. Sandro knows where I work, but none of my friends have a clue. It's part of the conditions of my job. Peter, I convinced them I trust you and so they could trust you. They want me to ask you a couple of questions first."

"Fire away. Although it's all a bit cloak and dagger."

"Oh no! It's much more sophisticated than that."

"No. It's an English expression. It means secretive like a spy."

"I know. It is."

I was a little taken aback. If Costanza was a spy, which seemed somewhat unlikely knowing her politics and strong stance on ethics and moral issues, her bosses would hardly involve a foreigner like me.

"Pardon?" I said.

"I'll come back to that. First the questions I must ask you. Are you still a practicing Catholic?"

"Yes." A slightly odd question, although less out of place in Rome than it would have been in London.

"Are you still vegetarian?"

"Yes, of course." Costanza isn't vegetarian so it couldn't be a pre-requisite for the job. Another odd question.

"Do you still refuse to work on military projects?"

"Absolutely!" Well, that would finish this conversation off.

"Good. I told them that was the case. Okay I'm allowed to involve you and get your help. But I can't explain what we have to do here. Walls have ears."

"What? But…" This was the strangest job interview I'd ever had.

"Please trust me, as I told them I trust you. Get some things – wallet, passport, those awful mints you always eat – and come with me. We can't talk in the car. Even the

Carabinieri aren't privy to this discussion."

"At least tell me where we're going." I said as I stood and scooped up my wallet and passport from the bedside table. I looked out the window, across the piazza and down the Spanish Steps which seemed to have more tourists and fewer flowers than I remembered.

"We're going to visit your patron saint" she smiled.

I gazed over the tops of the buildings in the city that lay spread out before me to the dome that dominated it all. We were going to St. Peter's?

Vatican City

I've always avoided driving in Rome. The traffic and individualistic way that Romans interpret road signs and signals would be bad for my blood pressure. However being in an Alfa driven by the Carabinieri seems to make traffic part before you like the Red Sea in front of Moses. The blue flashing light and irritating siren help too of course.

In no time at all we were crossing the Tiber and heading towards the Borgo, the apartment filled streets around the Vatican that had survived the Goths but were now being homogenised and defiled by marauding tourists. We drove around the outside wall of the Vatican City until we reached the south side of St Peter's. We came to a large gateway where we were saluted in by one of the Swiss Guard. They always make me smile. The only army in the world with a uniform designed by an artistic genius. Their Michelangelan multicoloured doublet and hose is perfectly finished off with a black hat, always set at a rakish angle. But don't let the medieval uniform fool you, the Swiss Guard are a force to be reckoned with and they have more up to date weapons than the ceremonial halberds that tourists see at the gates.

We drove through two or three small piazzas and courtyards, around the bulk of St Peter's, suddenly moving from the blinding heat into the shadow of the basilica. The lush green of the gardens and the cooling spray of the fountains was very enticing. But we drove on, past the Mint and finally through an archway in the palace into the Cortile del Belvedere. Costanza and I got out of the car, and no sooner had we shut the doors behind us than it immediately sped off out of the courtyard. I looked around me. I had glimpsed this courtyard before from inside the Vatican Museum. It seemed a shame that such a delightful old building should now be enclosing a car park!

Costanza lightly touched my shoulder to regain my attention and said "Over here" as she started to walk towards a nondescript door in the western wing.

"Isn't this where the Vatican Library is?"

"Only one or two public rooms. But most of it isn't here any more. You know the Cortile della Pigna?" she asked, pointing to her right.

"Of course." The Pine courtyard was the other main courtyard within the Museum complex and its perfectly clipped lawns were open to museum visitors. "I usually spend a while dozing on the steps outside the new wing for a break whenever I'm visiting the museum. Mind you I don't like that dirty great bronze sphere they've stuck in the middle now."

"You remember when that sphere appeared?"

"Fourteen or fifteen years ago?"

"That's right. That was when they finished moving the library. It's now under the Pine courtyard in an underground complex centred beneath that sphere."

"So the sphere is …?"

"There were jokes at the time, apparently, that it was to hide the vents from the environmental control system. Or a secret escape route in an emergency. Or even some defensive system designed to protect the Library. But the truth is that it's just a work of art."

"Not my idea of art though!" With all the beautiful sculptures in the Museum from classical times and the renaissance I could never understand why they had commissioned a new work for that courtyard.

We had reached a rather inconspicuous door. It was not locked and Costanza led us in and through a couple of corridors into a panelled room with a ceiling that had been the victim of a 17th century artist, with angels, putti, flowers, urns and all sorts of clutter. Murals along the walls showed various events in the history of the Church. The numbered panels were obviously cupboard doors. Desks and chairs were positioned at intervals, but they were all empty. Part of the way along one side was a gap where a desk appeared to have been forgotten. Costanza walked up to it and opened the panelled door in the wall. Instead of a cupboard there was a corridor. But this was obviously much more recently installed and had a plain white ceiling. We walked along this short passage until we came to an apparently blank wall with a translucent panel to one side. Costanza pressed her palm against it. A few seconds later it responded with a small green light.

A slight hiss startled me and I turned to see a glass panel sliding across the corridor, sealing it behind us. Then, ever so smoothly, the floor beneath us began to sink. The end of the corridor was a lift and we were slowly going down in it. Costanza saw the look of surprise on my face.

"I told you the Library is underground now. It's also a lot more secure than it's ever been. The whole area is enclosed in a huge Faraday cage so no-one can eavesdrop on us. Which also means your mobile phone won't work down here either."

"We're going to the Library?" I asked.

"My part of it. Yes."

"Your part of it? That's very possessive!" I grinned.

"You know what I mean. I just work in it. One bit of it. The most interesting bit, of course."

"You work for the Vatican then?"

"Yes."

"Back to the family business!" I grinned. Some years before, at the launch party for a particularly gruelling project, we all had a lot of wine to drink and Costanza had mentioned that in the past her mother's family had been one of the more powerful families of Rome with a number of Cardinals and at least one Pope in their number. We had laughingly suggested, as an insult, that it was the Borgia family; she had looked wistful and said that unfortunately her family had not been that rich or powerful, and anyway the Borgias were Spanish. I knew she still had an uncle who held a high position within the Jesuits.

"Are you working for your uncle?"

"No, no. He's a Jesuit."

"I thought all the science, technology and research in the Church was carried out by Jesuits."

"Almost all. But the early Church Fathers had realised, long before Ignatius set up the Jesuits, that cryptographers were rare and special. More to the point, ever since classical times some of the best cryptographers have been women. So the early Church set up a society, an order for lay people, specifically for what we now call cryptography, crypt-analysis and steganography. All this work is in the control of that society."

"I've never heard of such an order. What's it called?"

She smiled, "First rule of the society was to keep it's own existence hidden. In fact it was probably the first Christian secret society. It's called the Society of Thomas, named after our patron Saint Thomas the Twin, or Doubting Thomas, who wouldn't believe what was hidden until it was revealed to him – the name was probably the first official Christian joke too!"

"You said 'our patron'?"

"Yes. I am a Thomasine, Peter. As I said I need your help. I need you to become a Thomasine too."

"I'm not taking holy orders."

"Of course not. I told you it's a lay society. Sign an oath of truth and secrecy. That's all."

"Really?"

"It's no different from the NDAs that you sign every

day working for banks or other big companies. Except that breaches will be punished in the next life rather than this one." She grinned.

"No celibacy or abstinence clauses?"

"No" her eyes twinkled. "I'll let you into a personal secret to prove it. The reason you thought I looked different when we met earlier is probably because I'm pregnant. My mamma tells me I'm glowing – she guessed I was pregnant two weeks ago, I only found out for sure yesterday. No-one else knows. Apart from Sandro, of course."

"Congratulations." Costanza had always wanted to be a mother and I was sure she and Sandro would make great parents.

"Thank you. But back to business. So, will you sign up to help me?"

"I still don't know what you want me to do." I had almost forgotten we were moving, but just then the gentle downward movement of the floor abruptly stopped. The glass partition slid back with another hiss and a further corridor stretched away in front of us. This was much more utilitarian than those in the building above us. The ceiling was obviously formed from concrete blocks. Small lights were placed at intervals providing sufficient but low-level lighting. Polished stone floors were disfigured by coloured lines in plastic tape, obviously identifying specific routes or zones.

"We'll follow the yellow line for now. I'll explain what we have to do and then you can decide whether you'll stay. If you do I'll show you the other zones. For now, just be aware that the environment in this whole complex is carefully controlled. These lights give out no heat. The air is filtered and dehumidified and the temperature is closely monitored. In fact the only uncontrolled components of this environment are people. So don't wander out of the yellow zone." There was an air of warning and menace in her tone; but, as with everything else about this woman, even menace was soft, like an ice-pick cushioned within a crimson velvet glove.

She walked away down the corridor and it took me a few seconds to gather my wits and follow her. Most of my work was in England where security guards are not armed, private armies are illegal and the building itself enforces security. I had worked in some very strange buildings in my time: software development labs where entry was through an individual-sized airlock – too many take-away pizzas and the programming staff would have been unable to leave; data storage vaults in large nuclear bunkers in the middle of nowhere; computer rooms behind triple-glazed bomb-proof glass. But this underground complex already felt much better protected than any of the places I had ever worked. For a start it's buried beneath one of the world's holiest sites, providing both legal and, hopefully, divine protection; there is one of the most technologically advanced, if small, armies in the world providing physical protection; and, more to the point, virtually no-one knows it exists, let alone where it is.

I caught up with Costanza as she reached and rounded a corner. We had turned into a small atrium. Behind a desk sat a Swiss Guard. As we approached he looked up and smiled at Costanza.

"Signora" he said.

"Ciao Tomaso. Signor White is here at the request of Cardinal Bianchi and with his express permission. You should find all the necessary authorisations in your system."

In front of Tomaso a keyboard was set into the desk. It appeared to be touch sensitive and gently illuminated from within. A low wooden panel at the front of the desk separated him from us. As his fingers played across the keyboard he was staring intently at the flat screen that was evidently embedded in that panel.

After a few seconds his eyes flicked up to look at me and back down to his screen. Again, twice more. If they were using my passport photo to identify me then no wonder he was dubious. Taken almost ten years ago, it showed me with considerably more hair and no beard.

"I have known Signor White for many years," said Costanza, "I can verify that this is him".

"Si," said Tomaso, "I too believe it is Signor White." He looked at me. "But Signor, please to give me the number."

Costanza looked confused. "Number? What number? I wasn't told to give him any number."

"No Signora. Signor White already knows the number."

Costanza looked at me. "What is he talking about?"

"I'll explain in a minute." I smiled as I leant forward over the panel and spoke quietly to Tomaso.

As I stood upright again, Tomaso looked up and saluted me. He handed me a red badge, motioned us both towards the door beside his desk and quickly played his fingers again across his eerily silent keyboard.

Costanza was still looking confused when the door slid open.

"Why has he given you a red pass? He should have given you a yellow pass. Red passes are for the Swiss Guard and other security operatives within the Vatican's Vigilanza. I don't understand."

"Don't worry. Tomaso won't get into trouble, he hasn't given me the wrong pass." She turned to me as I spoke, raised one of her elegantly defined eyebrows and waited. "Some years ago I did some work for the Vatican. Advising them on security procedures, that sort of thing.

In the process I was given an honorary rank in the Swiss Guard, and as a result a Papal medal."

"So you already knew everything I just struggled to tell you?" she said, looking a little hurt.

"Actually, no! A lot has happened since then. I really didn't know that the Library had been moved and no-one had ever told me about you Thomasines. Rule number one, remember. What the military call 'need to know'. Your bosses needed to be sure I was still loyal which is why they were interested to know whether I turn down military projects. As an officer in the Swiss Guard I can hardly work for any other military organisation. If I had I would have been a spy, albeit only in a legalistic sense, and therefore outside the protection of the Geneva convention. Not that those rules seem to matter to the big boys any more these days."

"So the number that Tomaso wanted?"

"He had my name, what he wanted me to confirm was my rank and serial number."

"Rank?"

"Mmm."

"Well?"

"Commander."

Costanza's eyes widened.

"I didn't realise there were any Commanders in the Swiss Guard. I know most of the Guard by name, but I've never met a Commander."

"I told you it's an honorary rank. Reserved for special occasions or old has-beens who still need to feel important. In my case it's a bit like being in the TA."

"TA?"

"Territorial Army. In Britain there are people who volunteer to be trained as a soldier or officer but then go back to normal civilian life. Every now and then there are exercises where they play at being soldiers. If there's a war they're called up to fight for real. Most countries have something similar, usually called reserves or reservists."

"Ah yes, I understand. But you've never been called up?"

"Not until now."

"Signora!" said Tomaso, trying to remind us to enter the door that he was still holding open. We walked through into yet another corridor, with the inevitable yellow line running down the centre. The door slid shut behind us.

Costanza shook her head slightly and recovered her composure. She led me along the yellow line around two or three corners and finally to another touch panel in an apparently blank wall. She palmed it and soon the now familiar green light had appeared. I was waiting for the hiss of a glass door and the movement of the floor, but instead the end wall of the corridor slid sideways and we walked in to a large office.

About twenty workstations were dotted around the room. A variety of chairs were arranged among them, including two long sofas. On one wall was a whiteboard that must have been ten metres long. One end was covered with mathematical equations and calculations, but most of it had been wiped clean. What was missing from this office were people.

"Welcome to our office. Commander" said Costanza. "No-one works here on a Saturday, especially not in August. Which means there will be fewer questions about you, luckily."

"I see you're using G5s" I said smiling.

"Of course. All dual 2.5GHz G5s with the latest version of system ten. Widescreen displays too. No point in being vulnerable to a virus however careful we are."

Like most security professionals I was a confirmed fan

of the Mac. As PCs have the bulk of the market for desktop computers, most viruses are targeted at Windows. Not only were Macs inherently more secure by design but they were hardly ever under attack anyway.

"It gets better," she said, grinning. "We have our own proprietary four level firewall running on an array of G5 Xserves. In the DMZ we've got a web server with a fake intranet system that appears to an outsider to be concerned with document management and we have a honeypot to catch anyone who manages to get in."

"And if they do?"

"This is a sovereign state. One of the advantages of working here is that we have our own laws. We're allowed to retaliate if necessary. We've developed some very neat anti-hack tools that trace the hacker back to their own machine and infect them with a virus that slowly replaces all of the files on their hard disc with multiple copies of a penitential prayer 'Pray for me, for I have sinned…'. We've only ever had to use it once, no-one else has got through the firewall."

"Who got through?"

"We don't know for sure. It seemed to be coming from somewhere in Cheltenham in England. Could have been the British SIS via GCHQ. Whoever it was they didn't come back and we fixed the hole they came through."

"So what are you protecting?"

"The Library."

"No. I mean with the firewall, DMZ, honeypot. What is it to protect?"

"As I said. The Library. We've digitised it all. Behind the DMZ there's a different four level firewall running on some more Xserves."

"And behind that?"

"The biggest supercomputer in the world. An array of

Xserves in a cube 1024 by 1024 by 1024." Her eyes twinkled as she watched me.

"A billion processors?" I let out a slow breath.

"Two actually. They're all dual G5 Xserves."

"But how could you get that many without anyone knowing? Without Apple knowing and wanting to tell everyone?"

"Companies are happy to keep secrets when they're bound by NDAs. Anyway, we get kit through a dozen research institutes around Europe. No-one knows it's us buying the machines and no-one knows they're all in one array. An additional plant was built just to supply European demand. Our demand. We get a good bulk discount!" She smiled again.

"Apple has already done some work with other researchers to make large arrays a reality. We've just redefined large." she added.

"I'll say. For large, read vast. But you don't need all that power just to store digitised images."

"No we don't. The images are kept in an array of Xserve RAIDs. We have backup archived storage in a secure facility deep below St. John in Lateran."

"Outside the Vatican. Isn't that risky?"

"It's all encrypted. But anyway the Lateran is extraterrestrial."

"Alien?"

"No. Oh, I mean extra-territorial" She grinned again. "Vatican territory even though it's outside the City. Our jurisdiction."

"This is all very impressive. I know you're trying to get me interested enough to stay around a while. But you still haven't told me what you want me to do."

"Okay. Sit down on this sofa and I'll tell you what's been going on. It started in Brazil…"

Sao Paolo (36 days ago)

Cardinal Eduardo Figueras was a tall, striking man. With his full head of black hair he didn't seem to fit in with most people's image of an 80 year old. Still sprightly and with a strong voice that needed no amplification even in the largest basilica, he was a well known figure in all of South America. Never afraid to be outspoken against governments, big business or criminals who preyed on the poor and social outcasts, he was a friend of the people and a pariah to the establishment. If he were still merely a parish priest he would have been disappeared long ago. But now he was an internationally respected figure and the world's media was always paying attention to him.

It was Friday morning. The Cardinal rose at 5 am as usual and had his customary cold shower. His deep baritone voice echoed around the tiled bathroom as he sang his favourite hymn†, dried himself and put on his tracksuit and trainers. He opened his door and padded along the corridor; tapped lightly on the door of Monsignor Vargas, who came out into the hall in his own running gear; and the two of them set off down the stairs for their daily jog. Concerned for his safety, the Cardinal's staff had convinced him to stop running around the streets of Sao Paolo early in the morning, so now he and Vargas confined themselves to the residence gardens and once around the basilica when it opened at 6.

By six thirty the Cardinal had showered again and dressed in his black suit, shirt and dog collar. He was ready for his breakfast of bran flakes, skimmed milk and orange juice. Today, being Friday, he would only be having a snack for lunch and a fish supper in the evening.

---

† *"The God of liberation / has challenged us to fight / injustice, exploitation / and sins against the light / by state or corporation / or any seeking gain / from human degradation / or profit wrought from pain"* Patrick Lee, Stephen Dean

So, as every Friday, he allowed himself a cup of coffee before starting the day's work. Only yesterday a parishioner had given him a special blend that was supposed to be perfect for breakfast. But he knew today would be busy, so he carried his cup with him as he went into his study and sat down at his large oak desk – an intricately carved affair that was one of the few reminders here of the Imperial origins of Catholicism in South America.

By nine thirty, when no-one had been summoned to transcribe letters from the Cardinal's bold handwritten notes onto a word processor, his staff were starting to worry. Monsignor Vargas knocked on the study door but got no reply. He tried again. Still no reply. He turned the handle and cracked open the door. He called out but there was still silence. He could just see the Cardinal in his chair, but something didn't look quite right. Vargas pushed the door wide open and ran in. As he got to the Cardinal's desk, he dropped to his knees, crossed himself and murmured "Oh Dio!". The Cardinal's head was slumped onto his left shoulder, eyes staring, mouth open. His hand still held the pen with which he had been writing. He was obviously dead.

The noon news bulletins in Brazil carried the solemn obituary of a well-loved and holy man who had died unexpectedly of a heart attack that morning.

Vatican City

"I remember Cardinal Figueras dying a few weeks ago. There was a lot of news coverage about the funeral. Some dispute about the government being there if I recall."

"That's right. Most people in Brazil were convinced that he had been murdered by the government or some corrupt cartel. The doctors were adamant he had died of a heart attack, even though he had no history of heart problems and was incredibly fit and healthy for his age."

"So what's that got to do with us?"

"Patience, Peter. The story continues in Boston in the United States…"

Boston, USA (25 days ago)

Archbishop Bernie O'Leary was not a popular man. After recent successful class actions against his diocese for child abuse by various clergy and other staff, he had declared the diocese bankrupt, with the result that no punitive damages would ever be paid to the victims. The bulk of his clergy, who were innocent of all charges, were now not only starved of funds for anything, but also themselves the victims of much verbal and, in some cases, physical abuse.

So when, on a bright spring morning, the Archbishop drove his car into a brick wall by Boston Common while attempting to turn from Beacon Street into Park Street, there was no-one who mourned his death. Even his mother had been so disgusted at his latest shenanigans that she no longer returned his calls, and had taken to going to Mass at St Joseph's across town, even though it meant taking two separate buses, rather than to her own son's cathedral which was within walking distance of her home. The autopsy showed he had suffered a heart attack while driving and was probably already dead before he hit the wall. For once, he didn't take anyone else with him.

The funeral was surprisingly well attended, considering no-one was sad to see him go. Cynics, and media pundits, suggested that most people who came to the cathedral that day wanted to make sure he was really dead. Some wanted to know where his grave would be so they could return later in their dancing shoes. There was much talk of Divine retribution and poetic justice – although not from the pulpit. A particularly vociferous group of abused ex-parishioners staged a protest outside, demanding that he not be buried on hallowed ground. Some even suggested he be 'tossed to the dogs' - although none of them had actually thought to bring any suitable dogs with them, apart from one little Shiatsu who was clearly not up to the task. Many mutterers said that a sudden death from a heart attack was too good for him, and that he had been let off lightly. For the first time in living memory, no-one from City Hall attended the funeral, even though a large proportion of the staff and the elected representatives were Irish Catholics who knew where their duties were supposed to lie. Media coverage was unusually understated, especially for a city that revelled in its religious heritage and enjoyed being the east coast's spiritual capital. For most of the city it was just another day. There was no large procession blocking the streets. No overflowing emotion threatening to drown the city in tears. No lines of police horses leading the catafalque. Indeed, no catafalque. No lying in state for the faithful to file past. Just a simple coffin, brought in through a side door at the start of the requiem, and taken out of another to the private courtyard reserved for episcopal burials. The dancers would be thwarted, there would be no public access to the concrete slab covering his last resting place.

Vatican City

"I didn't hear about that, although I knew there'd been some dodgy things going on in the US Church."

"The Church in America is completely out of hand. The gossip here is that it's only a matter of time before it's cut off. Ironic really, just as we're healing the schism with the Eastern Orthodox Church we'll have a new one in the West. The only reason it hasn't happened already is because a few members of the Curia are American and they argue that you can't punish the entire Church in America for the actions of some of the clergy."

"So why not just deal with those clergy?"

"They've tried, but short of threatening excommunication it's very difficult. The US Church is financially independent and legally established as a string of separate US-based charitable organisations. They've even tried to register the cross as a trademark!"

"No!" I frowned, still not sure of the relevance of all this.

"Apparently, 73% of all US citizens believe that Americans are God's chosen people. They are demanding that the next Pope should be an American. If that happens it would be a disaster for the Church as a whole. The Americans want to turn it into a multi-national corporation based in New York. We would lose our special status in most of the world. The Church would become just another employer and landowner, like the Church of England. We would probably lose many of the faithful too. It would open the way for another schism with a traditionalist break-away church, probably based in France or Italy. At the moment there are too many members of the College of Cardinals who don't want that to happen. But that's changing. Let me tell you what recently happened here in Rome…"

Rome (3 days ago)

Cardinal Bramante spent most of his time in Rome. As an active official in the Curia he had little chance to visit any of the dioceses for which he was spiritually responsible. He relied on his bishops to tend to the flocks. It was years since he had even confirmed anyone, let alone baptised a baby. These days his life was full of committee meetings, working groups, hearings and paperwork. Lots of paperwork. In his younger days, as a newly ordained priest, he had been keen to progress up the hierarchy. Having graduated from Pisa University with top marks in Theology and Philosophy, and then obtained his doctorate from Oxford, his family knew he was destined for greatness. He was already being noticed from the vaulted corridors of the Vatican. As a bishop he had been renowned for his thoughtful and well-researched epistles, although his delivery of them from the pulpit did tend to last rather longer than most parishioners found comfortable. When he received the scarlet, he had come to the Vatican and had never really escaped. He had quickly settled in to the bureaucratic lifestyle. Fluency in the three main languages of the Church (Latin, Italian and English) was an obvious advantage, as were his friendships developed at Oxford with theologians who were now very senior in the Anglican communion. He had been instrumental in bringing to fruition the rapprochement between Rome and Canterbury and was ever hopeful that the Church of England could be persuaded back into the fold of the One True Church. But his encyclopaedic knowledge of Canon Law, and ability to rapidly assess and respond to any situation with chapter, verse, case law and corollary had made him the perfect Devil's Advocate.

At 50 years of age, he was one of the youngest of the Cardinals. Some thought he would be an ideal choice for

Pope at the next Conclave, but there were still many old-school members of the Curia who were dubious of such tender youth and felt his time would be more likely to come at a Conclave further into the future. Some, however, mindful of St. Malachy's cryptic (and officially unaccepted) prophecies of future Popes, were inclined to see him as the likely holder of the office of Holy Father - as the only Roman among the Sacred College of Cardinals he was the obvious choice to fulfil the prophecy as 'Petrus Romanus', Peter the Roman, the 112th and final entry in Malachy's list. Pope John Paul II, number 110 on the list, was not expected to survive much longer and most of the bookies' favourites for his successor were relatively old and unlikely to remain in office for more than a handful of years.

Guiseppe to his friends, Peppino to his mother, the Cardinal still made time for those he loved.

"Peppino. You look pale. You should get more sun and fresh air. Stuck inside your dusty office all the time isn't good for you."

"Mamma. I'm not pale, I'm fine. I get plenty of sun and fresh air. I go for a walk every lunchtime in the Vatican gardens. Today, I ate an apple in the rose garden and then rested for a few minutes in the spray from the Eagle fountain. I have a sensible diet, I don't smoke. I had a check up with my doctor only yesterday. Perfect results. Stop worrying."

His mother looked unconvinced, but she nodded and smiled.

Ten minutes later, after his mother has stopped fussing and left to go home and make dinner for the rest of her family, Guiseppe Bramante lay down on his bed for a late siesta. He would never wake up.

Vatican City

"When did he die?" I asked.

"Last Wednesday. They found him when he failed to turn up at a committee meeting and didn't answer his mobile. He never switches, I mean switched, his mobile off. He was notorious for receiving and sending text messages during meetings – there's a story that once he even sent a text while celebrating Mass, but I don't believe it. So when he didn't answer they knew something was wrong and sent some Guards round in a car. They found him lying on his bed. The Rome coroner said it was a heart attack, the Vatican medical staff agreed that it appeared to be a heart attack but were very dubious because he had had a full medical the day before and everything had been fine. They suspected some other cause but were at a loss to know what it could be. That was when Cardinal Bianchi got involved."

"Who?"

"Cardinal Bianchi was a good friend of Cardinal Bramante, although older he was like a brother to him. The senior doctor confided his suspicions and he decided to investigate."

"Why, who is he?"

"He's the head of the Society of Thomas. My boss."

"But what's all this got to do with cryptography?"

"I'm getting to that."

As she had been talking she had made terse notes on the white board. Names, dates, locations. I looked for an obvious pattern in what she had written or the way she had written it. I couldn't see any link.

"I can't see any connection between the events you've described apart from the glaringly obvious, they were priests and they had heart attacks."

"They were priests, yes. They all appeared to have heart attacks, yes."

"Are you saying that they didn't have heart attacks?"

"We can't prove anything at the moment. The deaths all appeared entirely natural to the local coroners and so there has been no criminal investigation in any country. We're the only ones who have been suspicious at all. But we don't have jurisdiction in any of the cases so we can't take any direct action. Interpol aren't interested in unsubstantiated theories, they have enough trouble co-ordinating police force co-operation across boundaries when there's plenty of evidence and even outstanding arrest warrants. The security services don't co-operate at all, despite what you might think from James Bond films. None of them co-operate with us because we have a somewhat different philosophy when it comes to the use of force – no one here is 'licensed to kill'!"

"I still don't understand what this has to do with you. Or me?"

"Cardinal Bianchi was convinced that Guiseppe Bramante did not die from a heart attack. As we had lost two other senior clergy recently to sudden, unexpected, heart attacks he asked us to find any link we could. We treated it like a cryptogram and looked for a key."

"And that's where you came in?"

"Actually that's where our system came in. The Cardinal is a smart man and has his own access to the system. He knows how to formulate a query and initiate a search. So he did. The system searched our archives and the Web for any link between the victims."

"Victims? So you're sure they were victims?"

"At that point it was still an open question. VICI found no significant connections in our own databases or archives so …"

"VICI?"

"Oh yes. Sorry. The system is called VICI, in English it would stand for Vatican Information and Cryptographic

Interface, although it sounds better in Latin. Another little joke. Vici, as in Caesar's comment ..."

"Veni, vidi, vici. I came, I saw, I conquered."

"Exactly. Anyway, VICI searched the Web."

"Using which search engines?"

"None. It doesn't rely on search engines being updated, commercial pressures dictating what does and doesn't appear. If we want to know what's appearing on the web, we search it directly."

"What, dynamically?"

"Yes."

"In real time, no indexes?" She nodded.

"But that would take forever, unless you had a massive supercomputer." She raised an eyebrow.

"Ah yes. But you'd also need a very high bandwidth connection to the Internet's backbone." She raised an eyebrow again.

"The Vatican has it's own PTT. As an early participant in international network research we have been providing part of the European Internet backbone for years. We don't need access to the backbone, we own part of the backbone. We have as much bandwidth as we want. We even have our own communication satellites to provide alternate routing that avoids the trunks that are being snooped by the CIA. Why do you think our senior clergy have all developed a taste for satellite TV? They don't get it to watch football. Well, not all of them. Not only do we beam Vatican TV around the world, but we use VSAT technology that can piggy back on the same dishes to give us secure, high speed communications with any of our Cardinals or Bishops at their cathedral houses. But we're getting away from the point here."

"Sorry."

"Okay. VICI searched for a potential connection and found two. All three of them had been to Rome in the last year for meetings with the Pope. But that's not unusual for Cardinals or Archbishops, and Cardinal Bramante met with the Holy Father regularly. In fact, over half of all Cardinals had a meeting with the Pope in the last two years, and a quarter of all Archbishops. So that seemed to be irrelevant."

"And the other connection?"

"That proved to be more interesting. Do you remember 'Dial M for Murder' and 'Murder Inc.'"

"Vaguely. Films where assassins were available anonymously, so they can't be traced from, by or to their clients."

"More or less. Using the state of the art technology of the time, telephones. Now there's a similar service around, but this actually is anonymous and there isn't even really a client. Just a victim. Using today's state of the art technology. Based on a theoretical cyber-crime scenario dreamed up by an English academic when the Internet became commercial, it uses a combination of anonymous remailers, blinded signature electronic cash, message boards and a web site that's sitting on a server in a recently democratised state with no up to date legal system, no treaties with other states and no restrictions on online gambling."

"Gambling?"

"Yes. That's the apparent mechanism for the 'service' that makes it seem to be legal and legitimate, if tasteless."

"Now you've lost me."

"The service is called DeadBet.net – I think it's supposed to be a pun in American. Deadbeats?"

"Except that puns should be funny!"

"Indeed. The site works like this. They run a betting service where you can bet on the time, place and manner of death of 'celebrities'. If the celebrity dies in the place you said, when you said and how you said you win all the money bet on that celebrity – minus a commission for the service provider."

"So if enough people bet on a celebrity dying, eventually somebody will decide it's worth the risk to kill them to win the money."

"Exactly. They decide when and where and how they will kill them. Then they place a bet with the details and when they carry it out successfully they win the money."

"But how do they get the money? A transfer can be traced, even into a Swiss bank."

"That's where the crypto comes in. All the people making bets submit their stake in electronic cash. Anonymised electronic cash using double blinded digital signatures. The service provider can validate the cash but doesn't know where it came from. The banks that issued them can't trace where they were issued or who spent them. All the money staked against a celebrity is held by the service provider. When someone submits their bet they provide a public key with it. After the celebrity has died, the winnings are encrypted with the public key of the winner. The encrypted cash is then placed on the web site. Everybody who made a bet agrees to download the file, but only the winner has the private key with which to decrypt the electronic cash. They can then use it like any other electronic cash or convert it into funds in a bank account. Because of the blinded signatures on the cash it can't be traced when it's spent. As every player has downloaded the file, no-one can tell who was the winner from looking at web server accesses. All in all it's a cynically clever service. The original idea was mooted as a ridiculous example of the way that technology can lead to the development of ways of committing new crimes, not just new ways of committing old crimes. But no-one paid any attention, and now somebody has set up a service to do it. What's worse is that plenty of people are logging onto the service to take part. Mostly, of course, they're students and geeks who think it's all a game or just a weird form of bet. And most of the celebrities that they're betting on are soap opera stars (usually the unsympathetic characters and the bad guys) a few science fiction characters (some of the players really haven't grasped the point of the game they think they're playing) and various world leaders. Plus a few particularly unpopular people like Pinochet, Milosovich, David Beckham. Included on the list were Cardinal Figueras, Archbishop O'Leary, and Cardinal Bramante."

"Why? What's the common factor that would motivate someone to want them killed."

"They've all made enemies. The common factor is that there is no common factor, if you see what I mean?"

"Not really."

"Okay, imagine there was someone, or a group, who wanted to assassinate various people. Their motivation would presumably be some cause or other. They would choose victims that are the natural targets for their cause. The victims would be very obviously linked. Most of the targets on the deadbet website fall into the categories I described, soap stars, world leaders, sport celebrities. Some don't fall into any category. Cardinal Figueras was loved by ordinary people but despised by the politicians, corrupt businessmen and criminals in most of South America. Any of them would have willingly made a bet if it would get rid of him in a way that wasn't attributable to them. Archbishop O'Leary had become deeply unpopular with almost everyone in Boston. I'm sure there were some people who bear a grudge deep enough to encourage his murder – we are talking about America, violent crime capital of the world. Cardinal Bramante is a bit more confusing though. His only real enemies were other Cardinals in the Curia who wouldn't consider murder a suitable course of action – and most of them have enough trouble reading their email, they certainly wouldn't be capable of generating a key pair or handling electronic cash."

"But even if they were wished dead by unconnected groups of people, they all died in the same way. Presumably by the same hand. Was there a successful bet in all three cases?"

"Yes."

"Was it the same person placing all three bets?"

"We can't tell. We downloaded the encrypted winnings and used a brute force attack to find the keys. The first two have already been found but we haven't finished looking for the key to Cardinal Bramante's killer's winnings. The first two were not the same, but that doesn't mean the killer didn't just use different online accounts and different key pairs."

"You brute forced the keys already? What size were they?"

"Trivially small, only 1536 bits. It took 24 hours to do each one, using all the processors."

"What? That's amazing. Even with this much processing power it should take you, oh at least a week or two to break the key."

"I've been doing some very interesting research for the last few months and I've found ways to improve the efficiency of the general number field sieve. We can now do it significantly faster than the special number field sieve."

"Wow." Now I was really impressed. Deciphering an encrypted message without having the private key is like guessing the combination lock on a safe. The basic brute force approach means you start with the first possible combination and try it, if it fails you try the next combination and so on until you find the right one. If you start at 0000 and the right value is 9999 then you would have tried every possible value before you succeeded. Of course, if you'd started at the end and worked backwards you would have found it straight away (which is why you don't set a combination code to be too near the first or last possible value). On average, therefore, you would have to try half the possible combinations to find the right one. But some codes are more probable than others, codes in the middle of the range of possibilities are more likely, as are meaningful sequences like 1234 and significant numbers like 1066. So you try the most likely values first before you adopt a systematic approach. Breaking a cryptogram is very similar, but instead of a 4 digit combination code it uses keys that are very large numbers, numbers with over 1500 digits. Trying every combination would take an unbelievably long time – millions of years. The keys in a public key system are generated by some complex mathematics based on the unique characteristics of very large prime numbers. If you multiply two large primes together you get another very large number. But if you have only been given that very large number it is incredibly difficult to work out which two prime number were used to generate it, and it's the two prime numbers that you need for the key. This process, called factoring, can be speeded up by some very clever maths that lets you discard useless values based on what you've already tried (in other words sieving the possible values remaining to remove useless possibilities). Over the years it has been refined by various mathematicians and crypto-analysts, but was now thought to be as efficient as it could be – short of a major breakthrough in the underlying maths. If Costanza had achieved the speed increase she claimed, then she had made that significant breakthrough. But there had not been even a whisper of it in the outside world.

"So you're no closer to finding out who won the funds?"

"Not really."

"What are you going to do now?"

"That's where you come in." she smiled again, turned to the white board and wrote four names on it. "There are other target names on the betting system. They're getting to have quite high totals and we think one of them will be next."

As I read the names she had written on the board my mind raced ahead to imagine the consequences of their death, especially if foul play became suspected.

"There would be a series of unmitigated disasters. The Israelis would nuke Arabs. The Arabs would bomb Israel. The US would attack the Arabs."

"And the Universal Church would be taken over by American capitalists." She put down her marker pen and sat down gently on the sofa next to me.

"Cardinals Bramante and Figueras would both have been impediments to the election of an American Pope. But with them out of the picture it becomes a much closer contest. In fact, the most likely candidate is Cardinal Pietro Pescosolido."

The Cardinal was one of the five names Costanza had written on the board.

"If he suddenly dies of a heart attack, there's only one realistic candidate left. Cardinal John Thomas."

"Is that really his name?"

"Yes, why?"

"No reason at all. Carry on." A stupid schoolboy smirk tried to spread across my face, but I was alert to it and forced it back.

"He's the main American candidate. Originally from a Boston Irish Catholic family, he's been an archbishop in

Los Angeles and Washington. He's managed to relate to both the East coast Europeans and the West coast Hispanics. Surprisingly he has a lot of popular support despite his background in corporate America. His brother owns a large consultancy in San Francisco and his father is a partner in one of the big four accountancy firms. There are also suggestions that he worked for one of the Agencies while doing his national service. He has a sister who supposedly works for the US State Department, but we know she actually works for the NSA. And don't forget how important religion is in American politics."

"So you think that this is all about getting him elected as the next Pope?"

"I think so. Cardinal Bianchi doesn't want to believe it, but is determined to find out the truth behind Bramante's death. There's one more piece of information that I think is significant. One of the last people to see Cardinal Bramante was in fact Cardinal Thomas. They had a chat just before lunch, Thomas gave Bramante an apple. Bramante went into the Vatican gardens by himself, as usual, ate the apple and meditated for a while in the sun. He went back to his office and spent the next couple of hours doing paperwork. He went home early, spoke to his mother for about half an hour, and that was the last time he was seen alive."

"What are you suggesting?" I asked, slightly shocked, "that he was murdered by Cardinal Thomas with a poisoned apple? It's a bit far-fetched don't you think? Straight out of a fairy tale – Snow White eating the Queen's apple. Or rather the King's apple. Or is Thomas a queen?"

"No," Costanza looked very serious, "Thomas may be a prince of the church but he's no queen – he's one of the few senior American clergy who isn't gay. If there is an evil Queen, we have no idea who she might be."

I laughed. "Maybe we need the magic mirror on the wall." I looked back at the whiteboard, as did Costanza.

"Oh. There's one more name on the deadbet list that is getting a high total." She stood again, walked back to the white board and added something to the list. She was standing in the way so I couldn't see what she had written. Slowly putting the cap back on the marker pen, she turned, walked towards me and sat down.

I stared at the white board. The list now read:

Cardinal Pietro Pescosolido
Rabbi Chaim Cohen
Yasser Arafat
George Bush
John Paul II

Naples

By most people's reckoning Cardinal Pietro Pescosolido was an old man. In any other career he would have retired five years ago and now be living in a quiet villa, with olive trees, fig trees and vines to tend. His family had been reasonably wealthy before the second world war; but they had lost many of their possessions during the German occupation and much of their land had been destroyed. Since then they had lost more land to compulsory purchase by local socialist town halls to provide prime locations for the construction of comfortable villas for the party faithful. Even so, he would have been able to find a quiet hillside with a hectare or two of his family's land to see out his days.

Born four years before the start of the war, he had been steered towards the second son's traditional career in the church. After the war, he was packed off to the seminary, one less mouth to feed. Smarter than anyone had realised, he had made his mark there, quickly picking up Classical Greek and Aramaic and becoming the resident expert on biblical sources. Not wishing to see his talents wasted as a mere parish priest, Monsignor Valetti, the Principal of the seminary, had arranged for him to become the personal assistant to the Bishop of Naples. His sermons, though very erudite and liberally sprinkled with references, were spellbinding for the congregations who were lucky enough to attend his Masses. The Bishop, too, benefited from his talents, with a sudden increased finesse to his own sermons and diocesan letters, ghost-written, of course, by Fr. Pietro.

His abilities were soon more widely appreciated, especially once he had accompanied the Bishop to Rome for a series of meetings, including one with Pope John XXIII. He impressed everyone in the Vatican and was pressed to stay, leaving the Bishop to return alone to

Naples where his sermons soon drifted back to their old dull style. For some years he was very busy in Rome, where he was granted access to the earliest manuscripts of the Gospels and Epistles. His research was profound, producing new insights into the early Church and Christ's message to his followers. He was asked to join the Society for the Propagation of the Faith as doctrinal adviser, but declined, preferring to work in the dusty rooms of the Vatican Library where he could avoid public gaze.

Nonetheless, he was 'promoted', becoming a Bishop in his fifties. By the time he was almost sixty, the Bishop of Naples died and to popular acclaim Pescosolido was asked to fill the man's shoes. This time he could not decline and he moved back south from Rome to Naples. The real wrench for him was not Rome but the Vatican Library which, although only 150km away, was entirely out of his reach. He became an advocate of new technology, keen to see his beloved manuscripts made available outside of their carefully controlled reading room. It was he who persuaded Cardinal Bianchi that the imaging technology that was being employed in other well known collections, such as the British Library, should be used to record, preserve and make accessible the contents of the library. Once convinced, Cardinal Bianchi had quickly set about identifying suitable candidates to perform the process and the small Society of Thomas had suddenly become rather larger.

Four years later, when Bishop Pescosolido was given the scarlet to become Cardinal Pescosolido, he was also given a DVD-Rom by Cardinal Bianchi. It contained high resolution images of all the manuscripts he had been working on for so much of his life. Bianchi even gave him a Titanium PowerBook with which to view the disc. For most onlookers, it was difficult to tell which made him happiest, becoming a Cardinal or having access to his manuscripts again. For his closest friends, of which there were not very many, it was no contest. He would have been happy to have just stayed a priest all these years, but to have access to the manuscripts again was wonderful beyond words.

The Cardinal had always been a mass of contradictions. He was very popular, his sermons and now letters were well received and were even helping to raise the general level of education and debate about many matters in his diocese. His sermons were even being transcribed onto web pages, translated into many different languages and used all around the world. Yet, at the same time, he himself sought to avoid the limelight. He would often prefer his sermons to be delivered by someone else, his personal assistant or one of the cathedral's many resident priests. He only wore distinguishing robes when he absolutely had to, the rest of the time looking like any other priest. He even took to wearing gloves whenever he could, to hide the Cardinal's ring that he wore.

This, of course, only endeared him to many of the faithful, who saw in him some of the same qualities that they had loved in Albino Luciani the Patriarch of Venice who, as John Paul I, had been Pope for only 33 days in 1978 before dying unexpectedly of a heart attack.

Vatican City

After a few seconds, Costanza broke the silence.

"We think we know how."

"How what?"

"How the assassin kills them."

"Inducing a heart attack?"

"Indirectly. Some years ago the CIA developed a poison that could be introduced into a victim's food. After being swallowed, it's converted by the gastric juices in the stomach into a precisely targeted muscle relaxant that only affects cardiac muscles. It's absorbed into the blood stream and carried to the heart; when enough of it builds up there it causes arrhythmia, ventricular fibrillation and hence the failure of the heart to supply appropriate pressure to the blood. To all intents and purposes it looks like a heart attack. But when the muscles stop contracting for good it disperses back into the blood and quickly degrades into the usual waste materials you find in the blood stream of a dead person. It takes about two hours to kill someone and ten minutes to disappear without a trace."

"How do you know about it?" I asked.

"Our doctors deduced its existence and operation in September 1978. But they couldn't prove anything. Since then an ex-CIA agent called Daniel Browne made a full confession."

"What happened to the inviolable privacy of the confessional?"

"He Confessed to a priest who persuaded him to repeat it outside the confessional to the Vigilanza."

"What, here in Rome?"

"In St. Peter's. He came in to the basilica, stood before Peter's tomb for about three hours and then asked a nearby priest to hear his Confession. Luckily the priest, who spoke English, had his wits about him and steered

Browne to a quiet confessional by the altar of St Joseph. When he heard what he had to say, he convinced him to tell the authorities, went and found one of the stewards who brought them to the Vigilanza. Afterwards Browne went back into Rome and flew home to America. Two days later he was found floating in the Delaware River."

"You think the CIA are behind these deaths too?"

"No. If they were, they wouldn't be messing about with the deadbet website. They don't need extra funds to assassinate people around the world, that's what they're paid to do."

"So who then?"

"We don't know, although one of our theories is that it's a rogue agent who's gone freelance and taken some weapons with him."

"The heart attack poison?"

"Exactly."

This was very far removed from anything I usually dealt with. Hackers, sniffers, viruses, black hats and worms all paled into insignificance beside this. But I still didn't see what Costanza expected me to do.

"About five minutes ago you said this was where I come in. I still don't see what I have got to offer to help with any of this." I looked at Costanza as she sat on the sofa beside me. "What is it you want me to do?"

"We want to put a tracer into some electronic cash, submit it as a stake against each of the names on this list and wait."

"But that will only help when the assassin picks up the winnings."

"I know."

"Which means…"

"One of these people is soon going to die of a heart attack." She bit her lip. "We've run out of options. We've… I've… run out of ideas. I've looked at the

52

electronic cash and I can't work out how to put a tracer in it. I was hoping you would have some ideas."

"Well actually there is a way. When I was involved with the development of electronic cash systems we looked at the possibility of introducing a digital dye, like the explosive dye they put on bundles of cash to deter thieves. There was a lot of pressure from the US government to remove anonymity. When we wouldn't do that they insisted that we at least implement digital dye or they would make electronic cash illegal in the US. So we did. I'm sure that any other electronic cash systems would have come under the same pressure. As they're still claiming anonymity I assume they had to introduce the digital dye too. But to find out we need to look at the code and to do that we need to break the crypto that protects the money, which will require massive resources and lots of processing power ..." I looked at Costanza's raised eyebrow. "Oh yes. Okay. So when do we start?"

"Now would do" she said, "there's a machine free over here. I was pretty sure you'd say yes so I've already set up an account for you, with the same privileges as me. And there's a form on the desk for you to sign to be bound by the rules of the Society of Thomas."

Capri

In a twenty minute helicopter ride from the international airport in Naples, a group of conservatively dressed men were ferried to the island of Capri. Despite being a popular tourist destination, mostly for day-trippers from Naples, the Amalfi coast and various passing cruise ships, few visitors actually stay on the island. Most venture no further than the town of Capri itself, unless it is to be rowed into the justifiably famous Blue Grotto or to climb the steep road to the ruins of the Imperial Roman villa with its superb view across the island and out to sea. Even this far out into the bay of Naples, the brooding bulk of Vesuvius still dominates the horizon and perpetually draws the eye to it like a moth to a flame.

The men disembarked from their helicopter and walked, hair and jackets blowing about wildly in the rotor downdraft as they kept their heads down, across to the liveried footman waiting to lead them into the hotel. They were not the first delegates to arrive at this international gathering, nor would they be the last. Over 120 men and women, mostly from the northern and western hemispheres, were coming to Capri for this year's secret Bilderberg meeting. They had hoped that the relative inaccessibility of the hotel, and the restrictions on road traffic within the island, would mean that they were more likely this year to remain unmolested by journalists and protesters. As usual, however, certain so-called radical journalists had managed to divine the location of the meeting and had found rooms in other hotels on the island; some in Capri itself, but most over the backbone of the island in the quieter Anacapri, from where they could attempt to carry out their surveillance and investigations into the participants, agenda and discussions at the meeting. Some, convinced of the inherently suspicious nature of any organisation like

Bilderberg which conducts its activities shrouded in secrecy, were determined to try to raise awareness of the Group and its annual meetings which had been going on since 1954. Others, purveyors of conspiracy theories to the great unwashed, were happy to enjoy the delightful weather, cuisine and local wine at the expense of their tabloid editors, while revelling in their apparent exposés of the latest incarnation of the Zionist cabal secretly controlling the world and pulling the strings of most world governments.

Tim Shah was a freelance journalist whose writing was more widely read than most of the other media leeches currently in Capri. Having become too radical for most of the UK dailies, his columns were published in a variety of newsletters and newspapers on the Web, reaching an international audience that traditional daily newspapers envied. After trying to get into the hotel where the meeting was taking place, only to be turned away not just by hotel staff but by two horse-mounted Carabinieri, he had gone for a walk along the slope of the island's central mountain until he had reached the belvedere with its stunning views over the cliffs and natural bays. Looking across the string of weathered rocky outcrops, like the irregular teeth on a decaying jawbone sticking out of the water, he watched a five-masted schooner appear around the headland and sail smoothly and silently across the azure blue sea. Here and there the wakes from motor boats and launches marred the serene surface, a reminder of modern technology in this otherwise timeless scenery. To his right and below was the lighthouse that helped to protect boats and their crews from the potentially treacherous rocks hidden just beneath the surface. He contemplated the view, breathed in the fresh air, and ignored the slight vertigo he felt from being so high above a sheer drop down the cliff face. Suddenly, he gasped, clutched his chest and started to gag. He looked around for help, but the quiet English couple who had been here minutes before had already left to walk back into Anacapri; the two Italian teenagers, who had been canoodling at the railing had disappeared into the trees as soon as Tim had arrived. The tall blonde woman he had seen in his hotel lobby this morning had been walking along the path in front of him; he had hoped to catch her up and get to know her, but now she was nowhere to be seen. There was no-one else around to help. He sank to his knees, feeling unable to breath. The pain in his chest felt like a steel band being tightened around him. He couldn't bear it much longer. His eyes shut and he fell sideways to the ground. As the blood stopped being pumped around his body, his arms fell back, his tongue lolled out of his mouth and a warm wet patch started to appear in the crutch of his cream linen trousers.

Vatican City

For twenty minutes I had been working at the problem of cracking the code protecting the electronic cash. Only twenty minutes, but already Costanza had put the massive power of the Library's supercomputing array at my disposal, so I was now looking at the raw code.

"Hungry?" asked Costanza as she walked over and stood behind me.

I had been so absorbed in what I was doing that I would have jumped with surprise if it hadn't been for the dulled, but telltale, reflection of her red silk scarf in the brushed metal stand of the flat screen.

"Actually, I wouldn't mind something to eat. I was expecting to go out for a meal when you arrived, not to come into secret underground tunnels and be working at the largest supercomputer array in the world." I looked up at her and smiled, hoping she wouldn't take offence – I wouldn't have missed this for the world, certainly not just for a meal.

"Pizza be alright?"

"Sure. Straight Margherita. But where can you get it from? Surely there isn't a canteen down here too?"

"No. But the new canteen in the Museum above us offers the nicest pizza around. They won't bring it down here though."

"Why not?"

"They can't"

"Why?"

"Because they don't know that 'down here' exists. But I'll go upstairs, get some pizza for us and bring it back. Luckily we are allowed to eat and drink in the yellow zone, which is just as well or most of my staff would have starved to death by now!" No sooner had she spoken than she turned nimbly on her heels and walked back out of the room the way we had entered half an hour before.

Alone for the first time, I looked up from the screen and surveyed the room. In front of the sofas, next to the whiteboard, I had failed to notice a flat screen TV. It was currently switched to standby and was sufficiently large that it could be easily watched by someone at any workstation in the room.

I tried to imagine the people who normally worked here. Some, dedicated and motivated, like Costanza, working towards laudable goals; others, enjoying the challenge of solving apparently intractable problems, stretching their intellectual muscles; a few, Catholic fundamentalists, keen to see long-held secrets protected. But they were all signed-up Thomasines, so presumably all focussed on delivering the means of making the hidden visible – but not necessarily visible to everyone (or even anyone?). Thomasines. They, or I should now say we, having signed up before sitting down at this desk, had a long tradition to live up to (or escape from, depending on your perspective I guess). But with the use of this latest technology the breadth and depth of the Thomasines' work had exponentially increased. I thought about all the long-lost documents that were probably languishing in the archives, what secrets they were concealing, what secrets they may yet reveal. I immediately half-remembered late night TV documentaries on conspiracy theories, missing documents, rumoured artefacts, hidden evidence of the true history that was buried beneath political misinformation mixed with lies, later fabrications and embellishments. The Holy Grail, Dead Sea Scrolls, forbidden Gospels, secret Royal treaties. Who knew what may be in here. Of course, now, even if I saw everything in these archives I couldn't breathe a word of it to anyone, or even write in my diary (and as for including anything in an, as yet unplanned, autobiography...!). The irony was not wasted on me, having spent a good part of my life protecting secular secrets with a reputation based, at least partially, on my deep spiritual and moral convictions, here I was, on behalf of the religious establishment, breaking the protection for something at the very core of that self-same secular world (and for many people in the fashionably un-spiritual Anglo-Saxon culture that I normally inhabited, the nearest thing to divinity that they could conceive of) - money itself, the great god mammon, the all consuming numerology where size matters, bigger is better and less is definitely not more.

I looked back at the screen, "where was I?" I thought to myself, "Ah! Yes. Here's the obvious place to switch on the dye. Oh, there's a skipped instruction here. Let's see what that skip achieves. Hmmm. That's interesting..."

I was still looking intently at these particular few lines of code when I heard the door open and Constanza glided across the floor towards me. In her left hand she had a large paper bag; peeping out of the top I could see a bottle of Tè Freddo. But the smell of the melted cheese and bubbling tomato arrived at my workstation even before she did. I watched as she unpacked two large rectangles of pizza and put them on a paper napkin next to my keyboard. Two more appeared from the bag and were placed on another napkin on the other side of the desk. The bottle was now standing on its own, between the two napkins. Costanza picked up the empty bag and walked over to a waste disposal unit on the wall. On her way back she detoured to a water cooler further along the wall retrieving two small plastic cups. Dragging the chair from the nearest desk for the last 2 metres, she sat down facing me. Putting one cup next to my pizza and the other next to her own, she picked up the bottle and carefully turned the lid, releasing the pressure slowly. Having poured drinks for both of us, she put the top back on the bottle and took a sip from her cup.

"How's it going?" She picked up a slice of pizza.

"Not bad. In fact I've found the best place to switch on the trace. There's already a position marker in the code, exactly where I'd put it, obviously set up to make it easy to do. And a few lines further on there's something else too. I think you'll be interested to see this."

While Costanza put down her own pizza, stood up and walked around the desk to stand behind me, I took a bite from my pizza. She daintily dabbed at the corners of her mouth with her napkin.

"What?" She looked at the screen.

"See this string embedded in the code here? What does it look like to you?"

"A dotted quad."

"Yup. I did a reverse DNS lookup and it's the IP address of a server in Langley in the US. The whois entry suggests it's a small import/export business, but this address is one of a large subnet range that is registered to that same business. I've run a port scan, nothing unusual, but nothing you'd expect either; no web services, no mail, ftp or even gopher. It does accept packets into one custom port though but doesn't even acknowledge them. With that size of subnet it looks like a fairly major Service Provider, but they don't actually seem to provide any services. Or, … it's our agency friends in the US."

"How is the IP address used in the code?" she asked.

"That's what I'm trying to work out. It would be so much easier if I had the source code rather than having to reverse engineer this mint software. Anyway, as far as I can see it's used down here." I scrolled the window down and the few lines of the code appeared that I had highlighted moments before Costanza had returned.

"It seems that if the dye is switched on then the money sends I'm Alive Messages every time it is spent, validated or banked."

"To the CIA."

"So it would seem. But, of course, we can change the address so the money we mint will send the IAMs to us here. Do you have any spare IP addresses we can use that won't be traceable back here?" I looked up to find Costanza leaning forward avidly reading my screen.

"Yes of course. In fact all our public connections here use one NATted IP address which is registered to a telecoms company in Rome; it's actually owned by the Vatican PTT, but nobody is aware of that."

"Okay. If we insert that address and switch on the dye, we can mint some cash and submit the bets. Then we wait." I didn't like that last bit. Waiting was not something I was good at, especially as in this case we were waiting for someone to die.

Costanza reached forward and grabbed the mouse, moved the cursor to the bottom of the scrollbar and scrolled the display down. She was obviously looking for something and soon stopped the slow scroll. Towards the end of the code was a block of variable assignments, where the program's data is stored when it's running. Some were initialised to their default values, some were obviously useful constants.

"Did you see this?" she asked, with a frown on her face.

I looked at the lines she was pointing to.

"Sneaky!"

Hidden among the data was a sequence of numbers in an array. To all normal observers it would just look like any other data needed in the calculations to create the electronic cash. But Costanza had noticed something that I had previously ignored. Before the call to the code that used the CIA's IP address to send IAMs, was a jump. I hadn't got round to seeing what it did because it followed the pattern elsewhere in the code of validating data before actually using it – I had assumed this was yet another data validation routine. But Costanza had noticed that the address was in the middle of what should have been data not code and had followed the jump.

She selected the relevant data with the mouse and then the F5 key. A new window appeared with the selected data displayed, but this window treated the data as if it were programming code and showed us what it did.

"Sneaky's right" said Costanza.

This piece of code was indeed sneaky. It was a classic piece of misdirection, as beloved of virus writers. The I'm Alive Message is sent to a different IP address, then amended. The message sent back to the CIA would be altered, it would identify the money correctly but include spurious data in place of the location details of the transaction. Somebody else was getting the real messages.

I gently took the mouse from Costanza, called up the network assistant and typed in the new IP address from the sneaky code. It was assigned to GCHQ in Cheltenham. They weren't even bothering to disguise their identity.

"Another example of the special relationship." I grinned. "This is where we make the change."

"No, we have to change both. We don't want either the CIA or SIS getting any messages, genuine or spurious, from our money. We want to track it ourselves. They haven't helped us or even been prepared to listen to us. So we cut them out of this particular loop. In fact, when we've finished I would be very tempted to replace the public mint software with a modified version that undermines both of them with invalid messages."

"But for now," I said, "let's get on with the job in hand. I'll make the changes and then we can mint some cash. I'll need the IP address to use for our IAMs." I looked down and saw the forgotten pizza, still hot and beckoning me. "But I've got pizza to finish first!".

Costanza smirked, but nonetheless went back to the other side of the desk to retrieve her pizza before walking over to her own workstation.

While I was editing the file, Costanza set up a port to receive our messages and instructed the firewalls to let them through and direct them to her workstation. We both finished about the same time. I created some money and then paid it back to myself. Immediately a gentle ping from Costanza's workstation told us that the I'm Alive Message had arrived. She read it and turned to me.

"Thomas Peters' money has been paid to Thomas Peters. Thomas Peters?"

"Well? My new identity as a Thomasine. What name did you want me to use, Vatican?"

"Or Vatican 2. This time it's personal." Those twinkling eyes were back along with the infectious grin.

"Vat69. Just when you thought it was safe to go back in the pulpit."

"Okay, by comparison Thomas Peters is a good name to use. Well, messages seem to get sent and received. But I only got one message, did you completely disable the other?"

"No, I took out the corrupting code and changed the IP address. Just in case something happens and the messages don't get through to you here, the second message goes to a little server I have stashed at a hosting site in England. The message is identical to the one you get, except it's enciphered so no-one will know what it's about even if they intercept it. It gives us a backup, if we need it." I shrugged. "Oh, and if you need to retrieve them without me, the deciphering key is the same as we used for our testing in Venice two years ago."

"Err. Oh yes. 'Timsatwat'"

"Well remembered" I said.

"How is Tim?" she asked.

"Same as ever I think. I've had nothing to do with him since then, but I've seen the name Tim Weevil on various conference flyers, billed as a Cryptographic expert. I assume it's him."

"Please God. Don't let there be another!" Costanza said, looking pleadingly to heaven with her hands together in prayer.

"Last I heard he was working on new comms standards for ISO. Probably trying to make steam radio secure." I laughed.

Costanza's prayerful expression gave way to a grin. But then her face became serious again and she looked at me with those deep eyes that could, at times, penetrate into your very soul.

"Right, let's make our bets..." she said.

"...and lie on them." I finished. She was momentarily confused, then looked at me scoldingly. "I knew there was a reason I have to leave a gap of at least a year between seeing you. It's to get over your dreadful puns. I won't grace them with the title of humour."

I shrugged again. Looking back to the screen I opened the web browser and went to the deadbet website. We looked at the list of targeted celebrities, in potential winnings order. At the top was some American soap star I had never even heard of. Immediately below was Israel's Chief Rabbi Chaim Cohen and below him George Bush, then Yasser Arafat, John Paul II, and Cardinal Pescosolido. Two places further down the list was Cardinal Danziger.

"It'll look a bit odd if Thomas Peters suddenly turns up and puts bets on all the top targets. Shouldn't we be more selective?"

"Okay. Let's concentrate on the relevant ones. Ignore the top four. Bet on the Holy Father and the three

Cardinals."

"Three? Who's the third?" I asked.

"Right at the bottom of the screen. Cardinal Clean."

"Oh. I thought that was a joke or a TV character."

"No. It's the nickname in the Italian papers for the archbishop of Milan. He's very smart and hugely popular. He has a history of heart problems, so no-one would be surprised if he had a heart attack."

"Why didn't you include him when you told me your list of likely Papal candidates standing in the way of John Thomas?"

"Because he's a Jesuit."

"So?"

"No Jesuit has ever become Pope."

"Why is he on this website then?"

"I guess there's always an outside chance."

"Okay. Who's Cardinal Danziger?" I asked.

"French. Son of Jewish refugees escaping from the Nazis. He was educated by nuns and decided to convert to Catholicism in his teens, much to the chagrin of his family. He became a priest and has been a frequent visitor to the Apostolic Palace, especially in the last twenty years. But, too many of the Cardinals look down their noses at converts, for him to be elected. Anyway, it might be seen as a precursor of the imminent End of Days if he was."

"In what way?"

"The conservative doctrine is that, at the Second Coming, all the Jews will finally recognise Jesus as the Messiah even though they didn't the first time round. They will therefore be saved, as will the Catholics. But the other so-called Christian sects will be cast down to eternal damnation for the heresy of abandoning the One True Church."

"So, if a Jewish convert to Catholicism became Pope,

it would presage the Second Coming?"

"Exactly. And no-one wants to start another apocalyptic panic. Things were bad enough in the run-up to 2000!"

"Okay, four bets then. Here goes."

I spent the next five minutes minting some of our traceable money and using it to place the four bets on the deadbet website. When I was finished I let go of the mouse, sat back in the chair and looked at Costanza.

"Now we wait."

"Yes. Meanwhile, why don't you go back to your hotel, freshen up and meet me and Sandro in Via Margutta at 9 o'clock this evening. There's a vegetarian restaurant there that I think you'll love."

"Sounds good to me. How do I get out?" I started to get out of the chair.

"Follow me, I'll get you back out to the Cortile. If we ask Tomaso on the way past, he can arrange a car to take you back to the Hassler." She stood up and led me to the door.

The journey back to the lift seemed much shorter than it had in the other direction. We stood as it slowly went back up to ground level and this time the panel's hiss didn't make me jump. We retraced our steps through the passage, out into the panelled room and back to the nondescript door. Before she opened the door, she stopped and turned to me.

"Next time you come here, make sure you have your pass with you. It's got an encrypted RFID tag built into it that activates the lock on this door."

"I wondered why it had been left unlocked when we got here."

"It wasn't, it unlocked automatically once I was closer than 2 metres. Not great security, but it keeps out the nosey and doesn't attract unwarranted attention. Any casual observer would assume, like you, that the door had been left unlocked. Unlocked doors obviously aren't protecting anything so why would anyone bother trying it? If they do it happens to be locked." She smiled.

"The corollary to my favourite aphorism: 95% of the effectiveness of security is achieved by the impression of security." I said.

Costanza turned back to the door, grasped the brass handle and pulled the door towards her. After spending the last two hours in an air-conditioned room, the sudden onslaught of the dry afternoon heat hit me in the face like a battering ram. But as I walked through the door into the courtyard I was enveloped and felt bathed in soothing warmth. One of the reasons that I always felt so comfortable here in Rome was the dry heat. Venice had always been too humid, the heat there was sticky and uncomfortable. The same was true almost everywhere hot that I had ever been. The only other place I had ever felt comforted by baking heat had been at Giza in Egypt. Inside the pyramid had been unbearably hot, sticky and uncomfortable, not to mention cramped, smelly and full of other sweaty tourists (as I said, smelly!). I remember walking out of the pyramid into the mid-summer noonday sun of the Egyptian desert and being relieved to have a chance to cool down and dry off.

We kissed goodbye, left cheek, right cheek, left cheek.

"Ciao," I said "Via Margutta at 9 o'clock." I strode towards the waiting black Alfa, got into the back and turned to wave as the driver immediately accelerated away.

Leeds Castle, Kent

Security was tight at Leeds castle. Security was often tight at Leeds castle. Many significant events had been staged here. Events of global importance. Peace conferences, summits, inter-governmental negotiations. Robert had attended a few of them. He worried that no-one seemed to consider the impact on the local police force. While the county of Kent was world-famous as the garden of England, it was also the nearest part of the UK to the mainland of Europe. Twenty five miles of water (or underground rail-link) separated the main entry and exit ports of England and France. Illegal immigrants were a significant problem. Being on the doorstep of the London crime scene didn't help. But the people of Kent weren't made of money – or at least not enough to support the strength of Policing that was really needed. So yet another high-profile event at Leeds Castle added significantly to the workload for Robert and his busy colleagues from nearby Maidstone. Especially as this summit had been arranged at short notice, and no one had thought to give a heads-up to the Chief Constable, let alone any of his staff.

Robert sat in the mobile control van, parked on Penfold Hill, overlooking the estate. He gazed at the array of screens in front of him. Luckily he was one of the younger members of the force, and wasn't afraid of all this technology. Too many of the older officers wanted to have nothing to do with computers, video cameras and digital links. As a result many of these jobs were being taken by 'civilians', which just alienated the officers even more. But Robert rather enjoyed it. Secretly, he often imagined himself as Capcom at mission control in Houston, talking with Neil Armstrong on the moon or calming the apparently stricken astronauts of Apollo 13. Today was especially exciting. There was a no-fly zone imposed over a large area around the castle and indeed much of the heart of the county. The only things in the air below 2,500 metres were the Police helicopter and the UN Chinook that was ferrying VIPs from Heathrow airport. Of course the media had their own helicopters, flying less than 2 metres above the exclusion zone. But they wouldn't get to see much. Robert, on the other hand, had a fantastic view. The nose camera of Kent Police Force's main surveillance helicopter was being beamed straight into his van. He leant back in his chair, swivelled to watch the monitor to his left, and drew in his breath as the helicopter took off and he saw the ground falling away beneath. He couldn't afford fancy holidays, most summers were spent in a caravan on the South Downs, but he had flown once – a standby special to the Costa Brava with his wife before they had become the proud parents of a noisy, hungry, expensive, four-legged addition to the family. He had loved the experience and hoped to do it again sometime. He had applied to work with the airborne police squad but hadn't been accepted – his wife said it was because his face didn't fit in. Still, on days like this, he had a perfect view from the helicopter, which was almost as good as being there. As he watched, the rolling countryside flashed by on the screen. Fields of rape seed, fields of cereals, and the occasional field with a red sheen caused by wild poppies. Too few trees he always thought, but then he had grown up in Surrey, a county that, while only a few miles away, was so different from Kent it might just as well have been a separate country. Surrey consisted of woods and forests, interspersed with houses. Or at least it had been when Robert was small. His memories were of wisps of smoke rising from the chimneys of unseen houses hidden behind tree-lined winding lanes, green arches of leaves filtering the summer sunlight and creating dappled shadows on the ground. Now in Surrey, like everywhere else, successive governments had encouraged developers to destroy the environment, building ever more 'choice communities' of executive homes, with four bedrooms each too small to swing even a kitten and a postage stamp sized square of poorly laid turf laughingly called a garden. Kent had suffered too, but, luckily, much of the county, cleared of trees in ancient times, was still productive agricultural land and local councils had managed to fend off attempts to reclassify it for residential purposes.

Robert thought of archetypal country lanes as he watched the images from the helicopter slow down. Leeds Castle itself hove into view. No wonder the owner always claimed it was the loveliest castle in the world. The aerial view of this magnificent piece of English history, fortifications crisply defined in the bright summer sunlight while the moat twinkled like a magical defence, was quite breathtaking. Kings and Queens, Knights and Ladies had all relied on these defences in the past. Now presidents and prime ministers, patriarchs and potentates came here to talk in private – happy that these ancient defences were still as effective today. But, even so, they needed the help of Robert and the rest of the Force to ensure that those defences would go unchallenged. The helicopter would soon start flying around the perimeter of the massive grounds, looking out for intruders or anything out of place. He made sure the recording equipment was working correctly, adjusted the gain slightly on the monitor and returned his attention to the rest of the screens. Apparently indecipherable messages scrolled up on one side as the feed from the RAF ground radar stations came in, ready to alert him if the air-space was compromised. He could hear the various units on the ground checking in with each other, and occasionally with him, as they patrolled surrounding roads or monitored gateways and drives. So far nothing untoward had been reported and he felt sure it would stay that way. He looked at his watch. It was lunchtime. He was hungry. He had forgotten to bring any sandwiches with him. He was called this morning and told to start his shift two hours early and had completely forgotten about lunch when he heard that there was another 'security event' at the Castle. All he had was a packet of mints that had been left in the van by a previous driver. Better than nothing. Maybe.

Inside the Castle, the morning's introductory session had finished and everyone was enjoying a light lunch in the Banqueting Hall. The Queen had opened the Salaam-Shalom peace summit, speaking about the importance for religious leaders to take the initiative in peace. The Pope's Envoy had expressed His Holiness' concerns and hopes for a peaceful solution to the situation in the Holy Land. After lunch it would be the turn of Rabbi Cohen from Israel and then the Palestinian Imam Ben-Hassan. Once the political niceties were out of the way the real discussions could begin. Her Majesty would be leaving before the evening reception, but everyone else was here for the next two days.

Chaim Cohen was looking at the food on display before him with trepidation and longing. There were separate tables for kosher, halal, vegetarian and omnivorous dishes. For years now, doctors had been telling him to watch what he ate. He was supposed to be on the verge of a heart attack at any time and wasn't allowed to eat unhealthily at home. But he was here on his own this time and was going to indulge. Even so, he felt guilty as he helped himself to more vol-au-vents and the potato salad. What would Rachel say if she could see him? 'Chaimy, you'll be the death of me, making me sick

71

with worry that you'll kill yourself like that'. She could always get her own way by making him laugh. As he deliberated on what else to add to his plate he felt someone come and stand beside him. He turned and looked into the eyes of a beautiful blonde waitress in a black uniform with an impeccably starched white pinafore. She was holding a silver tray with a single glass of white wine. She smiled at the rabbi and he was reminded of his Rachel, over forty years ago when they first met as she served him a glass of wine at her father's funeral. She too had been a beautiful blonde dressed in a black dress. She still was a beautiful blonde forty years on. This waitress, young enough to be his granddaughter, brought a tear to his eyes. He smiled back and took the glass.

"Thank you" he said.

She walked away with her empty tray. He thought of Rachel again and decided that maybe he wouldn't eat the things of which she would disapprove – he wouldn't want to be taken from her any sooner than God had planned.

New York, USA

A tall gray-haired man stepped out of the lift and walked purposefully along the plushly carpeted corridor. His dark Armani suit was impeccably cut with no misplaced creases. He had clearly not travelled here by subway. His leather briefcase was well buffed, and the brass clasps shone like gold. He reached a door with a small brass plaque, took a key from his jacket pocket, unlocked and opened the door. Pocketing the key once again, he entered and gently closed the door behind him. The room was neat and tidy; two desks, mahogany inlaid with leather; a filing cabinet, also mahogany; two pictures on the wall, portraits of stern looking men in equally impeccable business suits, had brass lights carefully positioned above them – unnecessary at the moment as the sunlight was streaming through the large picture windows that looked out over Fifth Avenue far below. Behind one of the desks was a large leather chair, of the type that would be called Executive Deluxe in any office furniture catalogue. He sat down in the chair, carefully putting his briefcase on the desk in front of him. The scene could easily have been playing out anytime in the last 100 years, but for two items on the desk. A very modern telephone, with large display and multiple buttons for its various indispensable functions; and a flat screen monitor with a keyboard and mouse in front of it. Neither the keyboard nor the mouse had any visible connections. He reached down, having taken another smaller key from an inside pocket, and unlocked the drawer in the pedestal to his right. Sliding the drawer open he pressed a button and the screen in front of him lit up. Gliding the drawer closed again he watched the screen intently. After a while when the hieroglyphs and cryptic messages had ceased he was rewarded with a screen showing the same portrait as the picture on the wall behind him. Taking hold of the mouse, he opened his email and waited while the list of new mails was refreshed. Scanning the senders' names he selected a message that had arrived early this morning. As he read it he smiled and immediately picked up the phone handset. Dialling a number from memory he sat back in his chair to wait for the call to be answered.

"Good morning, Dawes residence."

"Good morning. It's Minister Rogers here. I'd like to speak to the Senator." His Texan drawl was in deep contrast to the clipped tones of Senator Dawes' butler which always made him wince.

"I will just see if he's available sir. Please hold the line."

You mean, see if he has bothered to wake up yet, Rogers thought. This Senator was the laziest person he had every met. Definitely not his idea of a hard-working, god-fearing representative of the people. But at the moment he served a very necessary purpose. Without funds the Campaign for the Denunciation of the Antichrist would not have made any progress. But thanks to the Senator and his friends, they could get on with their mission to pursue God's work.

"He will be with you in just a moment Minister. He's finishing a meeting."

"Thank you," he sighed, "an all-night meeting with his pillow most likely," he muttered to himself.

While waiting for the Senator to get up, he looked at his watch, took a pen from his inside pocket, removed the cap and wrote the time on the small notepad on the left of his desk. Then he added 6 hours to the time and wrote Rome next to the result. He had originally had grave reservations about the team that had been sent to Rome. He had always mistrusted blondes and was concerned that she was sending his foot-soldiers into the Antichrist's territory, like Daniel into the lion's den. Yet look how that had worked out. With God on your side even the enemy's lair was nothing to fear. What's more they already seemed to have made astounding progress. His thoughts were interrupted by a click on the phone.

"Good morning Minister Rogers, or can I call you Roy?" The same joke every time.

"Good morning Senator. I was just calling to inform you that we have had some good news from our friends in Rome. This afternoon they have made some progress and believe that they may be able to obtain the package within a few days."

"This afternoon? But it's not even ten yet."

"Indeed Senator, but it is already mid-afternoon in Rome."

"Of course. Well that's great news there Roy."

"Ray."

"Yeah. Well keep me informed."

"When they do manage to get the package they will need some help bringing it back here. Can you arrange for it to be carried in the diplomatic bag?"

"Of course. When you're ready, call me and I'll get our people at the embassy over there to play ball. Goodbye." He hung up.

"Good... Oh. Goodbye then. Nice to have spoken to you." He had noticed lately that same hint of sarcasm, tinged with irritation, entering his voice whenever he was forced to talk with the Senator.

Pleased with the swift progress his people had made in Rome, but angry with the Senator's offhand treatment of him, he was now unsettled. Maybe he should have one of his pills. He just knew that his ulcer would be playing up again by the end of the day. Especially if he had to talk to Dawes again. Once a day was more than anyone could stand, even a saint. Still, once they had retrieved the manuscript, the Senator would become dispensable.

The manuscript, however, would not be dispensable. Quite the opposite. Mere rumour for hundreds of years, it had been kept under lock and key away from prying eyes. Even the Campaign had only become convinced of its existence in the last twenty years. As recently as three months ago there had been no concrete evidence that it was anything more than a fanciful rumour, and no idea where it could possibly be, if it really did exist. But that had changed with the discovery of the diary of a 16th century Austrian countess that mentioned the manuscript and even described it. Her diary told how the manuscript had been brought to Europe from Jerusalem during the Crusades and had eventually come into the possession of her cousin, a monk called Albustensis. He had vowed to keep it safe and stop it falling into the hands of the enemies of Christ. As a result of the revelations in this diary, the manuscript had now become known as the Codex Albustensis and was a hot topic in many internet conspiracy chat rooms. According to general consensus, the manuscript dated back to the 1st century AD. It described a scandal involving St. Paul. At the time Paul was in conflict with the other disciples in Jerusalem over his plans to take the good news of the Messiah to non-Jews. James, head of the church at the time, was adamant that Jesus had been preaching salvation for the sole benefit of God's chosen race, the Jews. Peter, still in Jerusalem, was quite vociferous in his disagreement with Paul. In the historically accepted version of events, Paul won the argument, took the message to the Greek and Roman world and effectively created the Universal Church which, ironically, Peter then embraced to become head and first Pope when he too arrived in Rome. However, there is much controversy still raging about that argument between Peter, James and Paul. The Codex

Albustensis allegedly described the events at a meeting between them where Paul managed to blackmail the other two into supporting his position. No-one knows exactly what he did to blackmail them although conspiracy theorists have had a field day speculating, with suggestions ranging from the obscene to the ridiculous. Many people had been keen to read the document and find out what happened that day, not least Minister Rogers and the rest of the leadership of The Campaign for the Denunciation of the Antichrist, who were convinced that discovery and publication of the manuscript would lead to the destruction of the power of the Church of Rome with both its founding fathers, Saints Peter and Paul tarnished beyond recovery. This would leave the way open for fundamentalists such as The Campaign to establish a much more rigid and hard-line church and to move against other cults and religions.

It was recently that their luck had seemed to change. Their research tracked down the last movements of the monk Albustensis who had gone into permanent retreat in a remote, desolate church in the Swiss Alps where he had eventually died. They had dispatched people to the church. It was still in use, although only for one Mass a week from a peripatetic priest based in a parish some twenty miles away. They had taken the opportunity to search through the church itself, and even raided the tomb of Albustensis who had been buried beneath the floor of a side chapel. But to no avail. Meanwhile they had discovered that immediately prior to going to Switzerland he had been summoned to the Vatican by Pope Gregory XIII. It was then, they believed, that he had passed the manuscript that now bore his name to the Pope and hence into the Vatican secret archives. Gregory's subsequent rabid anti-Jewish stance was, they were sure, driven by what he had read in the manuscript.

The manuscript must still be in the secret archives to this day.

At that point in their research the Campaign felt they had reached an impenetrable barrier. The secret archives of the Vatican had remained inviolate for nearly 2 millennia. They were unlikely to be able to find and remove the manuscript from such a well guarded location. Like everyone else outside the Curia they didn't even know the archives' location. Most people assumed that they were in the Vatican. Visitors were shown around parts of the Library and certain rooms were designated as the repository of the secret archives. Apparent catalogues of the secret archives were available for perusal on the Vatican website, while facsimiles of various of the most notable contents were even on sale in the Vatican Library gift shop. But despite the size of the publicly announced 'secret archives' there were still many items that were rumoured or even known to exist in the Vatican's collection that didn't appear on any official catalogue or website. There must be a part of the archive that was still secret. The Campaign had been unable to infiltrate the Library's staff and the best they had managed to do was keep the buildings under surveillance to try and identify theologians or scholars, who may be visiting the archives, to see where they went. For some time this had achieved nothing, but a few hours earlier today they had seen a woman who they suspected of having something to do with the Library being driven into the Vatican in a police car. She had been accompanied by a man who they had subsequently quickly identified as a high-tech security consultant from England. They had a good feeling that these people were somehow relevant, so they had decided to keep tabs on both of them for the next few days to see what they did and where else they went. If their hunch was right they could use one or other of these people as leverage to get into the Library and obtain the Codex Albustensis. Their email to Minister Rogers had consisted of the codephrase "Prepare for Thanksgiving, we have sighted a turkey."

Rome

After showering and changing into a cool cotton shirt and linen suit, I strolled out of the Hotel and over the road to the top of the Spanish Steps. It was early evening and lights were coming on across Rome as the sun finally decided to give up for the day. The air was filled with the almost uniquely Italian cacophony of cutlery clattering on china, glasses clinking, and all the generations chattering away as they sit down to an evening meal. Here above the city I was insulated from the background sound of TV that otherwise permeates most residential areas of Rome. Even after dark, the air was so warm that no-one could bear to keep their windows closed, air conditioning still being a luxury ill afforded by most ordinary Romans. The setting sun, glinting off the domes of the myriad churches sprinkled throughout the city, also caught the spines of the ubiquitous gaggle of aerials plastered over the highest point of every visible roof. Behind me, the chirruping of the crickets in the gardens reaching a crescendo; below, the persistent sound of splashing water from that famous fountain. Running water is one of the most characteristic sounds in Rome. Wherever you are there is always a fountain nearby – yet even the ornamental fountains that grace almost every piazza or courtyard, usually overly ornate and ridiculously monumental in stature, are outnumbered by the constantly running drinking fountains that keep residents and visitors alike cool and hydrated, often emptying into stone troughs that were originally Roman sarcophagi.

Here, in one of the busiest parts of Rome, voices coming from the nearby exclusive restaurants brought me snippets of conversation in almost every language under the sun. The famous steps themselves were carpeted with people; couples, young and old, sitting together, talking and laughing, holding one another; students, in groups, discussing the state of the world, unshakeably certain of their own particular solutions to all the big issues; tourists, families, strolling up and down, around the fountain, looking into the tea rooms or wandering off to window shop in Rome's most chic streets; young men arguing about the relative merits of Lazio, Roma and FC Milan, while their girlfriends rearrange their skirts and hair to look just right for the benefit of anyone who happens to be looking.

I picked my way down the steps, between the patchwork quilt of flowers and people who littered it. At the bottom I slowly wandered across Piazza da Spagna and headed towards Via Margutta where I ambled along glancing into the antique shops and glamorous galleries.

A gentle tap on my shoulder turned me around to find Sandro and Costanza standing there smiling. After the obligatory triple kisses, Costanza linked her arms with my right and Sandro's left, and the three of us walked together down the street towards the restaurant.

Costanza had booked a table and we spent a very pleasant evening, Sandro and I drinking Frascati, Costanza sticking to mineral water for the sake of the new life growing inside her; eating a variety of vegetarian gourmet dishes and remembering days spent in London, Venice and Florence. It was strange how almost all our recollections of days gone by revolved around eating and drinking.

"Do you remember that restaurant in Venice, right near the Ghetto. They made the best pizzas and we'd go there on Friday nights to start the weekend. What was it called?" asked Sandro.

"Vesuvio." Costanza and I both chorused simultaneously.

"There were two of your colleagues who came along sometimes. A girl…"

"Dawn" said Costanza.

"Oh that's right. There was a man too."

"Tim." I answered.

"Do you ever see either of them?"

"No." I said. "Dawn married her fiancé and moved to Paris. I think she's working for a bank there."

"And Tim?"

"Don't see him at all." I shook my head. "Wouldn't want to anyway. It's because of Tim that the project ran late and we all lost our bonuses. He was the worst manager I have ever had the misfortune to work for. But I don't think he's a manager any more. I think he's a consultant. Makes me feel sorry for his poor unsuspecting clients."

Costanza was nodding.

"Tim was a disaster from the outset." She said. "But let's not talk about him any more. Have you tried these grilled zucchini? They're delicious."

One or two courses later we had moved back in our memories to Florence and my apartment on Piazza di Signoria. It was perfectly sited at the heart of the city and had been equipped with a superb espresso machine. Many an evening's passagiata had finished with a coffee in my lounge, gazing out of the window over the square, watching the world go by.

"We went to the Uffizi one weekend. The café opens out onto the roof of the Loggia and we could see your windows through the balustrade. It made us realise that the coffee wasn't as good as yours." As Costanza spoke, Sandro was looking thoughtful.

"I'm normally too lazy to make espresso first thing in the morning, but that machine was terrific. I'd always find time to have my morning fix before I had to leave. Then I'd walk over the bridge, pick up some focaccia at that little bakery and wander along to the office." I still remembered that focaccia, I'd never found anywhere that made tastier bread.

"You never did tell me what you guys were doing there. All top secret." said Sandro.

"Indeed it was" said Costanza.

"And still is." I added.

"If we told you…" she started.

"…we'd have to kill you!" I finished with a serious look at Sandro.

I could see that Costanza was having trouble keeping a straight face. Originally, we hadn't been able to tell Sandro what we were doing in Florence because we had signed a Non-Disclosure Agreement that forbade us even admitting that we were doing any work at all for the bank. For a while we had been suspicious of our paymasters and even got to the point of believing them to be criminals, laundering drug money through an apparently legitimate bank. But we weren't sure that they even had the intelligence to set up such an operation. Eventually it became clear that they really were as dull as they looked, yet another small financial institution run by bean-counters. The NDAs were in place to protect them from prying eyes and the tax authorities (who are treated with disdain by all Italians as a matter of course). Now, those NDAs had expired, but it still amused Costanza to keep the secret from Sandro. The work we had been doing may have been secret, but it was far from exciting. Maintaining the secret and letting Sandro's imagination try to fathom out our work was much more exciting for her.

"Sorry, still can't tell you," said Costanza, "but don't forget, the work in Florence paid for our villa, so don't knock it!"

"Even so, I don't like all this secrecy" said Sandro.

"It's what we do" laughed Costanza "but just because it's secret doesn't make it exciting, or even interesting enough to talk about to you …"

"…or dangerous?" asked Sandro.

"Or dangerous. I promise you. Especially now." She glanced down towards the, as yet invisible, growing life in her womb.

"So, Peter," Sandro looked at me, "you came to Rome for a holiday and Costanza has roped you into doing some work for her?"

I looked at Costanza, not sure how much she had told Sandro.

"You know me, I find it difficult to turn down a challenge even on holiday."

"A challenge?" asked Sandro.

"Costanza wanted my help with a little technical problem. I think it's sorted now, so…"

"Back to your holiday?"

"Well, I'm not really here on holiday. I was asked to come by someone I once worked for. I'm not sure why as I haven't seen him yet."

"I thought you were here on holiday," said Costanza "that's certainly the impression I got from your email."

"I was told to let people think I was here on holiday, meet up with old friends that sort of thing, while waiting for instructions."

"And you just did it without question?" Sandro looked incredulous.

"Yeah, well. It's a very trustworthy client. Goes back a long way." I glanced at Costanza who had the beginnings of a knowing look slowly appearing on her face.

"Anyway, let's stop talking about work. What about you two? Have you decided how to decorate the nursery yet?"

Sandro immediately brightened up and the frown that had been deepening on his face over the last five minutes miraculously disappeared. For the rest of the meal we talked about the merits of primary colours over pastels, animal motifs versus numbers or letters, and the finer points of cots.

Costanza was good-humouredly battering Sandro for his inability to remember an apparently beautiful wooden cot she had seen in Venice.

"I think it was in the shop with the wooden life-size motorbike in the window" I whispered to Sandro.

"Ah yes!" now he remembered the shop Sandro could feign a memory of the cot that had obviously made such an impression on his beloved.

While Sandro defended himself, I felt a gentle vibration in my pocket. I reached in and retrieved my phone. I had set up my news service to send me text alerts whenever a significant story broke. I flipped it open, pressed the menu button to select messages and scrolled through the short item. Quietly I closed the phone and put it back in my pocket.

"I just got a news alert," I said, trying to keep my voice steady, "apparently Rabbi Cohen has died of a heart attack."

Costanza stopped beating her husband and looked at me in shock.

"So there should be a trace waiting...", she put her hand to her mouth.

"No, we didn't include him." I shook my head.

Sandro was now looking worried.

"What are you two talking about? What has some Rabbi got to do with you?"

"I can't tell you now. Look, Sandro will you settle the bill. Peter and I need to go to my office right now. Thanks. I love you." She was already rising from her chair as she spoke. She kissed Sandro on the cheek, turned and glided across the room. I was only a little way behind her as she made her way down the stairs and out into the street.

I have never seen Costanza run, but she was walking very fast now, across Via Margutta and along the main road looking for a taxi. Eventually we found one parked between Santa Maria's two churches in Piazza del Popolo. It would only be a short journey to get back across the river to the Vatican.

Vatican City

For the second time that day I found myself being led through corridors and passages and going down in the surprising lift. By some good chance, or unconscious precognition, I had put the red pass I had been given earlier in the pocket of my suit, so we quickly got unhindered into Costanza's office. She switched on the TV on the wall and flicked through the various news channels until she found one that was reporting from Jerusalem.

As we listened, my eyes flicked to the list of names still visible on the whiteboard. Only hours before we had, calmly, been discussing these people as possible targets of an assassin. Now one of them was already dead, how long till another?

"I think you need to talk to other agencies. There's two more significant names on the list who we didn't place bets against and neither of them is in your jurisdiction."

"Maybe you're right," she said, walking over to her desk and picking up the phone.

I carried on watching the TV reporter in Jerusalem interviewing senior members of the Knesset, while out of the corner of my eye I could see Costanza having an animated discussion on the phone. After a few minutes she slammed down the phone and walked over to me. I was somewhat taken aback by this uncharacteristic display of aggression and it obviously showed on my face.

"Well!" she started "you'd have slammed the phone down too. In fact you'd have used lots of rude words first, if I know you." She almost grinned.

"I take it they were less than helpful?"

"Helpful!? They weren't even interested. They said that the Rabbi's death was no surprise to anyone as he had a history of heart problems. It was just a question of time.

They aren't going to look at deadbet.net, let alone take any additional precautions to protect the president. And, of course, they aren't in the least bit interested in passing any warnings on to Yasser Arafat, in fact they said that if he had a heart attack it would be a very timely solution to their problems in the Middle East. Their problems indeed!"

"Actually, while you were on the phone, they were saying on the TV report that no-one was surprised by Cohen's heart attack. They seemed to think that he had been hanging on to life by the thinnest of threads for a while now. Apparently he was at a peace summit in England. They think he may have over-indulged in rich food. No-one suspects foul play."

"Apart from us."

"Well? It could be co-incidence. Or that people who were expecting him to drop dead soon were just using deadbet as a rather tasteless way to benefit. If he was likely to have a coronary any day, then it would be easy to make regular bets that he would die, and sooner or later it would happen. Meanwhile other people have been attracted to the site and place bets on him because he's running near the top of the list, building up the potential winnings. If, like us, they didn't know his history of heart problems, then they wouldn't realise that they were betting against someone who was backing a virtual certainty. All the while making it even more attractive to bet on his heart attack."

"So you don't think that these deaths have got anything to do with deadbet.net. We've been following the wrong leads?" Costanza looked forlorn.

"I didn't say that. Even if the Rabbi's death is coincidence, the others seem to be linked."

"So what do we do now? Our trace won't do anything until the money is collected, which won't happen until one of our targets has been killed. Any bright ideas?" she asked.

"Hmm. I'll work on it" I mused.

"Did you say he was at the peace summit in England?"

"Yes. At Leeds Castle, with the Queen and a Palestinian Imam"

"And a Papal Envoy. I'd forgotten about that. There was some discussion about it here the other day. I have the number of the SIS agent in charge, in case we needed to contact them about his security. I'll try and talk to them, see if they're more interested than the Americans."

Cheltenham

Even though it was late in the evening, Katie Cannon was at GCHQ when the call from the Vatican was routed through to the office where she was working. She never seemed to get home before midnight these days. Coming down here to Cheltenham hadn't helped, as she still had a two hour journey home to look forward to. But the people here worked ridiculous hours, and always had their brightest ideas, or biggest panics, just when she was hoping to leave. Standing in the doughnut shaped building, looking out of the window into the inner garden she was surprised to see people sitting there, talking, reading, even typing into laptops at this late hour. At least she wasn't the only one still working. There was something about the shape of this building that made it feel like a cocoon, so the cryptographers who worked here felt safe and enveloped - allowing them the freedom of expression that had in the past often led to groundbreaking results.

Katie was surprised to get a call this late from the Vatican. She had rarely had any dealings with the world's most secretive secret service. She knew little about them except that they had very different 'rules of engagement' from every other country's intelligence agencies – their motivation was neither political nor economic, and they didn't interact with the rest of the intelligence community unless they absolutely had to. As agent in charge of the security for the peace summit she had expected an advance call about the arrangements for the Papal Envoy, but now it was almost over a call seemed somewhat redundant. Although she had a gift for languages and was fluent in Japanese, German and Arabic, Katie had never bothered to even try and learn Italian. She was not interested in art, music, architecture, ancient history or food and had thus never understood the attraction of Italy to the English middle class. Having been to a modern Grammar school she had never been forced to study classics and so did not even have any Latin to fall back on. While she was waiting for the call to be put through she crossed her fingers and hoped that the Italians would be able to speak English. At last a rather refined woman's voice, sounding a little fed up, came out of the speakerphone.

"Hello? Is there someone there?" Costanza's voice resounded around the small office.

"Yes. My name is Katherine Cannon. And you are?".

"Ms. Cannon. Hello. May I call you Katherine? My name is Costanza. I'm pleased to talk to you at last. You're difficult to find this evening, I hope I haven't disturbed you at home."

"Yes, you can call me Katherine. And no, I'm not at home. Unfortunately. But I am away from my usual office so they had a bit of a job to find me here. Mobile phones aren't allowed at this site so they needed to find the right room to connect you with. But enough of that. What can I do for you Costanza?"

"We heard about Rabbi Cohen's death and I wanted to get some details from you."

"He had a heart attack. He was not a well man, apparently, and was under strict doctor's orders to be careful what he ate. He clearly wasn't careful enough. But I don't see how the Rabbi's heart attack raises any concerns over the security of your Envoy."

"We have some information that suggests that the Rabbi's heart attack was not caused by his overindulgence but rather induced."

"Induced? By whom?" asked Katie walking away from the window against which she had been leaning and sitting down at the chair in front of the phone.

"We don't know. We've seen three of our own senior

91

clergy die over the last five weeks of unexpected heart attacks. We've been trying to find the link."

"Well this was hardly an unexpected heart attack."

"I know. But there is a link between all four deaths. They're all on a list we have."

"A list?" Katie pressed a blue button on the phone; a small red light started to flash next to a miniature display that started counting up from 00000. "From where? Who?"

"I can't tell you at the moment, especially not on an open line like this. You never know who's listening." Katie knew from her tone that Costanza was grinning. "But it's a dead bet."

Katie raised an eyebrow. Although this Costanza's English was very good, almost fluent, it was idioms that let her down. Had she meant 'dead cert'? Should Katie correct her? She decided against it.

"There's no more I can tell you. The Rabbi had a heart attack in the afternoon about two hours after lunch. They believe he had had a good lunch. Or, as it turned out for him, a rather bad lunch. The doctors who examined him said it was a classic case of arrhythmia leading to ventricular fibrillation. Thankfully for him it was all over very quickly. The rest of the summit has been cancelled and your guy is going home in the morning."

"You said he died two hours after lunch?"

"Yes."

'Were there any unusual events at lunch? Security breaches?"

"No. Nothing. The Castle catering staff served lunch. Waited for the delegates to finish eating and cleared it away again."

"All the usual staff?"

"Yes. We had checked that there were no new faces,

sudden no-shows or replacements."

"Okay. If anything strange turns up will you let us know please?"

"If it seems relevant. About this list though, are there more names on it?"

"Yes. But no-one British, so you don't need to worry."

"Are they all religious leaders?"

"No. Although they're all leaders of one sort or another. And at least one of them thinks he's god! I better go now. Please call me if anything turns up. Goodbye."

"Goodbye!" said Katie as the speaker clicked. She pressed the blue button again and the red light stopped flashing.

"The only strange thing about this Rabbi's death has been your phone call, my dear." she thought aloud.

Rising from the chair she walked back to the window. She didn't really think it was worth taking this Italian bimbo seriously, but she did start to wonder whether there was any significance in the disappearance this afternoon of one of the catering staff at the Castle. Everyone else thought she had probably just skived off to enjoy some sunshine. Katie had ignored it because the doctors had assured her that Rabbi Cohen had died of very natural causes so there was no reason to be suspicious of a lazy waitress. She gazed out of the window.

"No," she decided. "just because they're paranoid, I don't have to get caught up in it."

She'd had enough for one evening. She picked up her handbag from the desk, walked to the doorway and out of the room, pulling the door closed behind her. As she made her way around the inner circumference of the doughnut towards the stairs, automatic sensors switched off the lights in the vacated office and the empty segments of the corridor. From outside the building a patch of darkness appeared to be spreading around the centre of the building.

New York, USA

Adam Sawicki was listening so intently on his headphones that he failed to notice Laurie Qureishi as she walked into the room and stood watching the flickering lights on his equipment. After a few seconds she shuffled her feet, and then gave a little dry cough into her hand. He was still oblivious of her. Tired of waiting and giving up on subtlety she stepped closer and tapped him on the shoulder. He reacted as if she had given him a 1000 volt jolt. Pulling the headset off he spun round and leapt to his feet.

"Oh, it's you." He said, sounding more disappointed than surprised.

"Why? You were expecting someone else?"

"No. But I'd lost track of the time out there in the real world. I've been listening to everything these guys are saying in the hope that we can nail them. But they're being very careful. Everything is 'case' or 'client' or 'victim', although they have been talking about dealing with the agency and there's been a lot of criticism of the government. Still, it's all too vague to reel them in yet. I hope you have better luck."

"Yeah. Well, there are advantages to the evening shift" she nodded.

"No dozing allowed you know" he grinned.

"No, I meant that as they get more tired they're likely to become careless and let something slip. They don't actually know we're listening to them, some of them think they're being paranoid and eventually one will blurt something out that will finger them."

"So far they've been very good at keeping to their cover story. If I didn't know better I'd almost believe they were social workers."

"Yeah and pigs will fly. Look an airborne hog's going past the window right now." She returned his grin.

"See you tomorrow morning." He picked up his jacket and draped it over his left shoulder.

"Don't be late" she called after him as he walked out of the door.

Laurie really did prefer to work the evening shift. That way she had an excuse for having no social life. She didn't want to admit, perhaps not even to herself, that she was more interested in furthering her career. She could blame pressure of work, especially when her mom nagged her about settling down and supplying the desperately awaited grandchildren.

"Sorry mom, I have no time to even meet a nice man, let alone settle down with one. I'm working all day every day and most evenings too" she had told her mom only this morning.

"But what is it that you have to do every evening? It isn't right that they make you work so hard. I bet your boss isn't working the same hours as you is he?"

"No mom. But if I work hard now I'll get to be the boss and then I can spend less time working." Even as she said it she knew it sounded ridiculous.

"Why not spend less time working now and don't worry about bossing people about?"

"You don't understand mom. What's the point in working unless you want to become the boss?"

As usual they had had to agree to differ. And as usual her mom had the last word.

"By the way are you coming over on Thursday. It's your uncle Mo's birthday and he wants to see you. The way things are going it'll be his last, the cancer's getting worse you know. So no excuses this time. See you Thursday. Bye darling" and so saying she had hung up.

Laurie hoped that this surveillance operation would be over by Thursday. If not she'd have to find a way to get out of it that evening. Maybe Adam would swap for a day? She couldn't not see Uncle Mo on his birthday if the cancer really was that bad.

She picked up the headset and carefully positioned it so she could hear without catching it on her earrings or messing up her thick dark hair which, as usual, was beautiful.

Adam was right, these people were obviously well trained to avoid mentioning any details in their conversation. It sounded normal, but then again it sounded too normal which was usually a sign of the exact opposite. After years of covert operations listening to all strata of American society, the NSA had come to recognise that anyone with nothing to hide usually didn't. Anyone being so careful about their conversation must be up to no good. There was a time when such people would have been accused of being commies, subversives or even anarchists. Now they were more likely to be labelled activists, fundamentalists, insurgents or terrorists.

It had struck her as ironic that she should be teamed with Adam for this operation. A Moslem and a Jew trying to bring to justice a group of Christian fundamentalists. What a sublime reversal of the last few hundred years. But even more ironic was the fact that these fundamentalists were responsible for killing other Christians not Jews or Moslems. Archbishop O'Leary had become extremely unpopular, even deserving of some sort of punishment, but it was still hardly keeping to the Christian ethic to kill him. At first her superiors had suspected the CIA of being up to their old tricks. Some twenty five years on from the Church Committee investigation into illegal CIA operations and President Carter's ruthless overhaul, the CIA had finally become less paranoid of their political masters and more likely to re-engage in black ops. The suspicious heart attack of

Cardinal Figueras had all the hallmarks of CIA poisoning, but the NSA couldn't get involved in the Brazilian investigation which had been only cursory and had completely bought into the heart attack explanation. The Brazilian government were fearful of the political backlash if it appeared to be anything other than natural causes. The CIA had been known to provide mercenaries for other governments in the past – plausible deniability being the watchword. Anyone caught would be labelled a rogue agent at best, but most likely a double agent. Without evidence the CIA could get away with murder. Literally.

But then, when O'Leary died in Boston, the NSA was able to take control of the investigation. While the coroner and police department had fronted the case and publicly announced that the Archbishop had died of a heart attack while driving, behind the scenes the FBI forensic team had acted quickly enough to gather what little evidence remained that cardiac arrest was induced by a foreign substance in the blood stream. Luckily no-one had insisted on an open-casket for the funeral, because there was little left intact after the comprehensive autopsy and dissection of most of the archbishop's vital organs. Laurie's boss had been watching this investigation with great interest. There was no love lost between the agencies and the NSA wanted to make sure that the CIA were reined in. Under Executive Order 12333 no agencies had the authority to operate in the homeland or against American citizens and the NSA would exploit any evidence that showed their rivals had been in violation. They knew that for years the CIA had been using a substance that causes a heart attack, usually against foreign governments or agents. If they were using it now at home then they could be discredited and maybe the NSA could finally get its own way and take control of all aspects of external intelligence. As the covert investigation had continued, however, disappointment set in. It became clear to Laurie that this wasn't the work of a professional agency, but more likely to be activists. After some concern that they too were now in violation, they had convinced themselves that they were dealing with terrorists and hence within one of the carefully constructed loopholes in the law. Adam's research had identified a shadowy organisation of Christian fundamentalists who were antagonistic to the Catholic Church. One of their supporters, a tall blonde woman called Rebecca Bedford, had been in Boston at the time of the archbishop's death, and had been in Brazil on vacation two weeks before. The coincidences were almost too good to be true. Now she was in New York and had been meeting with a number of small groups of people in her hotel room – obviously the organisation was divided into operating cells and she was their controller. They were planning a large meeting on Thursday. If Laurie and Adam could collect enough evidence before then the meeting could be raided and all the cells mopped up in one operation. Then she would be able to get to uncle Mo's birthday party.

SUNDAY

Rome

I lay on my bed, staring at the plaster stucco on the ceiling. I had taken my shoes off for the first time in hours and was enjoying the sensation of freedom that resulted. One of the few downsides to the summer heat of Rome, combined with the vegetarian plastic alternatives to leather out of which my shoes were made, was the amount that my feet seemed to swell. After a day's walking I was ready for a rest, although I was toying with the idea of phoning reception to ask them to arrange a foot massage for me.

I closed my eyes for a second, and immediately the phone beside the bed started to ring. I forced my eyes open and reached for the receiver. Somehow the room had got a lot lighter in that second.

"Pronto."

"Signor White. Your alarm call. It is eight o'clock."

I blinked in surprise, and looked at my watch. It was indeed eight o'clock. That second of shut-eye had actually lasted six hours.

"Thank you." I put down the phone.

"So much for a foot massage before going to sleep." I said out loud to no-one in particular, as I swung my legs off the bed and started to get undressed to have a shower. Hopefully the shower would refresh me more than the shut-eye had – after six hours I still felt in need of a good night's sleep.

I showered and got dressed again, phoned down for coffee and a newspaper and switched on the TV news channel. By the time the coffee arrived I was pretty sure that no-one else had been killed overnight – or at least none of the people on our betting shortlist. I drank the coffee, skimmed through the paper, picked up my keys and headed out of the room towards reception. While they got me a taxi, I waited in the air-conditioned lobby and read the paper. A small item on an inside page reported the death of Rabbi Cohen. The taxi arrived and I headed back towards the Vatican.

I don't really know what it was that first alerted me to the two men who were following us. Their car was dull and inconspicuous, just another dark Fiat like almost every other car in Rome. But at times it was driving just a little bit too close, and the route we took from the hotel was very definitely not a suitable route for any other destination. When we reached the Angel's Gate, I told the driver to stop early and paid him. I included a handsome tip and asked him if he could arrange some sort of incident with the car that had now stopped behind us, to distract them while I made the last 50 metres on foot. No sooner had I stepped out of the car than he reversed back into the grille of the Fiat, jumping out and starting to shout and gesticulate in that way that Italian drivers are so good at – even I would have been convinced that he was the injured party. But I didn't stick around to watch the charade. I slipped into the gathering crowd of bemused tourists, keeping my head down low, and got to the gate and the Swiss Guard in charge of it. Showing my pass I ducked under the pole and quickly made my way through the arch and round the corner out of sight. Even as I hoped that my final destination had gone unobserved by these unsubtle followers, I reasoned that they could only be keeping a watch on me because of my newfound link to the Vatican Library and therefore my destination would have been known to them in advance, anyway.

I walked through to the Belvedere courtyard and into that same doorway I had left only a few hours earlier. Making my way among the panelled rooms and corridors, I mused on the possible reasons that anyone could have to follow me. The slow descent of the lift gave me time to consider the potential candidates.

"One of the government agencies?" I thought aloud, "If they're refusing to take any of Costanza's warnings seriously then what would they be doing following me? Unless they're playing a bluffing game - deny being interested while keeping a close eye on what's actually going on? That fits with the way most of the agencies relate to each other – although usually the official denials are balanced by field agents working together behind the scenes. So it seems unlikely to be CIA, or SIS. If it's not the so-called 'good guys', maybe it's the 'bad guys'?"

The lift stopped and I walked through the door and headed towards the guard's station.

"Whoever is trying to rig the next Conclave would want to make sure that the Vatican didn't get wind of it and stop them. But why follow me? How would they know I was helping Costanza? How would they know about Costanza at all? Unless they were sufficiently trusted within the Vatican hierarchy to know about the Thomasines and their alternative rôle. But in that case they wouldn't need to have me followed to know where I was going. Why follow me?"

As I turned the corner I saw a Guard standing in front of the desk talking to the seated Guard behind it. As I approached they both looked at me with curious, even suspicious, expressions. The standing Guard straightened up and tensed. I pulled the red pass out of my breast pocket as I reached the desk and they both immediately saluted me.

"Who is following you, Commander?" asked the nearest Guard.

"What?" I said, instinctively looking behind me. There was no-one there.

"You said 'Why follow me?' as you walked in. Who were you talking to?".

"Oh!" I grinned sheepishly. "Myself. I was thinking

out loud. Someone followed me from my hotel, but I don't know why."

"Protection?" suggested the Guard behind the desk.

"From whom?"

"I don't know. You're an officer in the Swiss Guard. We have enemies. And not just Satan's henchmen." He looked me straight in the eye. I couldn't tell how serious he was.

"Maybe. I must say I had assumed it was more likely to be an antagonist following me, but you could be right."

The door slid open and as I stepped through I looked back at them.

"Thank you, err. I'm sorry, I don't know your names."

"Bandinelli, Paolo" said the Guard behind the desk.

"Fusco, Antonio" said the other.

"Thank you Antonio, Paolo. See you later."

I walked through following the yellow lines as the door shut behind me.

"Why protection?" Antonio asked Paolo.

"Because on the monitor here it says we must take great care of Commander White. As of last night there's even a special Avisso from Cardinal Bianchi placing a hands-off security blanket around him when he's outside the City. But if he's already spotted them, they're not being very hands-off." He picked up the phone built in to his desktop. "I'd better tell the Cardinal."

As I entered the Thomasine's office, my mental deliberations were almost concluded. The room was still empty, Costanza wasn't yet here. I went over to the whiteboard, picked up the pen and started to sketch out my argument with a spider gram.

Some thirty minutes later, when Costanza walked into the room, I had organised my thoughts into a considered, coherent and credible theorem. I had even managed to capture it succinctly on the whiteboard.

"Ciao bella," I said, "I have a theory to run past you."

She dropped her clutch bag onto her desk, kicking her ever-so-elegant Gucci shoes under her chair. Her jacket was already suspended on a hanger on the coat stand by the door. As she walked over to join me at the wall she scanned the bullet points I had written and frowned.

"What theory?"

"On my way here I was followed from the Hotel. I managed to lose them down the street but I'm sure they realised that I came in at the gate. The guards here suggested it might be some form of protection, but I don't know of anyone from whom I need protecting. So I've been trying to work out who else would be following me and why."

"I can see from your list that you've been, exhaustive!" from her tone and the twinkle in her eye I thought she was amused, rather than concerned – the reaction I had expected.

"What? You think I'm being paranoid?"

"Oh no. If someone was, or is, following you, then we should try to understand why. I was just amused at some of the candidates in your list. You seem to have considered everyone except Spiny Norman" she grinned.

When I first met Costanza, many years before, I had introduced her to the sketches, and films, of Monty Python, as a way of helping her to try to understand the British sense of humour. She had taken to it avidly, and we had spent many evenings in smoky bars or waiting for our results in empty computer rooms reciting the dead parrot sketch or the cheese shop sketch like nerdy adolescents.

Was she now making fun of me? Probably, but I knew that she cared about me and the humour was undoubtedly a deliberate attempt to underplay any potential danger.

"Well they are all possibilities, but, as you can see, I have discounted most of them. CIA, NSA, SIS, FSB, Mossad are all implicated if your deadbet assassin is true. Or even if they think it might be true."

"But then they would surely not be refusing to talk to me about it?"

"Exactly, unless they think we're behind it."

"Which is so unlikely as to be laughable. Even they wouldn't be suspicious enough to think we could behave like that."

"So they would have no reason to follow me. Anyway, if they were going to follow anyone, surely it would be you?"

"Or, they think that you're the assassin and that's why they're following you. Which is also why they won't talk to me because we're known to have a history and therefore I'm implicated. But..."

"That might fly as a theory if it was only one of them ignoring you, but they all are – and they would never share intelligence that widely. No they're ignoring you because they believe you're wrong."

"Or they know I'm wrong. Because they know what's actually going on."

"Right. In which case they wouldn't be following me. Because I haven't got a clue what's going on!" I grinned. "Which brings me to the next group of candidates."

"Cardinal Thomas et al?"

"Right."

"But you've discounted them too?"

"Of course. If it's an internal Vatican conspiracy, then they don't need to follow me because they could follow you and I am of no value to them. If it's an external conspiracy then they probably won't know that you're on to them, in fact they won't know you're even looking for them. They certainly would have no reason to follow me at all. The same is true for each of the other groups on this list. Which is why they're all discounted except the last."

"Okay. Enlighten me. What is POPU? Or who?"

"Person or Persons Unknown."

"That's very clear! I think I prefer Spiny Norman."

"I don't know who they are, but I think I know what they want."

"Which is…?"

"You!"

"Me? Why follow you to get to me?"

"Because they don't know who you are, they just know you must exist. They want something that's in the Library. If they can find someone sufficiently powerful within the Library organisation they hope that they can get what they want through subterfuge, blackmail, or duress. It's too difficult to reach any of the known public figures like Cardinals. They suspect that I've come here to help someone involved with the Library. I guess they figure they can either use me to get access, or at least to get to a suitable person that they can then use to get them into the Library."

"But why would they think you've come here to the Library?"

"They probably hadn't realised beforehand. But maybe they recognised me and put two and two together. If they have recognised me then they won't be long finding links to you and they may soon be following you. Or Sandro."

"Now I think you are being paranoid. Even though it's on my behalf."

"Just watch out; and you better tell Sandro to watch out too."

"I can't. Especially after his concerns last night." She sank down onto the nearest chair and looked thoughtful.

After a few moments she looked up at me.

"No, it's no good I need some help. Have you been to Mass yet?"

I shook my head.

"Come on. There's an English Mass at the high altar today." She looked at the watch on her slender wrist. "It starts in ten minutes. Just time to get there."

"But won't there be long queues to get in to St. Peter's?"

"Not the way we're going." She stood up, walked over to her desk and retrieved her shoes and bag. On the way to the door, as she lifted her jacket from its hanger, she glanced back at me.

"You really think Vatican staff have to queue at the door?"

As we left the room it was clear that we were following the red line that I had seen occasionally crossing the yellow route to which I had so quickly become accustomed. We turned corners I had never seen before and followed the red line along a corridor that started to become smaller and then clearly older. We reached a glass panel, which hissed aside to Costanza's touch, walked a little further around a curving passage and came to a bronze gate. It too opened at a touch and as we walked through I realised we were now in the crypt of St. Peter's. We followed the curve around and came to the narrow twisting staircase that leads up and out into the vaulted basilica. As we climbed the stairs we could hear the sonorous strains of the entrance hymn being played on the massive organ whose pipes bracketed the high altar. But even so, the sound of hundreds of tourists milling around in the main body of this great church welcomed us as we stepped out and past the warden protecting the crypt entrance from wayward visitors. We made our way to the pews in front of the altar, found two spaces and stood as a priest entered in procession with the oldest altar server I had ever seen – 80 years old if he was a day – carrying a thurible, and swinging it with gay abandon.

Capri

The hotel lobby was buzzing with conversation. The atmosphere positively dripped with wealth and power, while elsewhere the midday heat just made the atmosphere drip. Clusters of men and women sat around coffee tables drinking their martinis and planning the future of the world. Or at least the future of their world, if everything continued going their way. This year had been a particularly good conference. There was more consensus than usual, with much of it being directed against the delegates who were, unofficially, representing the New American Century. The death of the journalist Tim Shah yesterday had been unfortunate but had diverted much attention away from the delegates and onto the media themselves. However, a few of the delegates felt that the NAC contingent seemed to know too much about Shah's demise and were too pleased about it. Almost as if they were gloating. But however much trouble the media tried to cause for these meetings no-one had ever considered taking such extreme action. Surely, even the Americans wouldn't be that stupid.

The agenda for the afternoon had been amended at the last minute with a new topic inserted at the start. One word. 'Security'. No-one seemed to know who had tabled it, or exactly what aspects of security were to be discussed. This was not the way these things were supposed to be conducted. Everybody liked to be prepared for their discussions, with no surprises. Who could prepare for such a vague topic? Security could mean anything from worries about the pack of media hounds outside the hotel grounds, to the state of the ongoing supposed war against terrorism being peddled by the US and UK governments. With delegates here from most major states, representing a large proportion of the Judaeo-Christian world, and a few humanists thrown in for good measure, there was likely to be a mixed but not overtly hostile reception to a discussion about such matters. When it came down to it, though, as in previous years, the majority of delegates were more concerned about the effects of war on their balance sheets (state, corporate, or personal); while there was plenty of money to be made from arms dealing and post-war reconstruction, especially by those who were supportive, or at least not publicly critical, of the invaders, no-one was likely to be highly outspoken – even if it meant biting a tongue that wished to tell the NAC exactly what the rest of the world thought of them.

When the time for the session arrived, movement towards the meeting room started to work its way through the delegates with a coriolis effect. Those nearest were sucked into the room first, attracting the attention of others nearby, who themselves made a detour to grab a colleague, deposit a glass or retrieve a briefcase, all the while spreading the word to yet more. They, in turn, slowly finished their drinks and conversations before moving towards the room. Within three or four minutes only a few stragglers were left hurriedly downing their gin or dashing to the loo, before finally, with everyone inside, the room was locked like the Sistine Chapel at a Conclave, enabling and assuring privacy for the discussions that would take place within.

Two hours later when the doors were unlocked there was an uncharacteristic quiet hanging over the delegates. Most came out and went straight to their rooms, ignoring the customary gin and tonic to counter the effects of the afternoon tea. The bar staff, who had been polishing the glasses and tabletops exceptionally diligently for the last two hours were taken aback to find the expected deluge of orders reduced to a mere spatter. At least there were always a few old faithfuls who could be relied on to prop up the bar come what may. Only the American delegates walked out of the room in buoyant mood and came over to the bar to pop a few Buds.

The bar staff had been given large gratuities in advance to ensure that they carefully failed to listen to any of the conversations going on within earshot, but Mario couldn't help overhearing two of the smiling Yankees talking about Cardinal Bramante and an investigation into P2. Mario hesitated for a moment, remembering what his mother had told him about the Cardinal at the Vatican who had been a Godsend to the people of Anacapri when their local church was threatened by developers in the pockets of the Neapolitan Camorra. He was sure that had been Cardinal Bramante. But he had been paid not to listen. Mamma would understand, especially as she relied on his income now that Pappa was dead. He polished a glass and tried to think of other things.

Rome

As usual, for a summer's evening, Piazza Navona was full of life. Everywhere artists sat in front of their easels sketching podgy tourist kids while adoring parents looked on approvingly. Pigeons stalked the pavement around the fountains for crumbs of bread or scraps of pizza. The ever-present sound of splashing water filled the piazza, echoing from the fronts of the churches and palazzos. Affluent tourists sat at the café tables drinking their coffee and eating their ice cream. Outside the Brazilian embassy a small crowd had gathered around a man dressed as the Statue of Liberty in a long silver costume, standing perfectly still on an upturned box. Occasional forays by small children to drop a coin in the tin in front of him would elicit a mere wink or a shake of his torch. Although the sun had sunk behind the hills over two hours before, the air was still very warm. Despite the heat Liberty managed to keep remarkably still.

A tall blonde woman walked across in front of the crowd, almost kicking over the tin with its meagre contents of a few Euro coins. She skirted the fountain, causing a flurry of pigeons to erupt before her like the bow-wave of a speedboat oblivious to its surroundings. She headed for Tre Scalini, where she was quickly seated by an obsequious waiter eager to please this obviously powerful lady. Within moments a glass of water and an espresso had appeared on the table in front of her. She was aloof, and mysterious; her patently unnecessary sunglasses remaining fixed on her nose while she tossed back the coffee as if it were a shot of vodka or schnapps. Somewhat surprisingly, to anyone who had happened to be paying any attention, she smiled a little knowing smile as the tartufo ice cream was delivered to her table. Behind the dark lenses her eyes twinkled, unseen. How someone with such a figure would dare to eat rich ice cream like this, was a mystery to the waiter. But eat it she did. With obvious relish. As she delicately dabbed at her lips with the linen napkin, having laid the spoon on the now empty plate, the subtle smile once more played across them. She closed her eyes, took a deep breath and let it out slowly. Sipping the water, she beckoned to the waiter and handed him a 50 Euro note. As he scuttled away, she looked around at the people infesting the square. Mostly tourists, they, like her, were here to enjoy the atmosphere of a magical almost legendary place. A once-in-a-lifetime visit to the ancient centre of the world was not complete without stopping off at the modern day cultural landmarks – art galleries and museums seemed to be as full as ever, but the cafés, gelaterie and pizzerie seemed to be busier than at any time in the past - a tartufo in Piazza Navona was an essential part of the experience of modern Rome.

She stood up, smoothed down the crease that had appeared in her black skirt, adjusted her sunglasses and tucked a strand of hair neatly behind her left ear. Then she walked away, purposefully but still elegantly, cutting across the piazza in the direction of the Pantheon. Various pairs of eyes followed her progress across the square, all belonging to young Roman men, staying in Rome for the summer to provide various services to rich tourists; especially beautiful women; especially tall blondes. However, they all had the good sense not to pursue this one.

When she reached the Pantheon, she ignored the cafés, the horse drawn carriages and the scores of people lounging on the fountain or sitting around outside the great bronze doors. Walking past to the rear of this magnificent building she glanced at the elephant supporting an obelisk in front of the restaurant at which she had made her reservation. She went in and was shown to a small table in a corner, banks of geraniums on each side. She picked up the wine list and quietly perused it while waiting for her evening's companion.

To an observer, even one as professionally interested as the young men in Piazza Navona, this lady seemed confident and self-assured. She was obviously not Italian, but difficult to place – her height and blonde hair suggested Scandinavian or German, while her confident, almost disdainful air, suggested American. Her understated clothes, on the other hand, black and demure, suggested a Southern European widow. She was a conundrum for anyone who had the time or inclination to watch and wonder. They would be unlikely to guess her true identity. Helen Wates was the name on the passport she carried in her small clutch handbag. An American whose father and mother had met in Baltimore where his Danish parents and her Czechoslovakian parents had settled after they had escaped from Europe just before the second world war. Growing up in Baltimore had been a great constraint on her and she had determined that she would, one day, see the world – or at least the most significant parts of it. Being fascinated by history, especially tales of legendary heroes, great civilisations, and valiant adventurers, she considered the most significant parts of the world to be largely centred on the Mediterranean. She had spent some time in South America, but had remained entirely unimpressed by the remains left behind by Incas, Aztecs and Mayans – in comparison with Rome, Greece and Egypt they were late, and somewhat poor, imitations. Now she was here, at the heart of her world-view and determined to enjoy it. Nonetheless, she couldn't forget the reason why she had been forced to come here, and wore the widow's traditional colour as a reminder to herself and to others. The dark glasses, part of her black image, also helped to hide her most distinctive feature – stunningly green eyes that shone like cut glass and that pierced into the soul of anyone with whom she made eye-contact. Without the sunglasses she would have been one of the most memorable people in Rome for anyone who saw her. Given her current plans, she was keen to avoid being noticed, let alone remembered.

A short, dark man ambled over to her table, pulled out the other chair and sat down. She looked up, smiled gently and handed him the wine list, pointing to the Frascati Superiore. He nodded and signalled to the waiter. The lack of any demonstration of affection or even acknowledgement of each other, indeed almost diffidence, suggested either the most casual of acquaintance or a deep and secure relationship that needed no public affirmation. They both scanned the menu while the wine was being uncorked and poured for them.

"It's good to see you again, Anna. How're you keeping?"

"Pretty much as you'd expect I guess. It was difficult at first. I was angry and sad all at the same time. I suppose I needed to exorcise some ghosts, which I've been doing. Now I'm able to think about getting back to a normal life once I get home."

"You're going already? I thought you only got here this weekend?"

"Yeah. Well. I've seen what I wanted to see. Done what I wanted to do. I have one more day and then I'm going to New York."

"Can I take you anywhere, show you anything? Anything?" he grinned sheepishly. "You know how I've always felt about you. I'll do anything I can to help."

"For me or for Dave's memory?"

"For you of course. I knew you before Dave did. In fact I knew you before I knew Dave."

"Really?" the hint of a frown suggested itself above her dark glasses.

"Sure. I only met him after he started working at the Agency. I'd already known you almost a year by then."

"I thought it was you that recruited him. He once spoke about being persuaded by Manny to sign up. I assumed he was talking about you?"

"Nah. I was never any good at recruiting. Couldn't bring myself to talk about patriotism and duty. You have no idea how close I came to botching it when we first met. I would have been in so much trouble when we bought those houses from you if you'd even guessed we were a government agency, let alone which one. Hardly a great advertisement for a secret service. Nah, Dave was recruited by Manny Shadwell. He was one of the old school, ya know? Did everything by the book – Jeez, I think he actually wrote the book! Died last year of lung cancer. Too many smoke-filled rooms I guess."

"Oh. That's too bad." She reached down to the handbag hanging over the back of her chair, opened it and clicked something inside. She closed the bag, looked up and smiled again.

"Let's order."

New York, USA

Although it was Sunday afternoon, Adam was still busy with his surveillance of Rebecca Bedford. He had never trusted blondes, especially the tall leggy ones that always seemed so confident. Or at least he had not trusted them since sixth grade when Mary Shelly in his class had tricked him into show and don't tell.

"I'll show you mine if you show me yours" she had said.

Already fascinated with biology he had only seen drawings in library books and was keen to see for himself what made girls different. But she hadn't kept her end of the bargain. Instead she had laughed at him once he had dropped his pants. He had never even considered that being circumcised might make him different.

"But where's the rest of it?" she had laughed. "That's not what Patrick looks like. Or Sean. Or Michael. They're real boys. They don't have bits missing." Then she had run off.

Mary Shelly had been blonde and tall for her age. He had hated blondes ever since, the taller they were the more he hated them. He knew they were all scheming liars. So he was already pre-disposed to believe that Rebecca was capable of anything. He had been watching her since she came to New York. He had watched as she had met with various small groups of people in her hotel and elsewhere. He had watched as she had sat in Central Park reading her Bible; drinking a coffee; walking around the expensive streets of Manhattan and the grimy streets of the seedier parts of the city. She had been to a Baptist church; she had been to City Hall and the Metropolitan Library. He had listened to conversations with a Minister; someone she called brother; someone who had called her angel. He had heard her talking about a Senator; about the Agency; about victims; about making an example;

about forcing the government to change; about showing the city the true cost of ignoring them. He had no doubt that Rebecca Bedford was planning something terrible. But so far he had no idea what it might be. He knew she had come to New York to arrange an event that would demonstrate the power of her terrorist organisation. He suspected that whatever it was would be unleashed on Thursday as a result of the meeting she was apparently arranging with all of her various cells. If he and Laurie were unable to stop her before then they would have to raid the meeting – at least that way they should be able to contain all of the cells and sweep them up in one manoeuvre. Hopefully they wouldn't be too late to stop whatever she was planning.

Rebecca had spent today in her hotel room alone. She had woken up late, watched some TV, curled up on her bed reading various papers and a book. Adam was unable to tell what she had been reading, but that didn't matter. He didn't need to see what she was reading, he knew it would be subversive material, manuals for anarchists and insurgents, or a handbook of techniques for terror. She was obviously obsessed. In the few days he had been keeping track of her, she had never had any intimate contact with anyone. No sex, no kisses. She hadn't even pleasured herself as far as he could tell. She obviously wasn't normal. He couldn't spend that much time alone in a strange city without having to find someone to satisfy him. He'd never had to pay for it either, well only that one time in Denver and that was just to stop the bitch running to the police to complain about his little foibles. What had been her problem? Most girls thought it was cool when he got out his gun and used it to stimulate them. When he had commented to Laurie about Rebecca's low libido she had pointed out that most religious fundamentalists were either sex-obsessed or virtually chaste. Rebecca clearly fell into the latter category. Adam still couldn't comprehend such an attitude even if he did understand the cause.

"No wonder she's an embittered terrorist," he thought, "not only is she tall and blonde, she's probably never had sex with a real man before."

Whatever else you might think of Adam Sawicki, you certainly couldn't accuse him of being liberal.

Rome

In her hotel room, Anna sat at the desk and gazed into the mirror. She took off her sunglasses and shook her head to loosen the strands of hair that had become sweat-plastered to the side of her face. Lighting a long cigarette, she took a deep draw on it. As she slowly blew the smoke at her reflection, she raised an eyebrow.

"That was close," she now started speaking to her reflection, "nearly made a mistake there. You don't want to make a mistake. Not another one. You're getting careless. Making assumptions. You know that's dangerous. Make mistakes and they'll catch on. Then where will you be?"

She finished the rest of her cigarette in silence, eyes cast down towards the writing pad on the desk. She realised that she had been doodling. When had she been doodling? While smoking or before she went out earlier? Had anyone seen what she had written? The chambermaid? No. She was sure that she must have written it just now. Still. It was another careless action. She had drawn an apple and a cross. No-one would understand the significance, even if they had seen it. She picked up the sheet of paper and very carefully and meticulously folded it in half and then again into quarters. She ran her fingernail along the fold to flatten it, and then tore the paper into half a dozen strips which she dropped into the ashtray. She got out her lighter to set fire to them and then thought better of it, stood up and carried the strips of paper into the bathroom where she flushed them down the toilet.

An apple and a cross. Was this a guilty conscience trying to assert itself? She didn't believe that she had a conscience, certainly not a guilty one. So it was more likely an unconscious frustration with the one mistake she had made, and the second she had so closely averted.

That apple had been meant for Cardinal Thomas. She had given it to Cardinal Thomas. She hadn't expected him to give it away to Bramante. So it was his fault not hers. She had executed her plan faultlessly. She had managed to get an appointment to see Thomas. She had played the devout, yet frustrated widow (although she had made sure that he didn't realise who's widow she was). She had given him the apple as a way of saying thank you for listening and had only left because Cardinal Bramante had been passing and had stuck his head around the door to ask a question. When she was going out the door she heard Bramante comment on how nice the apple on his desk looked and Thomas tell him to take it as he didn't really eat apples. She remembered the unintended irony of his actual words "I don't eat healthy stuff like fruit – I'm sure it'll actually kill you". She had managed to get out without panicking, and after a moment's thought decided that, as there was nothing she could do about it, she could at least benefit. She headed for the nearest cyber café and placed a bet against Cardinal Bramante. At least she could get some more operational funds. It was his fault not hers. His fault. Not hers.

Not hers.

"Well Manny," she said out loud to an empty room, "at least you didn't suffer on someone else's account. Unlike Dave. Unlike me. But Cardinal Thomas" she spat the name out, "is going to. Oh yes. Make no mistake about that. He's going to pay."

MONDAY

Cheltenham

Tony Hey liked to get in early. Not to avoid the rush hour. There wasn't much of a rush hour here. He only lived 10 minutes drive away in a typically beautiful Cotswolds village. The road to get to GCHQ was never that busy, even at 8:30 in the morning when most people were expected to arrive. He liked to get in before everyone else so he could be sure that his phone had been hygienically cleaned and his coffee mug had been sterilised. He had an obsessive fear of being contaminated with the bacteria that he knew waited around for him to leave and then sneaked onto his possessions over night.

At school and university he had made no efforts to hide his fears and as a result he had virtually no friends. Most people though he was weird. The fact that he was a mathematical prodigy hadn't helped. Being two years younger than everyone else in his class had made life even more difficult. He was too young to go drinking in the union bar – not that he'd have wanted to anyway, too many bacteria in those dishcloths that the careless bar staff casually used to polish the glasses. When he wasn't in the computer lab experimenting with fractals or elliptic curves, he was in his room in the hall of residence playing and re-playing classic chess games from one of his collection of chess books. Most people had no idea that he could play chess at all, let alone that he would have been able to give most grand masters a run for their money. He wouldn't use anyone else's chess pieces in case they were contaminated. His own set was made from stainless steel and could be decontaminated before use in the small sterilising unit he had bought second-hand when a local cottage hospital was being demolished.

Since those days he had learnt not to stand out from those around him. Rather than broadcast his concerns, he chose to deal with them before others arrived. A sink full of boiling water and a sterilising tablet dealt with the coffee mug and teaspoon. He always made his own coffee so he could be sure to get his own mug and spoon. Bactericidal phone wipes had been a godsend to him and enabled him to use telephones almost with impunity. He wouldn't make a call on anyone else's phone without first wiping it clean. He always kept a few sachets of wipes in his trouser pockets and had developed a way of wiping a phone before using it without anyone else noticing. The wipes were now standard items in the stationery cupboard so others too had started using them, although not to the same exacting standard as him.

This morning, as usual, Tony had arrived half an hour before his colleagues. Plenty of time to clean the mug and spoon, wipe the telephones of all the nearest desks and, just for good measure, wipe the door handles. As he was cleaning the phone in the small office by the window, he noticed that a call had been recorded but not erased. This room was usually only used for small meetings or by visitors who needed a temporary base. Curious he pressed the play button and listened.

"From where? Who?" a slightly muffled echoing voice.

"I can't tell you at the moment, especially not on an open line like this. You never know who's listening. But it's a dead bet." The second voice was accented, Italian or Spanish.

"There's no more I can tell you." The first voice again, obviously English.

Tony listened to the whole of the short conversation and the abrupt goodbyes. By now he had recognised the English voice as agent Cannon who often came down here to talk to some of his colleagues. He had never spoken to her, but he knew her name. She had obviously been here over the weekend. He had no idea who the other voice belonged to, although he was sure that she was tall, dark and stunningly beautiful. Something in the recording had struck a chord but he wasn't entirely conscious of what it was. He had to listen to it again twice more before he finally realised.

"I don't think Ms. Cannon understood what she was being told. I better explain it to her," he muttered to himself as he walked out of the room and into the larger office he shared with ten other cryptographers. At his desk he tapped the mouse to wake up his screensaver and sat down as he waited for the online phone directory to respond to his request.

Five minutes later he was holding on to his phone while waiting for the call to be connected to Katie Cannon. At last there was a slight buzz and then:

"Hello, yes?"

"Ms. Cannon. You don't know me. My name is Tony Hey, I work at Cheltenham."

"Hello Tony. What can I do for you?"

"Were you here over the weekend?"

"Yes. Why?"

"Did you record a phone conversation with a foreign lady?"

"Yes."

"When she said that she couldn't tell you where the list came from because she couldn't trust the line, you do know she then told you exactly where the list came from, don't you?"

"What? She said she couldn't tell me, and she didn't."

"Oh yes she did. But if you didn't get the reference I think you better come down here and I'll show you exactly what she meant."

"You're having me on aren't you?"

"What? No. Of course not. I'm serious, quite

serious."

"This better not be a wild goose chase. If you guys are trying to have some fun at my expense there'll be all hell to pay."

"You better just get here and see for yourself." He put the phone down. He'd never spoken to a woman so forcefully before. In fact, he'd hardly ever spoken to a woman at all. But all the crypto team had a very low regard for the agents who lorded it over them. "Why are they the ones who are known as Military Intelligence, when we're so much smarter than them?" went the familiar refrain whenever another operational cock-up was inevitably blamed on technology or the back-room boys. These back-room boys and girls were fed up. But for a while now, the whole of the Intelligence community in Britain had been feeling the same way — a collective whipping boy for a government desperate to distance itself from its own actions, the 'secret service' was being readily and repeatedly blamed for providing faulty intelligence that led the country into a dodgy war.

Tony sat back in his chair and let out a long sigh. Ms. Katie Cannon was coming here to see him. A smirk played on his face for a while and then he leapt up, picked up his notebook and pen and almost ran back to the small office to make sure he had a transcript of the recording. It wouldn't look good if she got here and someone else had erased the conversation.

Vatican City

Cardinal Bianchi sat in his office and leaned back in his chair. This room was in one of the older parts of the building, close to the Pope's apartments. He looked up at the ceiling and considered the angels that were gazing down at him from all sides. They had the benefit of flight and supernatural vision. His own guardian angels, as he called his protection team, had to make do with mechanical transportation and human sight.

He had heard from the Swiss Guard that Peter White had spotted the angels and had tried to lose them. Perhaps he should have told Peter that he was being protected not pursued. If he had spotted the angels, then anyone else who might actually be watching him had probably noticed them too. They were obviously losing their touch. Maybe a shake-up was called for. He sat up straight again and lifted the phone, keyed 88 and waited. After a few seconds the ringing tone stopped and a voice answered.

"Yes your Eminence?"

"Pasquale. I hear that your surveillance of Commander White has been less than successful."

"Yes, your Eminence. I'm afraid so. He obviously spotted the angels and arranged an accident to distract them."

"Pasquale, you're slipping."

"I'm sorry Eminence. They may have been careless, or he may be very astute. I'm trying to find out which at the moment. If necessary they'll be retrained."

"Good, we can't afford any mistakes, lives may be at stake. I think you better put your best people on this job."

"Yes your Eminence. I have already replaced the team with Michele and Gabriele. You need not worry, I have every confidence in them."

"And I have always had every confidence in you, Pasquale. I hope neither of us will need to reconsider."

"Eminence. Will you be telling Commander White about the angels?"

"No. For the moment, if he doesn't know about them he will remain vigilant, especially as he now thinks someone is following him."

"Someone is following him, that's why you called on us."

"He doesn't need to know that for certain, but if he suspects he will undoubtedly be more careful."

"What about Signora D'Andrea-Mancini?"

"Who do you have looking after her?"

"Raffaella."

"On her own?"

"She prefers to work alone. She is the best angel we have and has never lost a charge."

"Good. I haven't told Costanza that you are watching her. She doesn't even know that your team exists. But she may become more nervous if Commander White relates his experience to her. You better warn Raffaella that her charge may be more aware."

"Certainly."

"And make sure that none of your teams are careless again."

"You have my word, Eminence."

The Cardinal put down his phone and looked back up to the ceiling. A little divine help wouldn't go amiss.

Naples

"Dottore."

Ernesto Gambraccio looked up from the desk with a pained expression. He had been here less than two minutes and already someone was in his office shouting. He wouldn't have minded so much if he didn't know that everyone was aware of his acute hearing and had been repeatedly asked not to shout around him.

"Inspector. What can I do for you?" he asked calmly – famed as much for his easy-going nature as for his aversion to loud noises.

A tall dark man with a large nose and very bushy moustache walked into the room and stood looking down at him.

"There was a death on Capri over the weekend. An English journalist. The doctor who examined the body when he was found diagnosed a heart attack. As he was a foreigner we need to be sure though, so I want you to get the body back here and check for yourself."

"Where was he found?"

"On the belvedere. Some kids found him. It doesn't look suspicious but we don't want to miss anything. Did I mention he was a journalist?"

"Yes"

"So we can't afford any mistakes or it'll be just another story about incompetent provincial police, just what Rome wants to add weight to their argument for central control."

"Who examined the body?"

"Fulcanelli."

"A good doctor, I know her. Young, smart and up to date. I think it unlikely she missed anything."

"That's as maybe. But I don't want our reputation to rely on some local doctor. I want one of our own to make sure."

"Now who's being dismissive of provincials?"

"Far from it. If I was taken ill on Capri I would like to be looked after by Doctor Fulcanelli. Oh yes!" he grinned, "she could look after me anytime she likes, as long as my Maria wasn't around. But that isn't the point," the grin vanished as quickly as it had appeared. "She, I lust. You, I trust."

He turned and walked out of the room, stopping momentarily to call back over his shoulder.

"A launch is waiting. I want you to supervise retrieval personally. I don't want any mistakes."

As the inspector disappeared down the corridor, Gambraccio looked at the pile of papers in his in-tray. Today he had been determined to tackle them; maybe this time he could actually make an impression in the paperwork before it all toppled over on top of him – physically as well as metaphorically. But today was now destined to be yet another crisis-driven day.

Later that morning, as he walked up the hill from the quay in Capri, Ernesto Gambraccio loosened his tie and undid his shirt collar. It was going to be a lovely day – weatherwise. He wanted to make the most of it while he could, as he suspected he would be spending much of the rest of it in a cold, artificially lit room in the company of a corpse on a slab. He arrived at Elisabetta Fulcanelli's office and rang the bell. Almost immediately the door opened and she was standing there herself. Her face lit up with a big smile.

"No one to open your door these days?" he asked.

"Only today. Lisa's mother is sick and needs looking after. I gave her the day off. Come in Ernesto, it's lovely to see you."

"Thank you. I'm here for the dead Englishman."

"And I thought you'd just come on a social visit – you haven't been here for a long time you know, I'm beginning to think you don't love me anymore."

"Elisabetta, I'll always love you. You were my best student. You know that Angela and I think of you as the granddaughter we never had. I've just been busy. This police work never seems to let up."

He walked through the door and gave her a hug, kissing her on both cheeks. Letting go he turned and entered a comfortable waiting room full of soft chairs and soft music but devoid of people. Elisabetta closed the door and followed him across the room.

"Sit," she said, gesturing at the nearest chair.

"As I said I'm here for the dead Englishman."

"I know. But why you? Not that I'm not always pleased to see you, but it's a straightforward case of a heart attack. I was expecting the funeral director not the coroner."

"You know Inspector Bettula?"

"Do I! I know he's supposed to be a good policeman but he's a chauvinist and thinks he's God's gift to women. I don't know how his wife puts up with it."

"What?"

"You're so naïve at times Ernesto. That's one of your many charms. He, on the other hand, is the exact opposite. Whenever I see him he tells me he has a swelling in his groin and would I look at it. Neither original nor funny. Anyway, what about him?"

"He's in charge of the investigation."

"What investigation?"

"Into the death of the Englishman."

"But it was a heart attack, what is there to investigate?"

"He's being thorough. This Englishman was a journalist so Bettula wants to make sure no one misses anything. If there's anything untoward he wants to know."

"What?" she exploded, and then, seeing his pained look, said more quietly "Sorry. Doesn't he believe my diagnosis?" She was still angry.

"Yes. But just in case others don't he wants it officially confirmed – a second opinion."

"What is this? Paranoia?" she asked.

"Maybe. I must admit I'm a little surprised myself. I haven't seen any details of what you found in your examination. Was there anything unusual?"

"No, nothing. No external wounds or trauma. All the usual signs of a massive heart attack. Cut and dried. Messy though."

"Messy? I though you said there was no external trauma?"

"That's right. Messy in the trousers." She looked at him with eyebrows raised. "As usual, but this one must have had a very full bladder."

"Oh. Yes. These days they've usually been cleaned up by the time I get to see them."

"So why is the inspector so nervous? Does he know something we don't?"

"Who can say? I've told you all I know. He says it's because this man was a foreign journalist. He doesn't want bad publicity."

"What bad publicity can you get from a heart attack. Natural causes. It could have happened anywhere, it just happened here while the guy was on holiday. So what?"

"He was a political journalist apparently. I don't think he was on holiday, he was here covering a story of some sort. I've never been interested in politics so I don't really know what he might have been here for."

"As I said, charmingly naïve." She smiled at him. "There's a big conference going on. Lots of journalists are here to cover it but apparently it has very strong security and strict secrecy. Already I've had to patch up a couple of other journalists who've had run-ins with the security guards. The dead guy was here to cover that I think. But he didn't look like he'd been a victim of their security. They're anything but subtle, or even intelligent. If this was something other than a plain heart attack it was induced by someone very clever - without leaving a trace."

"How can you be sure?"

"To tell the truth I was suspicious at first, as soon as I knew he was a journalist, given the other patients I've had. So I ran a few more tests than normal. Nothing invasive, I'll leave that to you. But I did some bloodwork and it came up clean. The guy was pretty fit, seemed to be healthy, wasn't noticeably overweight, no drugs or alcohol in his blood. No obvious natural cause, but heart attack it was."

"If you were already suspicious, why were you so angry that Bettula wants a second opinion?"

"As I said, in the end there's no evidence of any external cause. I'll be interested in your conclusions, but I'll be very surprised if you find something. I don't believe it's anything more than an unexpected heart attack in an apparently healthy man."

"But?"

"But what?"

"You didn't say it, but I heard a 'But…'"

"Okay. But, if the Inspector is so keen to check and double check I'm more suspicious. Especially as, if this wasn't natural causes, the most likely reason is political. The Inspector is a very politically aware man. If pressure is being brought to bear on him from above then there's probably something going on."

"Now who's paranoid?"

"No. Nothing to do with me. But you might want to take care when you announce your results, whatever they will be."

She stood up.

"Come, call your men and we'll go and get the body. It's in the morgue at the clinic."

He stood up and as he followed her to the back door, he took his mobile phone out of his inside pocket to call Claudio and Marco to meet him at the clinic.

Rome

Although it was Monday morning, Costanza had decided to leave home later than usual. After Sandro had gone out for the day, she started to look around their apartment carefully. If Peter was right then she may already be being followed. They may have been here searching through her things. She hadn't noticed anything out of place, but if they were professionals they could surely search an apartment and leave very little trace.

What would she do if she were searching an apartment. Obviously check in the study, see if there's anything written down on carelessly left paperwork. Check the bins. Check the computer. Look around the other rooms. Where would someone like her hide things? Probably in the bedroom. She had never had any reason to hide anything in her life and it seemed strange to even think about it now. If you had papers or a disc or even a chip to hide you would want to put it somewhere where an intruder would not think to look; or not want to look. She had seen enough Hollywood films to know that inside the toilet cistern was the first place to look – that was where the gun or drugs cache was always hidden! Perhaps in her underwear drawers?

She went into the bedroom and carefully opened her top drawer. The satin lingerie that she liked to wear and that Sandro liked her to wear all seemed to be unruffled and as smoothly laid out as ever. She flicked through them, nothing appeared to be missing. She looked in the next drawer. All her cotton knickers were there and nothing looked as if it had been disturbed. The bottom drawer with her socks was the usual jumbled mess. She closed the drawer. Was she being paranoid? Where else would she hide something? Where would someone not want to look? Of course, in the dirty clothes. She walked over to the metal basket and lifted off the wooden disc that acted as a lid. Putting it down she peered in. How would she know if anyone had looked in here? The clothes at the top were definitely the ones she and Sandro were wearing yesterday – his cream socks and grey boxers, her white knickers and bra. Beneath them was Sandro's shirt. Both she and Sandro had been here all night so last night's cast-offs should be undisturbed. Delving deeper she came across Saturday's underwear and beneath that Friday's. It was clear that no-one had looked in here for anything. Normally, when it was time to do the laundry, she was resentful of the fact that this basket was fixed in place and couldn't just be carried to the washing machine and upended in front of it. Now she had mixed feelings. If she couldn't upend it, then nor could anyone who might be searching through her possessions. They would be certain to disturb the order of the layers of dirty clothes in their search. The more she thought about it the more she realised that if she ever did need to hide anything this would be the ideal place, perhaps beneath a false bottom. For all his good points, Sandro never did the laundry, so she could hide anything in here without him finding it. She looked at the bottom of the basket and wondered how easy it would be to make a false one. The existing one didn't seem to fit that well anyway, there was a gap most of the way round between the bottom and the sides. She'd never noticed that before. It was almost as if it already had a false base in it. Intrigued, she quickly pulled out all the clothes, dumping them on the floor unceremoniously – this was the harshest treatment her lingerie had ever received. The bottom of the basket looked like it could be prised up, so she went to the kitchen and came back with a blunt knife and a spoon. The knife was too long and couldn't get any leverage, but the spoon provided a suitable mechanism to lever the bottom up enough for her to grasp it with her fingernails and lift it out. Beneath she found the original base of the basket and nothing else. Surprised, and not a little disappointed she was about to put the false bottom back down when she realised that it had a buff envelope taped underneath.

Carrying the wooden disc over to the bed she sat down and stared at the envelope. After a few seconds deliberation she decided that she needed to know what was in this envelope, and why it was there. She could only assume that it had been hidden there by Sandro, but couldn't conceive of any reason why. Picking at the tape with her fingernails, she managed to remove the envelope and open it. Inside was a CD-ROM with a scrawled title written on it in Sandro's handwriting: 'NAC'.

What did NAC mean? Costanza had no idea. It wasn't a word she recognised in either Italian or English – the only two languages that Sandro spoke. It wasn't even an abbreviation with which she was familiar. Intrigued and a little worried, she dropped the wooden disc on the floor, stood up and walked to the study.

As she inserted the CD into Sandro's computer, all sorts of possibilities raced through Costanza's thoughts. She waited impatiently while the disc span up to speed and appeared on the desktop. The disc was named 'NAC' on the screen too. She opened it to find a list of files which were all encrypted. Most of them were obviously e-mails that Sandro had saved, some had been attachments. They all had names like NAC001 or BILD001. This still meant nothing to Costanza. She knew that Sandro used PGP occasionally, so she tried to decrypt the files. When prompted for a password she stopped. She had repeatedly lectured Sandro on choosing strong un-guessable passwords, but she suspected that, like most people, he always chose something easy to remember instead. She hoped he wouldn't have been foolish enough, but tried anyway: Costanza. The password was accepted and the files were decrypted. The first thing anybody would have tried. She obviously needed to lecture him again. If this was how careless he was with something he needed to hide, how easy would it be to break into his online bank account?

Now she had decrypted the files she opened one of them. It was an email sent by someone identified as TS. It had come from an account at a remailer five days ago and was addressed to Sandro. The subject line was NAC.

"What is this NAC?" Costanza wondered out loud.

As she read the email she sank into the chair in front of the screen. The email was signed by someone called Tim. He was clearly known to Sandro, although the greeting was formal, almost business-like, not an email from a close friend. The message, written in English, was about a meeting of American politicians and business leaders. When she got to the end she finally discovered what the letters NAC stood for.

"New American Century!" she read out loud. "Typically arrogant. Now they think they own time as well."

She opened another email and then another. They were all from the same sender, Tim, whoever he was. More reports about meetings. Almost like a journalist's filed copy. But why would this Tim have been sending them to Sandro? She opened the web browser to search for more information about the NAC and accidentally opened the history window. There, before her eyes, was an entry for deadbet.net. What was that doing on Sandro's computer? She hadn't used it to look at the deadbet site. Nor had she mentioned anything about it to Sandro. Why would he have visited it? Where would he have heard about it? Sandro was a photographer and used his computer mostly for playing with images. He used the

Internet in a limited way, for researching subjects and for email to friends and clients. He never gambled and wasn't interested in the cult of celebrity. He was unlikely to have come across a site like deadbet by browsing. Somewhat shocked she closed the browser and put the computer back to sleep after ejecting the disc. She stood up slowly, took the disc and walked out of the room and into the lounge where she picked up her handbag and slipped the disc into it. Still a little confused she walked to the door having decided it was now time to leave for work.

Capri

Mario was behind the bar, as usual. He was polishing glasses, as usual. He had been thinking about football, as usual. He was now thinking about that tall blonde who had just come down to reception. He was imagining taking her to the Blue Grotto, all alone in a small boat in that eerie cavern, lit by the fluorescent blue light from beneath. She would be enthralled; he would sing to her, his soft voice echoing off the walls of the grotto; she would be putty in his hands. Just then an unsubtle cough interrupted his fantasy and he realised that there were two guests waiting to be served.

"Scusa, Signori" he said, putting down the cloth and glass.

"Yeah, about time," said the shorter, fatter of the pair, "two martinis. You do know how to make martinis in this country?"

"Martini is Italian, sir."

"So?"

"We know how to make them." He bit his tongue. He was used to dealing with rich and rude guests, that was the name of the game in an expensive hotel like this. What did irritate him though was when they were so obviously stupid and ignorant. How did such a moron get to be rich and powerful? He made the Martinis and delivered them to the table that the two men had occupied.

"Add them both to my room, will you." said the skinny one.

"Which room is that sir?"

"The Fields Suite."

"Thank you sir."

"Oh, hey. Tell me, why is it called the Fields Suite. All I can see out the window is the sea, no fields."

"It is named after Gracie Fields, sir."

"Who?"

"She was a famous English actress and singer who came to live on Capri and spent her last years here."

"Never heard of her."

Mario walked back to the bar, and rang up the price of the drinks onto the Fields Suite bill. He returned to his glass polishing activities but couldn't summon up the image of the blonde to complete his fantasy. After a while, noticing the two men getting up to leave, he walked over to their table to retrieve the glasses, in the hope of finding a tip. The glasses were empty as was the rest of the table. The only tip was that of a cigar in the ashtray. As the men were walking away he heard them laughing.

"Bloody journalists, always sticking their noses in. Well at least that Shah won't be bothering us anymore. Glad we got rid of him..." the fat one was saying as they ambled away towards the conference suite. "...the Senator will be happy." They both laughed again.

Mario had already heard about the death of the journalist on Saturday. The body had been found by two youngsters who lived next door to his mother. The whole of Anacapri was buzzing with rumours about his death. The coroner in Naples did not work at the weekend so there had been no official announcement yet about the cause of death. Mario was now convinced that it wouldn't be natural causes. What should he do? If he told the police what he had heard there would be an investigation and he would lose his job for breach of confidence. If he did nothing he would be, what do they call it on the TV cop shows? An accessory after the fact. He would need to get someone else to tell the police without involving him. He would be having his morning break in a few minutes time and he often went for a walk around the perimeter of the hotel grounds, taking in the view and the fresh air. He could easily walk a little way outside and chat to the journalists that were waiting out there.

Half an hour later, Mario was standing on the edge of a cliff looking out to sea. Next to him was a slightly built man with pale skin and a balding head. His name was Norman.

"So what exactly did you hear?" asked Norman.

"I heard them say that they were glad they had got rid of the journalist Shah." Mario replied.

"So you think that they killed him. Or had him killed?"

"Don't you?"

"Is it easy to hire killers around here?"

"How should I know? I'm a barman not a criminal."

"Well, with the Naples mafia just over the bay."

"This is Capri not Naples. I don't know who killed him, but it seemed like those people were behind it."

"Maybe they were just celebrating. They don't like us you know."

"No it was more like gloating."

"What else have you heard them say?"

"Them? Nothing."

"Others then?"

"Well yesterday I did hear someone talking about P2."

"That's very old news."

"No, a new investigation to be launched by Cardinal Bramante."

"Well that won't happen now."

"Why not?"

"Don't you know?" Norman looked at him as if he was simple. "Bramante is dead. He had a heart attack last week in Rome. He won't be investigating anything now."

Mario looked shocked.

"You don't think?"

"What?" asked Norman.

"That they killed him. A Cardinal. A good man too." Mario had checked with his mother yesterday evening and confirmed that it had been Cardinal Bramante that had rescued the local church. She thought he was a saint.

"Wouldn't be the first time" said Norman.

"No, it can't be true." Mario was still looking shocked. He turned to face Norman and shook his head.

"They wouldn't dare." He walked back to the entrance, waited while the security staff opened the gate just wide enough for him, walked through and on past the growling guard dogs in a daze.

Norman was talking hurriedly into his mobile phone.

"Yeah, inside source. Says they're all congratulating themselves on having dealt with Shah and Bramante. Let me know as soon as there's anything official on cause for Tim. And check up on Bramante too. I seem to remember there was surprise that he should have a heart attack – he'd just passed a medical or something. Okay. Thanks."

Some of the other journalists had been carefully listening to what Norman was saying. Within a few minutes the whole of the press corps had become convinced that the NAC had killed their colleague. They wouldn't let them get away with it.

New York, USA

It was getting towards the end of a long night-shift and Laurie was just stifling a large yawn when she heard Rebecca's phone ring. Pressing the record button on the tape deck in front of her, she picked up the headphones and had put them back on her head just as Rebecca answered the phone.

"Hello?"

"Becca, is that you?" a man's voice asked.

"Yeah. Do you know what time it is?"

"Er, no?"

"Six o'clock."

"Were yer sleepin'?"

"Yeah."

"Sorry, I've been up for a while, I hadn't noticed it was still s'early."

"Too late to worry now. What's the matter Jerry?"

Laurie made a note on the pad in front of her, 'Jerry (surname?) – Irish American accent.'

"There's a problem here in Boston."

Laurie wrote 'Boston' on her pad and drew a line linking it to 'Jerry'.

"What now? I thought everything was in hand. You all know what to do."

"Many of the others think that what yer doing in New York is just a distraction. They think we should strike here in Boston first."

"What's changed their mind? They were in favour when I was there before."

"I'm not really sure. Lots of things have changed now we're rid of O'Leary. City Hall is a different place now. The general view is that now is not the time for subtlety. We need to take more drastic measures."

Laurie wrote down 'O'Leary!' and underlined it three times.

"It sounds like you believe that too Jerry?"

"I dunno. I think yer a great girl Becca. I think yer an inspiration and if anyone can pull this off you can. But maybe it's too much even for you. Maybe we should start with a significant show of strength here."

"But Jerry, what I'm doing here in New York will be so much bigger and better. We'll get national coverage. The government will be forced to see things our way if we have public opinion behind us. A small strike in Boston won't even make the inside pages of the New York Times, but by the end of this week we'll be front page news across the country. Have faith Jerry. That's all I'm asking. Faith and patience. Try and convince the others too, I don't want them doing anything stupid on their own."

"Okay Becca. I'll try. We'll see how things blow up on Thursday and take it from there. See yer. Sorry again about waking yer up."

"Never mind. See you Jerry."

As Rebecca put down her phone, Laurie was adding to her notes. She wrote 'Blow up New York Thursday, then strike Boston.' Not only had she now got a connection between the Bedford woman and the death of O'Leary in Boston, but she had clear evidence that they were planning some sort of explosion here in New York followed by an attack in Boston, and who knows where else. Now it was up to her and Adam to try and find out the target and stop her. It was looking like Thursday would be a busy day this week.

Cheltenham

The clock on the wall of the crypto team's office flicked over to show 11:00 just as the door opened and Katie walked in.

"Tony Hey?" she said, looking around at a room full of surprised faces.

"Hello Ms. Cannon" Tony said as he stood up. "Shall we go to the other office?" He walked towards her with his notebook in one hand and a sheaf of pages of laser printer output in the other.

All eyes in the room were on him, as he held the door open for Katie and followed her out. As the door closed a collective out-breath broke the silence. Slightly embarrassed at their own reactions, everyone quickly returned to work.

Even before Katie had sat down in the room where she had spoken to Costanza less than two days before, she was starting to get irritated by this man. Who did he think he was? Typically arrogant crypto type. Thought he was smarter than her, and keen to prove it. And that posturing when she arrived, clearly for the benefit of the rest of the room. She had already decided he was not only arrogant and insecure, but also a bachelor (probably living at home with his widowed mother) and a virgin. Likely to stay that way too.

"So. Now you've dragged me down here, tell me what I'm supposed to have missed from our Italian friend." She slammed her briefcase down on the table in front of her so hard that the handset jumped from the phone cradle just as Tony was about to press the play button. Reseating the handset, he pressed play with a flourish and sat down opposite Katie in triumph.

"From where? Who?" Katie's muffled voice came out of the speaker.

"I can't tell you at the moment, especially not on an open line like this. You never know who's listening. But it's a dead bet." The Italian voice.

Tony pressed stop and looked expectantly at Katie.

"So?" she asked.

"It's a dead bet."

"So what? She isn't as fluent in English as she likes to think and misused an idiom."

"Which was a very clever way to disguise what she told you, so that any grunt listening would think nothing of it."

"Okay so now you're just trying to insult me. Tell me what I'm supposed to have missed for godsake."

"Dead bet."

"Dead cert?"

"No dead bet. Deadbet." He looked expectantly.

"What?"

"deadbet.net!" he almost exploded with frustration, as if talking to an idiot or the barman in that awful new pub that had replaced the traditional inn in his village.

"Which is what exactly?"

"Do you lot never read anything we send you?"

"I've got better things to do than try and decipher a hundred pages of drivel each week." She was really irritated now and had given up any pretence of hiding that fact. "You guys are supposed to decipher things to make it easier for us to analyse, not harder."

This wasn't going the way Tony had hoped. Katie was supposed to be impressed at how clever he was and how up to date. Instead she seemed to be treating him like an idiot. Just like all the other women he had ever talked to; there must be some world-wide conspiracy among them to treat him like this – well it didn't need to be world-wide, he'd never travelled outside the South of England so it could conceivably just be a national conspiracy, although even the women he had tried to talk with in

Internet chat rooms had behaved the same (except Sasha, and she had eventually turned out to be a man anyway). He took a deep breath.

"deadbet.net is a web site. It's a betting site where the bets are on people dying. It was first proposed as an academic exercise to illustrate how wide area networking could lead to the development of new crimes."

"What's new about betting on the internet? Come to that, it's not a crime anyway. At least not here."

"The new element, and indeed the crime, is what they're betting on and how potential punters can win. You bet on the time, place and manner of death of an individual, usually a celebrity. Each punter places a stake. If, and when, the celebrity actually dies, the bet with the closest details wins all the stake-money - minus a commission and tax."

"I still don't see the criminal aspect of it."

"If you want to be sure to win, especially if the pot is quite large for a particular celebrity, then you can make sure that your bet is the closest if you kill the celebrity yourself in your predicted way at your predicted time and place."

"So surely the plods just arrest whoever won the bet."

"That's where it gets clever. The bets are made with electronic cash. The winnings are paid out from that electronic cash. It's anonymous and untraceable. Everyone who placed a bet downloads the winnings file, but only the actual winner can decrypt it and spend it."

"Okay, very interesting academic exercise. What's this got to do with anything?"

"I told you, the idea started as an academic exercise, but now it's a real web site running a real service. I went and had a look this morning and found the following names of celebrities who had been bet on the site and have recently died." He slid a sheet of paper across the desk towards Katie. "As you can see Rabbi Cohen is the latest one to die. But there have been some others in the last three months. The curious thing is that they have almost all died of unexpected heart attacks. Were any of these on your Italian friend's list?"

"I don't know, she didn't tell me who was on that list, although she said that they'd lost three senior clergy."

"That fits, there are two Cardinals and an Archbishop." She looked at the paper in front of her.

"Who else is on the list that's not yet dead?" Katie had almost forgotten her irritation as she started to see that maybe Tony really had picked up a hidden message in Costanza's comment.

Tony pushed another sheet of paper across the table.

"Ah! Now I see why they're worried" said Katie as she looked at the list.

"Who?" asked Tony.

"The Vatican."

"Oh yeah, I guess they would be."

Rome

As she made her way to work, Costanza's mind was reeling from her unexpected discovery. Who was this Tim? Why was he sending Sandro emails about an American political group. Why was Sandro hiding them? Who from? Why had he visited the deadbet website? It was all too confusing. She tried to piece together all the apparently unrelated facts, unrelated apart from having Sandro in common.

She had decided it would be better to walk to the Vatican this morning; it wasn't far from their apartment and the journey would give her some time to think. She crossed a road in a daze, safe in the midst of a crowd of people, but soon she was the only one in the side streets of the Borgo. She glanced in the window of a souvenir shop as she walked past. Among the plaster colosseums and neon sacred hearts there was a jigsaw puzzle of St. Peter's. The picture on the front of the box had one piece removed, a piece containing the Pope blessing the faithful, 'Urbi et Orbi' – the City and the World. She stopped and stared at the box. What was the missing piece in her puzzle? The piece that would bring the rest into focus and allow her to understand what was really going on? Was it too related to His Holiness?

By the time she had reached the Angel Gate she was no closer to a solution. She kept going over and over the same facts in her mind. Nothing made sense. Sandro wasn't interested in politics, not even Italian politics, let alone American politics. She walked through the security checkpoints on autopilot, everyone noticing how quiet and distant she was this morning.

Cheltenham

"So what should we do?" asked Tony as Katie looked at the list of names on the desk in front of her.

"Do?"

"Yeah."

"Nothing."

"What?"

"Is this website operating out of the UK?"

"No."

"No-one significant on this list is a British citizen that needs protecting."

"So?"

"So, there's nothing for us to do. It's not our problem. We've got too much else to do without going looking for problems."

"But people are in danger."

"Not British citizens."

"Even so, we should do something to help track down the killer."

"If there is a killer."

"Don't you understand how this works?"

"Yes. I'm not stupid you know. All you bloody boffins think you're so clever and that the rest of us are idiots. Just because I'm not interested in how big numbers relate to each other doesn't mean I'm simple. I got a first from Oxford. I have a life, unlike you. You may be able to speak algebra and differential equations, computer jargon and internet addresses. But can you speak any real languages? I'm fluent in Japanese, German and Arabic. And I can hold a conversation in Farsi, Mandarin, Korean, Dutch, Swedish and Danish. You may think you're so clever that you understood what our Italian friend meant when she said 'dead bet' and I didn't, but while you lot down here are busy having ecstasies over the latest prime number I'm out there in the real world trying to stop real enemies doing unspeakable things to this country. So don't tell me I'm stupid."

"I didn't."

"And don't try and tell me what we should do about some little 'click M for Murder' website."

Tony was taken aback by Katie's tirade. After a bad start he had thought she was warming to him. Clearly she had a low regard for him and everyone else in the crypto team. He looked down at his hands in his lap.

"I have a life."

"What?"

"You said I don't have a life. I do. We may not be as sophisticated here in the countryside as you Londoners. We don't have fancy night clubs and famous people to hob nob with. But we still have lives."

"So?"

He looked up from his hands and straight into her eyes.

"So, you think you're better than us, with your Oxford degree and your London home, and your nine languages. But when it comes down to it, you don't actually care about anyone else do you? You're not interested in doing anything to stop this deadbet murderer. Just because no-one that you're paid to protect is currently being threatened. But for all your airs and graces and fancy language, you don't have the imagination to see where it's leading. Even a 'bloody boffin' like me has imagination. I can see that it's only a matter of time before all the people you're trying to protect are threatened by this attack. What's more, we already had the imagination to see this coming. Even the yanks could see this coming. They hacked the software that generates electronic cash, so they could put a tracker into the money. Make a bet on one of the targets with the tracker switched on and they can find out where it goes when it's been won."

"Let them worry about it then." Katie glared back at him.

"It's too late actually. We hacked their hack some time ago, now any tracker reports to us and sends misinformation to them."

"What?" Katie was shocked.

"We can't have them undermining money can we?" Tony grinned "I've already submitted a bet on the website and the tracker will report back to me here when the money is retrieved."

"You don't have the authority to do that."

"As I said, too late."

"We'll see about that." Katie stood up and pushed the chair away with such force that it fell backwards behind her. She strode to the door muttering under her breath "Bloody boffins, always interfering."

As she opened the door she looked back at Tony and said "You'll wish you'd never come here from whatever poly they found you in."

"Actually I was at Cambridge. Kings. Double first."

Katie walked through the door with a shrug.

"And a PhD" he called after her.

"Hmm" he thought, "that could have gone better."

Vatican

Costanza walked through the door into a busy office. Most of her staff looked up to say hello, saw the look on her face and decided against it.

There had already been some consternation here this morning. The first people to arrive had been confronted by odd diagrams on the white board and me, a strange man, sitting at Costanza's workstation. No-one recognised me, but I was wearing a red pass so they decided not to challenge my right to be here. As the morning wore on and more people arrived the whispered speculation grew more outlandish, especially as Costanza had never been known to be late.

Now that she had arrived everyone became ostentatiously busy while managing to keep an eye on her desk to see what would happen. What did happen surprised all of them. Costanza walked over to her chair, the stranger stood up and she embraced him like a long lost brother. Instead of letting go she clung on as if for dear life and was apparently crying.

"What's happened?"

"I think Sandro must be involved somehow, but I don't know how. Or why."

"What! Why?"

"I told you I don't know why," she sobbed.

"No. Why do you think he's involved?" We were both whispering, much to the annoyance of a room full of curious voyeurs.

"I found some files. Emails. And Sandro's browser had been used to visit deadbet. It was in his history log."

"Just because he's visited the website doesn't mean he's involved."

"It's a bit of a coincidence, don't you think?"

"Coincidences happen. Do you really believe that Sandro could be involved in a murder plot?"

"No."

"Well, there you are then. Now, did you say something about emails?"

"Yes. I found a disc hidden in our bedroom with some encrypted files. They were emails from someone called Tim, about an American political group."

"How did you break the encryption? Do you have access to VICI from home?"

"No, I guessed his password. Pathetic, the first one I tried."

"Maybe he wasn't trying to hide it from you."

"It would have been the first one you'd try, or anyone else come to that."

"So what political group? I didn't think politics was Sandro's thing."

"It's not, especially not American politics. The emails were about some group called NAC. Apparently it's the New..."

"...American Century. Yes I've heard of them. Neo-conservatives, very right wing, even by American standards. Evangelical, convinced that the USA is the promised land and that Americans are God's chosen people. They are determined to put America in its rightful place as leader of the world and in the process wipe out all traces of dissidence or alternative culture, philosophy or religion. Just as totalitarian and psychopathic as the communists they claim to despise."

"I don't understand why Sandro would be getting emails about people like that. Or who would be sending them to him. Oh Peter. I'm so confused. And worried. For Sandro, the baby. I'm glad you're here. It must have been my guardian angel who sent you just when I need you."

"Not quite. I think it was more likely to have been your boss."

"What do you mean? He only agreed to let you help when I told him you were in Rome."

"But the reason I came to Rome was because I was summoned by the Swiss Guard. I was told to let people know I was coming here for a short break and contact my friends in Rome. I suspect that it was deliberately engineered so you would ask me for help without either of us realising we were being manipulated. A considerate boss who wanted to get you some help but didn't want to offend you by suggesting it directly."

By now, Costanza's tears had stopped and she let go of me. She retrieved a dainty handkerchief from her sleeve and dabbed at her eyes. Around the room, heads suddenly went down as everybody made sure they were busy and wouldn't be caught watching. I remembered why I don't like open-plan offices.

New York, USA

"Professor Smith?" asked the voice on the telephone.

"Speaking" she said.

It was unusual for Missouri to answer her own telephone. Despite having an office here in the university building she was almost never present. Even so it was, like everywhere else that she inhabited, a complete mess. Piles of papers on the desk were threatening to topple over and join the piles already on the floor. Stacks of books on top of the filing cabinet, window ledge and also on the floor were accompanied by bundles of essays from students, all awaiting marks but most destined to remain unread and eventually to join the archaeological layers of detritus that may one day be excavated – but only after the departure of the Professor to a better life. She was notorious among departmental staff for ignoring protocol, forgetting to mark coursework and abandoning papers halfway through to be finished by her co-authors. However she was also famously brilliant at her research (whether or not she ever published it), world-renowned in the fields of early Mediterranean history and archaeology, and legendary among students for her exciting, if unusual lectures.

Her excavation experience had come in handy when the phone rang, as she had no idea where it was, having not seen it for months. But the caller had been insistent and it had rung long enough for her to burrow through the strata of deposits on the desk and unearth it.

"It's Ray Rogers, Professor".

"What is?"

"Me."

"Sorry?"

"I'll start again. Professor, my name is Ray Rogers. We spoke some time ago about early Christian literature."

"We did? Oh yes. You were interested in the Pauline

160

Apologetic."

"No no. The Codex Albustensis."

"Same thing. Popular discussion is calling it that, but I'm more interested in its origins rather than who owned it a millennium and a half later, and anyway it's not a Codex. In academic circles it is known as the Pauline Apologetic. So, what can I do for you?"

"If someone claimed to have the Codex... I mean the Pauline Apologetic, could you verify its authenticity?"

"The Vatican have never even acknowledged its existence, let alone admitting they have it. So they'd never agree to letting anyone authenticate it."

"But what if the Vatican doesn't have it and someone else does? Someone who would be interested in finding out if it is genuine. Could you authenticate it?"

"It would be impossible to authenticate it as a reliable report of the event it purports to record. We could, however, determine if it was written in the right style and language for the time, using appropriate materials for the manuscript and inks which are authentic. We can date it. If it's a fake we can spot it. If it's real we can say it was produced at the right time in the right place but no more than that. Two thousand years on we can't tell the difference between a note that was made by a scribe who was present and propaganda produced by one of Paul's supporters who was not."

"But could you definitely rule out a later fake."

"We could spot anything produced more than about thirty years after the event."

"Good."

"But who is claiming to have it?"

"All in good time. But I believe it may come into my safekeeping in a few days time and if so I want to be sure that it is genuine."

"I told you, no-one can give you that assurance."

"Well then, I want to be sure it's no fake."

"Where is it?"

"I can't tell you. But it is headed this way. When I receive it I will contact you again and we can arrange for you to come and authenticate it."

"Hold on. It doesn't work like that. To authenticate it we have to run lots of tests on it. We need equipment, we have to take a sample of the materials and the ink. You would need to bring it to the laboratories here so we can run all the tests."

"And how long would that take?"

"If it's a fake we may know within half an hour, on the other hand it may take a few months to check everything."

"But I would need to know immediately. And I couldn't leave it with you for months."

"Nobody could promise to give you a result that quickly. We can take a sample for all our physical tests, use imaging techniques to obtain perfect copies under different wavelengths of light and x-rays, then give you back the original. We'd need it for about a day."

"That sounds a bit better. How soon could you do it?"

"Let me know when you have the manuscript and it'll take me a couple of days to get everyone together."

"Get everyone together? I thought you'd be doing the testing?"

"I need technicians to operate the electron microscope, the x-ray microscope, the spectroscope, to do the carbon dating, chromatography on the inks and..."

"Okay I get the idea. It's just that I don't want anyone to know we've got it until we're ready to make an announcement, especially if it isn't genuine."

"Of course, don't worry we're all professionals here. Everyone's used to not talking about our work until we're ready to publish."

"When the manuscript arrives I will call you again."

"Do you want to leave me your number now?"

"No. I'm calling from a public phone and I'm not sure where I'll be for the next few days. I have a lot of meetings with various groups of people and a conference on Thursday. I don't like mobile phones."

"Okay, but don't use this phone number. You were lucky you got through to me, I'm rarely here. Call the history department secretary and tell her where I should get in touch with you. It's Roy Rogers right?"

"Ray Rogers."

"Oh okay, sorry."

"While we're on the subject of names, were you really named Missouri by your parents?"

"Well, no. When I decided to become an archaeologist I changed my name to Missouri. You know, like Indiana Jones. I thought it sounded more cool."

"What's your real name?"

"Missouri is my real name. If you mean my original name it's Deborah, but I was always called Debbie. I grew up in Dallas, so that was another reason to change my name."

"Why what's wrong with Dallas?"

"You know Debbie. Dallas. Never mind. I've gotta go now. Students beckon. I'll talk to you soon then. Bye." She put the phone down, picked up the book she had come to retrieve and left her office. As tranquillity returned to the room the papers on the desk resettled around the disturbance caused by the extraction of the phone. Dust restarted its slow task of covering everything.

Rome

Despite my best efforts, Costanza had spent the rest of the day worrying, convinced that Sandro was somehow involved in the conspiracy we were sure we had uncovered. She had resisted the temptation to call him – if he was feeling concerned enough to hide his files from someone who might come looking, then those same people could be tapping his phone.

I offered to go home with her to talk to Sandro, but she was keen to deal with him herself.

"I don't want him to think I immediately came crying to you," she had said, dabbing the tears from her eyes with her handkerchief.

She failed to see the irony and I decided it would be better not to point it out. I had let her go home alone and she had been waiting there all evening for Sandro to return. About 10 o'clock she had phoned me.

"Peter. He hasn't come home yet. He's almost never this late, and he always calls me if he's going to be delayed. What if something has happened to him?"

"Was there any sign that your apartment had been searched while you were out?"

"No. Everything was as I left it."

"What did you do with Sandro's disc?"

"I took it with me. I still have it in my handbag. So anyone searching would have found nothing."

"There you are then."

"What?"

"If there was nothing to find anyway, what could be the problem? He's probably working late and hasn't noticed the time. You know what creative types are like."

"But if someone did come looking and found nothing, maybe they went after him."

"I think you're letting your imagination run away with you. I'm sure he's just working. Have you tried calling him?"

"Yes, of course. There's no answer from the studio and his cell-phone is switched off. Oh Peter. I'm so worried."

"Look, do you want me to ..."

"Hang on!" she interrupted me, "the phone is ringing in the bedroom. Don't go away."

I heard her drop her cell-phone and run across the room. The distant sound of ringing stopped and was replaced by a muted voice. After a couple of minutes the phone crackled as it was picked up.

"That was him. He's okay."

"Good. I shan't say I told you so. But..."

"Okay, okay. He's been shooting on location and the battery died in his cell-phone. He's just got back to the studio. He'll be home in half an hour. I was so relieved to hear his voice. He guessed."

"Guessed what?"

"That I had been worrying. He thought I suspected him of having an affair or something, especially as he'd been out with a model all day."

"He knows that you know him better than that."

"But Amadea, that's his Mamma, told him that I would be unpredictable and irrational now I'm pregnant, because of the hormones!" she laughed. "Maybe that's why I'm so worried about him tonight."

"Are you going to be alright until he gets home?"

"Yes thanks. I will now. See you tomorrow."

"Call me later if you need to. Whatever time, it doesn't matter. I don't mind if you wake me up."

"Ciao, Pietro."

"Ciao cara" I said and put the phone back on the cradle. I picked up the book I had been reading and lay back against the headboard.

The sound of the key being turned in the lock acted like a trigger to Costanza. Before he had got the front door fully open Sandro was being grabbed by his wife and hugged. Slightly bemused, but quite happy, Sandro reciprocated while slowly edging his way into the room so he could kick the door shut behind him. The two of them gracefully pirouetted across the room until finally they collapsed together onto the sofa.

"I was so worried."

"Why?"

"You hadn't rung or anything. I couldn't get through to you and I thought they had got you. I ..."

"Who'd got me? What are you talking about?" Sandro sat back looking at her as if she was crazy.

"Them. The NAC or whoever you were hiding the disc from."

"What? Oh. How did you find that? I thought I'd hidden it very cleverly."

"Pathetic actually."

"And I'd encrypted the files like you'd shown me once, how do you know what they're about?"

"Even more pathetic. Did you ever listen to anything I've ever told you about choosing passwords?"

"Er. Yes. I think so. You said don't use my name."

"or mine. It was the first thing I tried. But that's not the point. Who is Tim? Why has he sent you this stuff and how are you involved with deadbet?"

"Deadbet? What's deadbet?"

"A website that's in your browser history file."

"Means nothing to me. Anyway, Tim Shah is a journalist I worked with a few years ago – you remember that story in Morocco? Ah, no, it was while you were working in London. Anyway, I was shooting the pictures for a feature he did for a glossy – I think it was the New

York Times. We got on very well and have vaguely kept in touch ever since. He sent me an email a while ago and asked if I could keep some files for him as backup in case anything happened."

"Happened? Like what?"

"I don't know, he wasn't specific. I assumed he was worried about disc failures, viruses or something. So I agreed. He sent me some more emails recently with the files to keep for him. He suggested I burn them onto a CD and hide it. That's when I realised maybe he was worried about more than a disc failure. I did what he asked. I was going to ask your advice, but with the baby I didn't want to worry you."

"Well you've worried me even more in the end."

"Yeah. Sorry about that."

"So what now?"

"Wait for another email I guess."

Costanza leant forward and hugged him again. Sandro breathed deeply and looked at his beautiful wife.

"How about continuing this hug in bed…"

Langley, Virginia, USA

Even though it was early evening and most employees had already started leaving to go home, the Counter Intelligence Center Analysis Group was still busy. Or at least some of them were. Joel Schitzenberger had been very busy all day and was still at his workstation. Having only been working here for six months he was keen to impress his boss. He had seen a record of a phone call logged by the Office of Russian and European Analysis from somebody at SIS in England. The brief report had mentioned three separate keywords that had caused him to take an interest.

The first had been the inclusion of a reference to the Middle East summit that had been taking place in England at the weekend - although all official sources confirmed that the death of Rabbi Cohen had been entirely due to natural causes with no suspicious circumstances, any untimely deaths relating to the Middle East were always of concern to CIC/AG.

The second had been a reference to the deadbet website. It too had been of concern to CIC/AG who were convinced it was operated by a foreign intelligence agency as a cover for clandestine activities (although it had not occurred to anyone at the CIA that using a publicly accessible website to advertise what was essentially a contract killing service could hardly be seen as any sort of cover).

But most interesting had been the reference to the Vatican. Until today, Joel had been unaware that the Vatican even had an intelligence service. But within the space of a couple of hours he had seen two separate reports that referred to them. Over the weekend a call had come into the CNC from the Vatican themselves, the transcript of which also referred to the deadbet website.

Both calls had been handled rather poorly. The CNC

had been very offhand and dismissive to the Vatican, largely, Joel felt, because of a perception of their size and hence assumed professionalism. OREA had given every impression of being attentive in responding to the call from SIS, but the notes made it quite clear that no action would be taken. Joel knew that, despite public pronouncements about alliances and coalitions, the transatlantic 'special' relationship was very definitely one-way – any useful information that the Brits could dig up would be welcomed and put to good use, but nothing of any significance ever went in the other direction. "But hey," though Joel, "they are our oldest enemy after all. We had to fight a war to stop being a colony, why should we help them now?"

Nevertheless, Joel was inclined to believe that both these calls may be worth pursuing a little further. One of the common suggestions in both calls had been that someone was using the deadbet website to fund a campaign of assassinations and that in each case the victim died of a sudden unexpected heart attack. Although there had been no public disclosure of their weaponry, Joel knew that the CIA had, for years, been using a poison that could cause a heart attack and yet left no trace in the body. As far as the CIA was aware, no-one else, not even the KGB, had been able to reproduce this poison. If the deadbet victims were being murdered by induced heart attacks, and yet all of the victims had been declared as having died from natural causes, it suggested that the CIA's poison was being used. Unfortunately, it was standard field issue to every CIA office around the world, so it could have been obtained from almost anywhere. Office procedures were meant to ensure that no weapons were used without being signed out; records were kept to track usage and loss of weapons and ammunition in every office. Although most offices were supposed to submit their records to the Langley mainframe every month, lax attitudes to paperwork in various locations meant that the computer's records were often up to six weeks out of date. Luckily, one of Joel's co-alumni from Yale, Mike Probey, had started here at Langley at the same time as him. Mike worked in WINPAC and could probably get access to the records to see if any poison had gone missing. Joel called Mike's extension, but there was no answer, obviously Mike didn't feel the need to work late to improve his prospects. Turning to his computer screen, Joel clicked on the email icon and started to compose a message to Mike asking him to check the records. As he finished it and pressed send he heard someone walk up behind him. He turned his chair and found Assistant Director Hocke standing there. Flustered, he started to rise out of his seat.

"No don't get up Joel. I saw you here as I was walking through and thought I'd come and see what's so interesting that it keeps a young man inside here on a lovely evening like this."

"Well sir, I saw transcripts of two separate calls that had been dismissed by CNC and OREA, but seemed to corroborate each other and I wanted to try and investigate a bit further."

"And you were going to do this on your own?"

"No sir. I wanted to get more information before I brought it to anyone else's attention. Just in case it was a waste of time."

Sitting down on the edge of the desk behind him, Hocke looked interested.

"Start from the beginning, son."

"There was a call into CNC on Saturday evening from Vatican intelligence."

"Yes?"

"Before today, I didn't even know there was any such

thing."

"You better believe it. We rarely get to talk to them. They keep out of the politics and all the dirty stuff, but they exist all right. In fact, while there are no records, at least not available to us mere mortals, most senior intelligence agencies around the world suspect that they've been going a pretty long time. There's a reasonable likelihood that they've been around since at least the fifth century, possibly longer."

"But if they're so well established how come we hardly ever have anything to do with them?"

"As I said they're not interested in politics. They deal more in spiritual matters than worldly affairs. They have a different approach to everything and they're working to a different timescale, much, much longer term – no re-elections to worry about." He smiled.

"They have agents?"

"Yes, but not like us. They don't use guns or other lethal weapons. They collect intelligence at grass roots level, or so we think. Everywhere there is a parish priest they have a source of intelligence. One sixth of the world's population is Catholic, whatever nationality they are. If it comes down to a choice, many of them are more likely to help their church than their government. But having said that, they've never been a problem for us. Yet! But you said they called CNC?"

"Yes sir. They said they were concerned about a website that they thought was linked to the deaths of some prominent religious leaders."

"Catholic priests?"

"An archbishop and two Cardinals. But also Rabbi Cohen."

"The one who died on Saturday in England?"

"Yes sir. That's why they called."

"This website. What do we know about it?"

"We think it's a cover for a contract assassination operation. Probably being run by ex-intelligence officers from eastern Europe, working freelance now their governments have gone."

"So?"

"So CNC weren't interested and told them to go away. Politely of course."

"Why are you interested?"

"Because all the deaths have been caused by unexpected heart attacks."

"So they weren't murdered after all."

"Unless the heart attacks were induced."

"But presumably there were autopsies?"

"Which showed nothing out of the ordinary."

"So?"

"The second call was from SIS in England. The agent in charge of security at the summit where Rabbi Cohen died."

"And what did he say?"

"She called OREA this morning and said that the Vatican had been in touch with her asking about the Rabbi's death. She also mentioned the website, but she seemed to know we were monitoring it. OREA told her that we were keeping a watch on it and hoped to get some leads soon. But they had already checked up on Cohen's death and found out that there had been no close enough bets."

"Hold up. Bets? I thought we were dealing with contract hits not betting?"

"We are. The website works by masquerading as an offshore betting service, but the bets are all to do with the time, place and manner of the death of celebrities. It's called deadbet. We've been watching it for some time now."

"Ah yes. Sounds familiar, I think I read a preliminary

report a while ago."

"So anyhow, they effectively gave her the brush off."

"You still haven't explained why you've taken such an interest."

"Two calls within a couple of days seems too much to be just a coincidence."

"It's not. You said yourself that SIS called us because the Vatican called them. Sounds like they're getting worried and calling anyone they can think of. Why should we worry?"

"There have been three senior Catholic clergy die recently, all on the deadbet victim list, all of unexpected heart attacks. Rabbi Cohen was on the deadbet victim list and died of a heart attack."

"But hardly unexpected from what I heard."

"Maybe. I don't think we should assume it's the Vatican being paranoid."

"What's your theory then?"

"Someone has got hold of some TA21and is using it to kill people."

"Why?"

"Money. The 'winning' bet gets all the stakes on the website."

"Okay. How?"

"That's what I wanted to research before I flagged it up to anyone else. I have a friend in WINPAC. I've asked him to check records and see if any TA21 has gone missing recently from overseas offices."

"Only overseas offices?"

"No, but it seems the most likely, they're generally less well protected and accessible to more people."

The AD stood up again.

"Joel, you may be as paranoid as the Vatican. Or you may be on to something. Carry on and see what you and your friend can find out. If you get anywhere bring it straight to me. Understand?"

"Okay, are you sure?"

"Look, if TA21 is being used out there it could be a rogue agent, it could be black ops. They're both containable, one way or another. But it could also be something much worse. If you're right and someone outside has got hold of it and sells it to another agency we're in real trouble. Either way I want to know so we can handle it right. You get on with the research. If anyone gets in the way, let me know. I can usually expedite things with a few well placed phone calls." He grinned and walked away.

"Keep me updated Joel," he called over his shoulder.

"Yes sir."

Joel wasn't sure whether this had turned out to be a good day or the beginning of some very bad ones. He hadn't even realised that Assistant Director Hocke knew his name. Was that a good sign?

TUESDAY

Naples

Inspector Bettula adopted his familiar pose, leaning against an open doorframe looking down his nose and through the upper reaches of his moustache at a victim. The victim was, once again, Doctor Gambraccio.

"Well Dottore?"

"Yes I am, thank you for asking Inspector." Ernesto replied without even raising his eyes from the papers he had been failing to read for the last half hour. This was just the latest interruption in an endless stream. He would never clear this damned paperwork from his desk.

"No. I mean what is your conclusion..." he sighed. "...as I'm sure you knew" he added.

Massimo Bettula had always been convinced that those people with a better education than him, doctors, lawyers, engineers, had been trained in ways to make him look stupid. He wasn't exactly paranoid, he told himself, it's just that they were all out to get him – at least he always made himself laugh with that one, even if everyone else thought it trite.

The doctor gave up trying to read his paperwork, reached up to remove his spectacles and looked at the tall figure blocking his doorway.

"Have you not seen my report? I sent it to you last night." He frowned slightly.

"Typical. I've seen nothing. These people are useless. They can't even deliver a piece of paper from one side of the building to the other. You kept a copy of course?"

"Yes, do you want to see it?"

"Not now. Just tell me what your conclusions are."

"Okay. There were no visible indications of external trauma, no contusions or punctures. The cardiovascular system showed all the expected evidence that is concomitant with arrhythmia and ventricular fibrillation."

Massimo was irritated that the doctor was doing it

176

again.

"Without all the deliberately confusing jargon, if you don't mind."

"He had a heart attack."

"That's it?"

"Yes."

"Why?"

"Why what?"

"You know what I mean. Why did he have a heart attack? Was he overweight? Sick?"

"No. As far as we can tell he was fit and healthy. He had no trace of drugs or alcohol in his system."

"So, as I said, why did he have a heart attack?"

"No idea. He may have a family history of weak hearts, perhaps he was just unlucky. People do have heart attacks without any prior warning and with no obvious cause. Natural causes, that's what I concluded in my report. Natural causes."

"Ha! You're sure?"

"Yes."

"Okay, well you better come along with me then."

"Where to?"

"We have a visitor from the British Embassy who want to know what happened to their fellow citizen. You can tell him."

"Why can't you?"

"If he asks detailed medical questions I won't be able to answer and you will."

"Is an embassy bureaucrat likely to ask detailed medical questions?"

"This one is. He's not a bureaucrat, he's a friend of the cultural attaché. He's also, apparently, a doctor."

"Okay."

Ernesto pushed his chair back and stood up, at the same time absentmindedly folding his glasses and putting them into his shirt pocket in one fluid motion. He ran his fingers through his hair and walked over to the hook on the wall where his jacket hung limply. Trying to manoeuvre his arms into the sleeves whilst following Bettula along the corridor was not very effective. Ernesto had never been the suave sophisticate that most Italian men modelled themselves upon. He had always been slightly clumsy, gawkish. Most people expected him to wear English tweeds and smell of mothballs. As Bettulla accelerated down the corridor, the doctor found it more difficult to keep up without trying to run. That was his biggest mistake. At the end he rounded the corner and collided with one of the filing clerks. Papers went flying, his glasses spewed out of his pocket and he slammed into the wall, sliding down it into a heap on the floor. Seconds later, having regained his breath, he was helped to his feet by the clerk, who handed him back his glasses. As he bent to pick up her papers she shushed him away and pointed along the corridor to Inspector Bettula who was standing impatiently watching while holding open the door to the staircase. Feeling foolish and conspicuous, Ernesto walked towards the large man who was smiling through his stupid moustache.

"Careful, Dottore. I don't want another dead body on my hands."

"Thank you for your concern, Inspector" he said as he walked through the open doorway.

As the Englishman left the Inspector's office, Massimo turned to face the Doctor.

"Thank you. As I said, I wouldn't have been able to answer his questions. Especially as I don't speak English. You seemed quite fluent."

"Most of it wasn't even English, it was medical

terminology. Greek, Latin, German. But the same the world over among physicians. He understood what I found and agreed with what I concluded. I think he'll tell the Embassy it was natural causes. You won't have anything to worry about."

"I've always got something to worry about." The Inspector shrugged and looked down at his desk where he noticed a handwritten note from Commissioner Tersigni next to the doctor's report, which had now appeared. "Typical!"

Ernesto, who was in the process of standing to leave, turned back to see what had caused the latest outburst.

"Ah. I see my report has now arrived. Better late than never." He smiled.

"What? Oh yes. But I wasn't referring to your report's miraculous arrival."

"No? What then?"

"I have a note here from the Commissioner. Apparently there's trouble brewing over on Capri. There's some conference going on. Lots of foreigners. Rich, powerful foreigners. Especially Americans. It seems that there are also lots of journalists; friends and rivals of the dead one. They've decided he was killed by some American group called the NAC. So now Rome is getting edgy. The Americans are putting pressure on them, they're putting pressure on us. So we have to have a press conference to announce that this Englishman died from natural causes."

"Good luck then," said Ernesto as he started to walk out of the room.

"Not so fast. I'll need you at the press conference too. They might ask the same sort of questions. In fact, I'm sure of it."

"But I hate press conferences."

"Goes with the job. I'll get it arranged for just before

lunchtime, so no-one will be keen to hang around or drag it out. Be back here in time."

Ernesto sighed heavily and walked out of the office.

Rome

Anna sat on the edge of her bed and gazed out of the window. She could see the warm yellow stone walls of the building across the piazza. She could hear the sounds of life in the streets below. Women chattering away, children laughing. The putt putt sound of a motor scooter as it passed by. Water burbling in the fountain in the middle of the square. The sound of the coffee machine in the bar next door. A chair being scraped across the flagstones as a tourist settled down for a drink in the shade.

She shut her eyes and took a deep breath. The smells of pizza, coffee, scooter fumes all mingled together in her nose. The smell of Rome. The sounds of Rome. She had always dreamed of being here, but not alone. Never alone. This was not the way it should have been. This was not fair.

Opening her eyes again, she picked up the TV remote that was lying on the bed next to her. Flicking through the channels she found CNN. A news report was due to start any minute. She could catch up with what was going on in the world. What was going on back home. While she was waiting for the news she idly watched the weather report. It seemed odd to be sitting in Rome watching the weather forecast for the US east coast. Apparently Boston would have fine weather tomorrow. Shame.

She'd never liked Boston. Too uptight. Luckily she'd managed to avoid having to go there very often. Once she had been forced to attend a convention there, her dad usually went but he had been ill and she had to go in his place at the last minute. She had been very popular; most of the other attendees were balding middle aged men, they were all very keen to make the acquaintance of the cute young girl from Baltimore. After a while it drove her mad. She escaped from the hotel and went to find refuge in the nearby cathedral. While there she had seen a young boy crying in one of the pews. He was alone so she had tried to comfort him.

"What's the matter?"

"I'm frightened."

"What of?"

"Being hurt."

"Hurt? Hurt by who?"

"Father."

"Where's your mother? Won't she protect you?"

"No. She makes me go to him."

"Why?"

"She says it's good for me. She says I'll go to heaven. She says I'm just being a baby."

"Isn't there someone else who can help you? Keep you safe?"

"No."

She didn't really understand why he was frightened. She had heard about abusive parents, although she had been lucky enough to have a loving family. None of her friends had come from broken or dysfunctional homes. She was out of her depth. She also felt a little uncomfortable trying to look after a boy who was, after all, only a few years younger than herself. So she went looking for someone else to help him. She found two nuns in a small side chapel and they said that they would look after the boy. They'd take him to see the priest who looked after the choirboys.

"Don't you worry. Father will know what to do with him," they said as they led the sobbing lad away.

As she walked back to her hotel the boy's words played on her mind until she had a sudden, awful realisation. She may have consigned him back to the very person of whom he was afraid. She couldn't sleep and the following day had gone back to the cathedral. But she had never asked the boy his name, nor the sisters to whom she had entrusted him. She saw no-one she recognised from the previous evening. She left once more, feeling guilty.

A few years later, when media coverage exposed the treatment of boys by some of the clergy and created a scandal, she had been subjected to that feeling of guilt all over again. When Archbishop O'Leary had manipulated the diocese finances to avoid paying damages to the victims she had felt sickened with him personally. She read in one newspaper article that he had been choirmaster at the cathedral earlier in his career. She vowed at that point she would find a way to exact some form of payment from him; payment for the hurt he had caused that poor boy and others like him. But she had no idea what she could actually do. Then events had taken an unexpected turn and she found herself with the means to deal with him.

The Archbishop had never been particularly sociable. He wasn't a popular sort of person. Most people thought there was something peculiar about him. In return, he didn't care for them either. Quite why he had ever entered this vocation was a mystery to almost everybody, except his superiors who had always been impressed with his facility for the commercial and administrative aspects of the ministry. So when he got a rare request for an audience from an apparently wealthy young widow who wanted some advice, he had plenty of room in his diary. Not that he was particularly excited about having such a visitor, he had never been interested in women; unlike his assistant, a newly ordained young priest, who had made a very conscious decision to follow his calling even though he had been looking forward to losing his virginity at college - a dream left unrealised by going to the seminary.

Anna had arrived at the Archbishop's house and been

let in by Father Kevin, who was almost visibly shaking with pent-up emotion. Anna had worn her sheerest stockings and a very short dress – decent, but only just. Father Kevin soon had to excuse himself to go off for a few minutes of calming prayer (and probably a cold shower, she thought). O'Leary had agreed to meet her in his library. While she was waiting for him she looked around at the hundreds of dusty tomes. The library clearly pre-dated the Archbishop himself, presumably it was a collection started by an early predecessor and expanded by the intervening holders of the office. There were many books of theological discussion and philosophical argument, the majority with Latin titles. Some of the authors were names she recognised, St Augustine of Hippo (that had always made her laugh – as a child she had imagined him like St. George but riding a hippopotamus rather than a white horse), Thomas à Kempis, Thomas Kuhn, Aristotle, Plato. There were plenty of old bibles too, English, Latin, French. But she was surprised to see works by Hans Küng, Sigmund Freud, Carl Gustav Jung, Carl Rogers and R.D. Laing.

The Archbishop came into the library, introduced himself, sat down and asked how he could help. Anna, or Helen as she called herself, told him how she had been widowed and could not come to terms with her grief. She had no close family to rely on. She had moved away from her childhood home when she had married and had made no new friends. She had no-one to confide in, no-one to lean on, no-one to help her grieve or recover. She had been unable to talk to the local priest where she lived, but had heard that the Archbishop would be a suitable person to approach.

O'Leary was rather surprised to hear this. He couldn't imagine anything further from the truth and assumed that whoever had recommended him to her had been playing a rather cruel joke. For once, he decided that maybe he should actually try and help, if only to gain some sort of revenge over whoever had sent her his way. So for two hours he sat, still and quiet, in his library while this beautiful young woman sobbed and moaned. After more than an hour, Father Kevin who had been returning to the library to see if he could offer any assistance, had heard her moaning on the other side of the library door. This had set him off shaking again and he had retreated once more to the safety of his room, praying for guidance and doubting more than ever the wisdom of his calling.

A few minutes after Father Kevin's near re-appearance, O'Leary, regretting his earlier decision, decided he needed a break. He suggested that he fetch them both a drink. When Helen protested that she never drank alcohol, he quickly pretended that he had been referring to tea or coffee. Helen never touched coffee either (nor did she smoke or take drugs, apparently). But she did like herbal teas. The Archbishop rushed off to the kitchen, too eagerly thought Helen, to make her a cup of camomile tea. He would have a cup of English Breakfast tea himself, even though it was mid-afternoon. He had explained that it was quite some time since he had had to make his own tea so it may take longer than one might expect, allowing for him to find all the appropriate ingredients and equipment. In case she should come in search of him, he brought a tray to the library with a plate of cookies, a small jug of milk, a bowl of sugar cubes, two cups and saucers and a teaspoon. He returned to the kitchen for the teas, requesting her to keep an eye on the milk and cookies in case any insects should try to land on them. He was sure that would keep her in the library while he hid in the kitchen. He felt safe to stay away a further ten minutes, by which time he couldn't justifiably drag out the tea brewing process any longer and he returned to the library. He poured her camomile tea, she declined the milk and sugar, but accepted a cookie. He poured himself some tea from the other pot and before he could stop her she had added milk and was asking him how much sugar he wanted. Then she stopped, burst into tears and apologised.

"I'm sorry. I'm so used to being 'Mother' and pouring the tea for everyone else, it just came naturally. Do you even take milk in your tea?"

"Actually I usually don't, but it doesn't matter. I can still drink it like this." He toyed with the idea of wasting a further five minutes in the kitchen retrieving a clean cup, but decided against it.

"The milk is good for you, it'll give you exactly what you need. It has calcium, vitamins and all sorts of things in it," she smiled a sickly sweet smile. "Oh I'm sorry, I'm doing it again."

"Don't worry. Really. It's fine. Look, I'm drinking the tea. I'll even have more milk. See."

Helen smiled again as he poured the rest of the milk into his tea cup and topped it up with more tea from the pot. She became somewhat calmer and the next half hour seemed to O'Leary to pass much more quickly. Finally she stood up to leave, apologising for taking up the whole of his afternoon. O'Leary decided to see her out himself rather than call Kevin. He escorted her to the door, said goodbye and shut it behind her with a huge sigh of relief. He called Kevin, who came downstairs quickly.

"Can you wash up our tea things please, Kevin. I'm just going out for a while. Have you seen my car keys?" and so the Archbishop left for his last fateful drive.

Kevin did the washing up, wrote a resignation note to the Archbishop and, removing his dog collar, walked out of the house and took a taxi back home to his parents, who were surprisingly pleased to see him. Some months later he finally achieved his dream, not at college, but nonetheless with a college girl.

Forcing Boston out of her mind, Anna refocused on the TV screen. The news had started. After a few reports from Washington there was a short item accompanied by a photo of Capri. She sat up and turned up the sound.

"...many of his fellow journalists are convinced that there has been a cover-up. They say that he was killed by the American delegates to the conference. There has been talk of secret societies, in particular the Bilderberg group, and political machinations from US neo-conservatives. Italian police have refuted all the allegations, saying that the coroner has examined the body of Tim Shah, the dead British journalist, and confirmed that death was from natural causes, apparently an unexpected heart attack. But a significant number of the journalists here are flatly refusing to accept this version of events."

"Tim was very fit. He wasn't old or overweight. He didn't smoke and hardly drank. Why would he suddenly have a heart attack?" said one of the journalists being interviewed outside a large pair of gates.

The voice-over continued.

"The British Embassy has confirmed that they accept the verdict of natural causes. The US Embassy has pointed out that there are no official representatives of the Administration at the Capri conference. It is a private-sector meeting, they said."

A stock ticker started to scroll across the bottom of the TV screen and the business editor appeared to talk about the day's market movements. Anna hit the mute button, dropped the remote, and fell backwards to lie on the bed again.

"Hmmm," she wondered aloud. "Maybe someone else is using this stuff too."

New York, USA

Adam was watching Rebecca walking down Fifth Avenue. She seemed uncomfortable, as if she felt she didn't belong, or was expecting something unpleasant to happen. She didn't look like a danger to society. Quite the opposite, she looked like your favourite aunt (albeit a young and ever-so-slightly trendy aunt). He thought about the gap in the Manhattan skyline and remembered that fundamentalists like this were capable of doing anything, however normal and innocent they appeared. He saw her go through the revolving doors of number 666, around the waterfall screen, across the lobby and into a lift, along with a number of other people who had been waiting there. By the time Adam made it to the bank of lifts he had no idea which floor she had gone to. The lift stopped on at least seven of the thirty nine floors. Making a mental note of the floor numbers he walked over to the board by the reception desk to see who had offices on those floors. This building seemed to be very cosmopolitan. There were shrinks, cosmetic surgeons, lawyers, accountants, even an escort agency. Big corporations and small companies. On the seven floors where the lift had stopped there was a total of more than 200 different organisations. Any one of them could be the front for an activist cell, Adam thought as he turned away from the board.

He looked across the lobby. What struck him immediately was the floor. It was like a Mondrian painting, white blocks with black lines and a few red. He had recently discovered art. At school he had had no interest in anything as sissy as art. He had enjoyed maths, physics and chemistry. He had almost blown up the science block in an out of hours experiment and that had started his interest in explosives. That in turn had led him to worry about how easy it is to make bombs. He had considered becoming a policeman, or maybe joining a bomb disposal squad, but that had all seemed too active a job. He decided that he would prefer work that involved more thinking and sitting. While at college he heard about the NSA and was introduced to them by one of his tutors. He was ideal material and they snapped him up. Since spending all of his time spying on people and using resources such as the internet he had discovered a world of experience beyond science and numbers. He had begun to listen to music. As a child he had only heard the music that his parents chose, although he had also heard traditional songs at family weddings and bar mitzvahs. He had never really paid any attention to modern music or even classical music, even at college when he was free from his parents stifling control. Now he had bought an iPod and downloaded music from rock bands, folk singers and even choirs. When he had read some of the sleeve notes on the albums he realised that many of these musicians were inspired by other arts so he had gone to the Met to see what he had been missing. He was not very taken with the Renaissance or with Post-Modernism. He had quite liked Dada and Surrealism, but most of all he had been very taken by the Impressionists. He looked at the floor again. He hadn't been impressed by Mondrian at all. He thought it too clinical, too anal. Here was a floor that looked like one of his paintings. What did that say about the nature of Mondrian's paintings – they were good enough for people to walk on? That about summed them up in his opinion.

There was nowhere to sit down, so he went outside and hung around looking in the window of the clothes store that flanked the entrance. He had no choice but to wait for Rebecca to re-appear. He was furious at having lost her. What was she doing in this building? She could be meeting more of her cells, staking out another victim, or conspiring with other radical groups for more concerted attacks. If Laurie was right, they were planning some sort of bombing campaign here in New York and elsewhere. St Patrick's Cathedral was only a few yards away, maybe that was their first target. The upper floors of this building would provide a perfect position from which to launch rockets onto the roof of the Cathedral. Personally he wasn't that bothered about Catholics being targeted. There was some sort of divine payback for years of pogroms against his Jewish forebears. But St. Patrick's was almost iconic for the whole City. An attack on it was an attack against New York. He couldn't let that happen. These madmen had to be stopped before they could do anything. He was no closer to discovering what was actually going to happen. It looked like they would have to raid the meeting on Thursday to have even a hope that they could stop whatever was being planned.

Langley, Virginia, USA

Assistant Director Hocke was returning to his office after a particularly good lunch in the executive restaurant. Today, most of the Directorates had senior team meetings and there had been a good choice of company. He had caught up with the gossip from three other ADs and had arranged a golf match with Bernie Clifton from the Operations Directorate. As he walked past his secretary she smiled at him.

"You gonna beat him this time?"

"What?"

"Clifton. You gonna beat him?"

"You know already?"

"Sure. He got his PA to ring me straight away to make sure it was diarised."

"Very efficient."

"How come he has a PA and you have a secretary?"

"It's the same thing. They just use fancier titles in Operations," he laughed.

"That's alright for you to say, you've got Director in your title. Me, I'm just plain secretary. Sure would look better on my CV if it said PA."

"Why are you worried about your CV, Marge?"

"If I want to get a job elsewhere."

"You think we'd let you go anywhere else?" he grinned.

"I'd get paid more than here!" she grinned back.

"Marge. You know too much. You wouldn't be allowed to go anywhere else. We'd stop you."

"Huh. You just try it Mister Assistant Director."

Hocke feigned shock and walked into his office. Behind his desk a large flat screen TV was showing CNN news.

"...Tim Shah, the dead British journalist, and confirmed that death was from natural causes, apparently an unexpected heart attack. But a significant number of the journalists here are flatly refusing to accept this version of events…"

He watched the news item, muted the TV, then sat down at his desk. Picking up the phone he pressed the intercom button.

"Marge. There's a guy out on the floor called Joel something. I want to talk to him ASAP."

"Joel who?"

"I dunno his last name. I spoke to him last night, there was a card on his desk that said Happy Birthday Joel. So I know his name was Joel. That's all I got. How many Joels can there be out there?"

"Okay I'll find him, do you want him up here or on the phone?"

"Just get him on the line. Thanks Marge."

"No problem."

Two minutes later his phone rang.

"I've got Joel Schitzenberger on one."

"Thanks Marge." He pressed the button for line #1.

"Joel. How's it going?"

"Okay thank you sir."

"Did you get anywhere yet?"

"No sir, Mike is still trying to get all the records in so he can check through them."

"Mike?"

"Mike Probey, in WINPAC."

"Oh yes, your friend. Can't he start checking them before they're all in?"

"Oh, er, I don't know sir. He said he'd let me know when he had an answer, but I can see if he'll, er,…"

"Expedite matters, Joel."

"Yes sir, expedite matters."

"You do that."

"Yes sir."

"And Joel."

"Yes sir?"

"Check up on Tim Shah, a British hack who's just died in Capri, Italy. Unexpected heart attack. There's some suggestions that it wasn't really natural causes. There's a whole load more hacks out there who're pointing the finger at the US. Now they're saying that the neo-conservatives are having people killed."

"Again?"

"Find out if it's true Joel."

"Yes sir."

"Good man."

Hocke pressed the #1 button again.

"Marge."

"Yes sir."

"Get me the personnel files on Mr Schitzenberger and also someone called Mike Probey in WINPAC."

"We aren't supposed to have access to WINPAC personnel files sir."

"I know. Pull a 171 internal investigation to get it."

"Are you sure?"

"Yeah. I need to know if I can trust these guys."

"But they work here, surely you can trust them?"

"Marge. How long have you worked here? Do you trust everyone out there on the floor?"

"Well, no probably not. Especially not that evil looking guy who always wears the brown suits."

"Exactly. Get me those files."

"Okay."

Rome

"Sandro" Costanza called from the lounge to the kitchen, the source of the delicious aromas.

"Your friend Tim, the one who sent you the files, what did you say his surname was?"

"Shah. Tim Shah. He's a Brit."

"Isn't it an odd name for an Englishman."

"What Tim?"

"No, idiot. Shah."

"His dad was a Persian émigré during the second world war. His mum was Polish, they met in Paris and escaped to England where they married and had Tim and his sister. Why?"

"Is he on Capri?"

"I think so, yes." Sandro walked out of the kitchen, carrying a wooden spoon from which he had just tasted the mouth-watering tomato sauce.

"Have you heard the news at all this evening?"

"No, not really."

"A British journalist called Tim Shah died on Capri while covering a secret political meeting. The other journalists there are convinced he was murdered, but Naples police say he died of a heart attack."

"Are you sure?"

"Yes. Definitely Tim Shah."

"That's awful. Poor man. Do you think he knew he had heart problems? That's why he wanted me to keep his files safe?"

"Maybe. What are you supposed to do with them?"

"I don't know. He said it would be obvious what to do if anything happened. I think they were the text of a piece he was writing about a political group."

"Haven't you read them?"

"No, of course not. He sent me the files to keep safe, not read. I just saved the attachments into a folder.

When one of them arrived it also opened up a web page, but I closed it straight away and didn't pay any attention to it. Maybe that was the one you were asking about."

Costanza gazed at him and smiled.

"You're such a decent man. It's obvious to everyone you meet. That's why he knew he could trust you."

"But if he's dead now what should I do with the files?"

"I think we should read them and see if it becomes clearer. Maybe he included instructions."

"Okay, I'll get the disc after we've eaten."

"No need, I still have it here in my bag. I'll have a look at the files while you finish cooking. Incidentally it smells gorgeous."

"Do you mind?"

"What? That the food smells good?"

"No," he smiled "do you mind looking at the files. You'll probably make more sense of them anyway."

"Of course not. Your friend Tim is dead, we should try and see if his files throw any light on what happened."

"I thought you said he died of a heart attack?"

"That's what the police said, yes."

"Okay, when you talk like that it means you know something."

"Like what?"

"Like 'That's what the police said' has an unspoken 'but I know better' on the end. It's all in the tone. What do you know that the Naples police don't?"

"You can't tell anyone."

"I know. I know. Security."

"No I'm serious. Really serious. You can't tell anyone. At all."

"Okay. Do you want me to swear?"

"Don't be silly."

"Well?"

"We know that the CIA has a poison that can cause a

heart attack then vanishes without leaving any trace within a few minutes. Any subsequent medical examination will conclude that the cause of death was a heart attack. We think that someone is using it at the moment in a series of murders linked to that website. If your friend Tim's investigation got too close to whoever is behind these deaths then maybe they got rid of him too."

"And they would be looking for his files?"

"Because they might contain damning evidence."

"In that case, let's get rid of them. I don't want them to come here looking."

"If they know he sent them to you they'll come looking whether the file are still here or not. But if you want I'll take them to our lab and we can read them there to see if there's any clues to what's going on."

Sandro breathed deeply and looked at his beautiful wife. Then he sniffed very dramatically.

"Oh no, I think the tomato sauce is burning."

WEDNESDAY

Error

Rome

Anna woke up to find herself lying on top of the bed, the remote still next to her, the TV still playing CNN. It was obviously morning. She must have been so tired she fell asleep where she was. Rubbing her eyes, she sat up, shuffled herself forward till her feet could touch the floor and carefully stood up.

Undoing the buttons on her dress as she slowly walked to the bathroom, she shucked it off her shoulders and stepped out of it as it fell to the floor. In the bathroom she shut the door, slid her knickers to her feet and kicked them into the corner of the room. Unclasping her bra, she disentangled it from her arms and dropped it on top of the knickers. After relieving her bladder, she switched on the shower, waited till she was sure it wouldn't be cold, and stepped in. She always enjoyed the sensuality of washing her hair in the shower. The gentle massage of the water spray on her head, the tingling as she worked the shampoo through her hair and scratched it into her scalp. Then the delicious feeling as the suds were washed off her head, over her shoulders, into the small of her back and between her buttocks to drip off onto the floor between her legs. She moved her head and now the suds were cascading down her face, over her breasts, across her stomach, through the soft hairs and down between her legs. She turned her face into the full force of the water, keeping her eyes tight shut. Reaching for the small complimentary bottle of shower gel, she squirted some into her left hand, put the bottle down and rubbed her hands together. Then she started to spread the gel across her breasts, on her neck, shoulders and under her armpits. No-one had caressed her since Dave had gone. She hadn't wanted anyone to caress her. But she had wanted to be caressed, so much. She shut her eyes again, and, as she rubbed herself with bubble covered hands, she fantasised that Dave was sharing the shower with her, standing behind her, rubbing his hands across her body the way she had always loved. Slowly she moved her hands lower down her body, gelling her stomach, her thighs, her buttocks, her legs. If only Dave really had been there. Fantasising was nowhere near as good as the real thing. With a deep sigh, she switched off the water and reached for her towels. She rubbed her hair with a small towel which she then wrapped around her head, then slowly dried herself with the large towel, enjoying the roughness of the material as it rubbed against her neck, her nipples, her thighs. Just then there was a knock on the door to her room. Roused from the fantasy into which she was gently slipping back, she came out of the bathroom and peered through the peep-hole in the door. It was a young man bringing her breakfast. She had forgotten that, as a final luxury, she had ordered breakfast in her room for the rest of her stay. Reaching down, turning the handle, she opened the door.

"Breakfast, Signorina."

"Thank you. Bring it in and put it on the desk please."

She had wrapped the towel around her, tucking it in securely at the top.

"Could you sign please?" the young man proffered her a pen and the breakfast bill.

She took the pen in her right hand and the bill in her left. As she went to sign it she lifted her arms slightly and the release of pressure, combined with a slight swelling of her chest as she breathed in, loosened her towel which elegantly fell open across her front and then dropped away to the floor. Taken by surprise she was too slow to catch it, especially as she had her hands full. For a split second she was even debating whether she cared. This young man was very handsome and maybe he could deputise for Dave in her fantasy. She knew she looked good, and the look on his face confirmed it. She saw his eyes involuntarily drawn downwards, his gaze palpable as it lingered on her breasts. Almost immediately he started to drop to the floor and she shut her eyes in anticipation. After a few seconds, however, nothing had happened and she opened her eyes again to find him standing in front of her, eyes averted holding up the towel as a barrier between them for her to reclaim her modesty. She decided to take her time. She finished signing the bill, reached around the towel, stuffed the pen in his breast pocket and the bill in his trouser pocket, enjoying watching him squirm as she did so. She could see that his trousers were getting tighter by the second. Finally she took the towel from his hands, wrapped it back around herself and gently spoke.

"Thank you."

"My pleasure," he smiled, making the briefest of eye contact.

"Indeed," she too smiled.

He walked past her, opened the door and stepped out of the room, leaving the door to close itself behind him.

With the towel still securely wrapped around her, Anna walked to the window and looked out. It was going to be a hot day. The sky was clear blue, not a cloud to be seen. The weather was never like this in Baltimore. But it reminded her of Sao Paolo. Especially her last day there. She had been to see Figueras, given him the gift of a special blend of coffee beans – she had told him it had been blended specifically for him by an Indian in the jungle, using astrology and native magic to produce the ideal blend for the Cardinal's breakfast. She had given him the gift to say thank you for the time he had spent over the previous few days consoling her. She had no friends in Brazil, no family, and when her husband had died she didn't know what to do or who to turn to. The

Cardinal had helped her so much it was the least she could do to give him this special gift before she went back to the States. He had been very touched and said he was already looking forward to his breakfast the next day, although he wasn't entirely sure that he should condone using astrology and magic on his behalf. She had gone straight from the Cardinal's house to the airport to catch her plane home.

She turned away from the window and caught sight of her reflection in the mirror. She moved closer and then, on a whim, took off the towel and looked at herself more closely. She was still a beautiful woman – in fact she still thought of herself as a girl rather than a woman. Dave had been the only person to see and enjoy her body. Together the two of them had learned about their own and each other's; had learned about love and passion; about restraint and about abandoning themselves to one another. Neither of them had ever had such experiences with anyone else. They had anticipated enjoying each other until old age removed either the ability or the desire. But they would never reach that point now. Could she ever achieve that type of experience with another man? Would she? Should she? Perhaps she should make do with her fantasies and the memory of Dave. Casting a last appraising eye up and down her body's reflection she walked over to the dresser, opened the top drawer and started looking for some appropriate underwear.

Vatican

When I got to her office, Costanza was already there, studying her screen intently. She looked up as I walked up to her desk.

"Peter, I'm glad you're here. I'm looking at the files on Sandro's disc. The emails from Tim Shah."

"Ah, now you know who they're from?"

"Yes, a journalist that Sandro worked with some time ago."

"I thought you already read through them?"

"No, I just skimmed through a few at random. Now I'm reading them properly."

"Why, has something happened?"

"Tim Shah was a British journalist who was covering a Bilderberg meeting on Capri. He died at the weekend."

"Oh."

"He had a heart attack. His friends say he was very fit, nobody expected him to have heart problems."

"Aah. You think there's a connection?"

"I've only read some of these emails but it seems like he was determined to do a thorough job of exposing how much control he believed the Bilderberg group have and how powerful the NAC have become in setting its agenda. He foresaw conflict with Cardinal Bramante who was about to chair an investigation into P2 and other organisations that may have been controlling certain interests and people inside the Curia."

"I thought the P2-IOR scandal was buried years ago?"

"Not really, many of those that were implicated publicly are dead. Calvi, Villot, Cody, Sindona. But most people are convinced that there are still plenty left in the Curia as well as in the Italian and American Governments. Marcinkus is still alive, skulking in America. Gelli is in prison. There's been a shift of power and those that stopped the investigation that John Paul the first wanted

202

to launch have finally been bypassed. That was what Bramante was about to do."

"So did this Shah think that Bramante was killed by the Bilderberg group?"

"I don't know. The last email that Sandro received from him was the day before the Cardinal died. If he wrote any more he didn't have a chance to send it."

"So let's get this straight. Bramante was going to open a new investigation into P2. P2's old members are now in the Bilderberg group and are supported by the NAC. So they kill Bramante. Won't someone else just chair the investigation?"

"No-one else would be as well qualified as he was. It will take time to find someone else suitable and get them up to speed. By which time we may have a new pontiff, directly under the control of these people, who would cancel the investigation."

"So it still comes back to a plot to make sure that their guy becomes the next Pope."

"Of course. It's all linked and it all makes sense. Stop any investigations, internal or external. Eliminate the likely contenders. Make sure that there's only one real candidate. Then dispose of the current Pope."

"Okay, what about Archbishop O'Leary and Rabbi Cohen? Where do they fit into this plot?"

"I don't know. Maybe they don't. Maybe they're collateral damage, or maybe they knew something and had to be silenced. Bilderberg has links into Israeli politics too. I'll do a bit more research into both of them. But even so I think we should go to see Cardinal Bianchi and tell him what we know."

"I still think it's a bit early yet."

"I'm going to talk to his secretary and arrange to see him. You're welcome to stay here and see what else you can dig up. Okay?"

Rome

Their vigilance finally rewarded, they watched as Peter White walked out of the Angel Gate and into the busy street teeming with pilgrims, tourists and all manner of people walking to, from and around the Vatican City. For once he appeared to be alone and intending to walk back to his hotel across the river rather than being driven there by the Police, Swiss Guard or Vigilanza. In this crowd they would have the perfect opportunity to block him and then hustle him away. It was unlikely that anyone would even notice, and certainly nobody would try to stop them.

The three men crossed the street, blending into the throng walking along the road, following the signposts to the Vatican Museum. They slowly split up and positioned themselves around Peter so that they could grab him when the right moment came. As the small knot of pedestrians approached the corner in the road and prepared to turn left along the tall defensive walls of the Vatican Gardens, they made ready to guide Peter out and across the road towards the tram shelter in the middle of the Piazza where they could quietly disable him and call Luca to bring the car.

But somehow it didn't quite happen the way they planned. As they tried to close around Peter he seemed to be replaced by a large blonde man in a dark suit. They looked around to try to see where their target had gone but he was now nowhere to be seen, as if he had never been there in the first place. Within seconds they realised that they had now become victims of the same ploy they had intended to use on him. They were being carefully manoeuvred across the road towards the tree lined shade of the tram terminus. At least four large men were behind and to the side of them ensuring that they couldn't double back. Ahead, beyond the number 81 tram that was about to leave there was an empty and quiet piazza where no-one would notice three men slumbering under the trees for a few hours. Convinced they were headed towards their own execution, the three of them simultaneously came to the same decision regarding their only possible escape. They suddenly broke into a run and leapt through the closing door of the tram just as it was departing. All three of them hit the far wall and turned, winded, to watch the reaction of their pursuers. But there were no pursuers to be seen. As the tram pulled out of the Piazza and headed down the long road towards the bridge to the heart of Rome, the receding tram terminus appeared completely deserted and quiet. Confused, they looked at each other. The shortest one shrugged. A cough from an elderly lady with a black shawl around her shoulders and a black lace scarf in her hair made them turn back. She was looking very pointedly at the ticket machine, and, knowing never to mess with old ladies in Italy, they all sheepishly started to search their pockets for a bus ticket to validate.

Half an hour later, in the shadow of Santa Maria Maggiore, the three men were sitting around a café table staring into their espresso cups.

"What happened?" the short one asked.

"What do you mean 'what happened'? You were there." The largest one looked up, irritated, and glared at the short man opposite him across the table.

"Sure I was there. But I still don't have any idea what happened. One second we were surrounding the guy and the next second he's gone. Then those goons suddenly turn up and hustle us off and when we make a break for it they've gone too. So I ask again. What happened?"

"Who actually saw White come out of the gate?" asked the third man, softly spoken and inscrutable behind his mirrored sunglasses.

"We all did." The short one spoke again.

"YOU said you did. I'm not so sure," said Large, still irritated and glaring at Short.

"We all seemed sure at the time," said the third man.

"What of it?" Large again.

"If we're not sure he actually came out of the gate then maybe he didn't disappear at all. Maybe he was just never there."

"But what about the goons?" asked Short. "I didn't imagine them."

"Are you sure?"

"Sure I'm sure. They were big guys in dark suits; shades, blonde hair, blue eyes, very white teeth and breath that smelt…" he shuddered.

"Yeah, smelt of incense. That was odd. Didn't that seem odd to you?" Large added, looking at each of them in turn.

"Uh … I guess … a little."

"Anyway how'd you see their blue eyes behind those shades?"

"They were … I mean … I dunno. I just know they had blue eyes. But I'm sure they were wearing shades. All of them."

"All of them? How many do you think there were?" asked the third man.

"At least four," said Short.

"Easily five or six," said Large.

"And they were right behind us when we got on the tram?"

"Yeah," nodded Short.

"Right behind," agreed Large.

"So, where did they go?"

"Dunno!" Large frowned.

"It's as if they weren't there at all. As if we just thought they were there. Like someone's messing with our minds." The short man was starting to get twitchy.

"Obviously doesn't take much to mess with such a small mind as yours," said Large, still glaring.

"Hey what's that supposed to mean?" Short said, glaring back.

"Proves my point." Large grinned.

"What?" Short was now more confused than ever. He gave up and stared at his coffee again.

"What if?" Short started again.

"What if what?" asked the third man.

"What if there was some sort of supernatural force at work here. Making us see White when he wasn't really there so we could be moved out of the way."

"What, you think the Vatican is employing ghosts?" Large laughed.

"Or angels. No, demons." Short involuntarily shivered. "I don't like this any more. I think someone or something powerful is protecting White."

"I think you're letting your usually limited imagination run away with you. These are just people we're dealing with. Ordinary people. Not ghosts or demons. No supernatural forces. People." Even speaking softly the third man could be very forceful.

"I don't know about that. Maybe they've lasted thousands of years 'cos they've got some sort of supernatural help. The Minister said they're the agents of the Antichrist, so surely they'd have satanic powers to call on?"

"Two," muttered Large.

"Two what?"

"Two thousand years. You said 'thousands of years'. It's only two thousand years."

"Two is more than one," said Small with a sneer.

"Well done, you can count!"

"So it's thousands. Plural." Small said with vitriol.

"Hardly."

"What, now you're a mathematician? Or a philosopher?" Small seemed to have forgotten his fear of the supernatural in his anger at the never-ending put downs from his larger companion.

"Big words. Did you swallow a dictionary?"

"Funny! Anyway, the church was based on the Jewish tradition which must go back a couple more thousand years. So it's millenniums old."

"Millennia."

"Whatever. And they had the ark of the covenant to attack their enemies with spirits and stuff. I know about that."

"That was a film."

"Yeah well, based on the Bible."

"No it wasn't. God you're such a moron."

"Who are you calling..."

The third man calmly grabbed the nearest arm of each man.

"Calm down both of you. You're getting off the point. Losing the plot. Name calling won't help us, only them. We have to think straight and make a new plan."

By now Short had defused his anger sufficiently to remember his fear.

"Plan? If they have got some greater power protecting White then my plan is to leave him alone. Why don't we find a softer target?"

"Funny you should say that," started the third man, "because I'd already been thinking along those lines too, as a backup plan in case we never got a chance to grab White. I did some checking on the woman that White has been meeting. The one we think works in the Library. Her name is Costanza D'Andrea-Mancini. I think we should concentrate on her now. I'll tell New York there's been a change of target."

"But surely whoever's protecting White will be protecting her too."

"I'm sure they are. But I'm also pretty sure they won't be protecting her husband. If we get him we can control her, through her we can access the Library and get our hands on the manuscript. We might even find some other things that we could sell to help recompense us for all this extra inconvenience. She's quite cute too. There might be some other ways we can be recompensed." He grinned and the sun glinted off the gold bridgework in his mouth.

New York, USA

It was late in the afternoon and Laurie was just waking up. The biggest problems with these all-night surveillance sessions was trying to adjust her body's internal rhythms to sleeping during the day. The curtains in her apartment were not thick enough to keep out all the daylight, especially on a bright sunny day like today. She never slept well in the daytime and that made her more tetchy at work overnight. Still this might be the last time for a while, if Adam was right about tomorrow's meeting. In some ways she would be sad not to be there, but she had to run tonight's surveillance operation.

As she was lying in her bed watching the digits on her clock slowly tick their way towards four o'clock, she snuggled under the covers and shut her eyes again. The alarm would go off in five minutes and she would have to get up, she would make the most of those last few minutes. Burying her face in the pillow she was suddenly surprised by a ringing sound. It couldn't be five minutes already. Sighing she rolled over and stretched out her hand to snooze the alarm. But it wasn't the clock that was ringing, there were still three minutes to go until four o'clock. She blinked and realised it was her phone. Kicking off the covers she stumbled out of the bed, tripped over her slippers on the rug, and made a grab for the phone which was lying on the seat in front of her dressing table. As she lay on the floor winded, she managed to flip open the phone and hold it to her ear.

"Hi Laurie, it's Adam."

"Hey Adam," she managed breathlessly, "what's up?"

"You okay? You sound out of breath. I didn't interrupt you working out did I? Or something more exciting maybe?"

"No. I was in bed and had to get up to reach the phone that's all." She had got her breath back now and had managed to sit up on the floor.

"You alone?"

"Of course I'm alone. I told you I was in bed."

"So."

"So mind your own business. What did you want? I'm just getting up, I'll be there in just over an hour."

"That's what I was ringing to tell you. Don't bother coming in. I don't think we need any surveillance tonight. Whatever they're doing is going to happen at the meeting. I think it would be more useful if you came along to the bust tomorrow rather than any surveillance tonight."

"Are you sure?"

"Positive. Rebecca's been calling various people to make sure they'll be there tomorrow. She keeps saying that what they're going to do – whatever it is that they're going to do - will be the best demonstration yet of the power of a determined group."

"Do you know yet what they are going to do?"

"Not for sure, but when I followed her the other day she went to a building which would be a perfect site to launch an attack against St. Patrick's Cathedral. I think they're going to bomb it, or fire a rocket at it or something like that."

"There's been no evidence that she's had any weapons delivered to her at the hotel."

"I don't think she's that stupid. I imagine it's been smuggled here by others. Maybe in pieces. I think we'll find it when we raid tomorrow's meeting. So don't get up, go back to sleep and meet me here tomorrow morning at nine."

"Are you sure?"

"Yes I told you. Get some sleep. See you tomorrow."

Laurie closed her phone. Get some sleep he said. But now she was wide awake. And hungry. She put the phone back down on the chair and, using the chair back to steady herself, she stood up. Looking down she saw that the tumble had ripped her night dress and her right breast was exposed.

"Lucky it wasn't a video call" she thought, "Adam would definitely have got the wrong idea."

Taking off her ruined shirt and throwing it on the bed, she turned, tucked her feet into the slippers that had caused the damage and walked naked into her bathroom. A nice bubble bath would do the trick followed by some supper. Then maybe she would be able to get some more sleep.

Twenty minutes later, as she luxuriated in the hot water, she heard a ring at her front door. She decided to ignore it. Whoever was there tried two more times. Then her phone rang. She had left it in the bedroom so she ignored that too. "If it's important they'll leave a message" she thought.

Outside Laurie's front door, Adam heard her voicemail prompt. Should he record a message or just hang up? Forced to make a decision by the beep, he spoke into his phone.

"Laurie, it's Adam. I was passing so I thought I'd see if you were okay now. I hoped you might still be awake and thought I might be able to help one way or another. Never mind, I guess you're already asleep again. Shame. Another time maybe. See you tomorrow morning."

Langley, Virginia, USA

It was almost time to leave for the day so Mike Probey was putting everything away in his pedestal drawers, in conformance with WINPAC's clear desk policy. Just before shutting down his workstation, as he was about to log out of the network, an alert box appeared on his screen telling him that the search he had initiated on the mainframe records had completed. Instead of logging out he clicked the OK button and waited for the results to display. Fully expecting a short message informing him that no anomalies had been found he was surprised when a screenful of data appeared. Pausing a second to recover, he focused on the summary line and immediately picked up his phone.

"Joel? Hi, it's Mike."

"Still here?"

"I was just about to go. You know that search you asked me to do. The TA21 records."

"You got a hit?" Joel suddenly sounded more interested.

"Sure did. The results just appeared on my screen a few seconds ago. To be honest I was expecting squat, so it was a bit of a surprise when it came up."

"What? Tell me."

"You may be on to something after all. The office in Sao Paolo, that's in Brazil,…"

"Yeah, I know where Sao Paolo is."

"Okay, well they just reported that they mislaid a dozen doses nearly 2 months ago."

"Mislaid? What's that supposed to mean?"

"It means lost."

"I know what the word means. But how do you mislay a dozen vials of lethal poison."

"Beats me. There are supposed to be strict controls on the use and issue of all weapons in field offices. But

213

most people here at WINPAC believe that no-one pays much attention except where guns are concerned. Or big stuff."

"Big stuff?"

"You know, rocket launchers. Tank-busters. C-4."

"But not poisons?"

"Small stuff. Only kills one at a time. Not a serious problem if it's misused. Especially abroad, only likely to kill foreigners, no-one important."

"So, getting back to Sao Paolo. Do they have any idea where it might have got to?"

"I guess not, otherwise it wouldn't be mislaid. Look, I'll dump the details from the search into a file and email it to you. There's some data about the last few visitors to the office prior to when the stuff went missing, but there were no locals, all our own people. No-one unusual. Anyway, you can see for yourself."

"Okay thanks."

"Later."

Mike dropped the phone back onto its cradle, quickly saved the search results into a file and emailed it to Joel as promised. Then he logged out, picked up his jacket and sauntered out of the building towards his new SUV in the car park.

Joel was waiting impatiently for the email to arrive. It should only have taken a few seconds to get from Mike's account to Joel's, but recent updates to the email system had apparently improved security, added much better spam filtering, yet made performance a joke. While he was twiddling his thumbs, literally, he was trying to imagine the possible scenarios under which weapons could be removed from a field office situated within an embassy. A ping from his workstation told him that

Mike's email had arrived and he printed out the file that had been included. As he read the report he realised that someone would need to talk to the office in Brazil to establish what happened. It was too late to call them now. Should he let the Assistant Director know straight away or wait until he had spoken to the Brazil office. As he considered his options he felt someone standing behind him. With a feeling of déjà vu he turned expecting to see Hocke there. Instead there was a short lady smiling at him.

"Joel?"

"That's me," he said, unsure whether he should stand up.

"Hi. I'm Marge. We spoke on the phone yesterday."

"We did?"

"Yeah. I'm Assistant Director Hocke's sec... PA." She had decided to adopt the title anyway.

"Oh, right."

"He was wondering if you had any new information on the matter you and he discussed."

"Actually I just got some right now."

Joel waved the sheet of paper in his hand.

"Good. In that case will you come with me please."

"I was just going to call him."

"That won't be necessary. Come with me."

They walked towards the doors at the end of the room, threading their way through the maze of desks, most of which were now clear and unoccupied.

"So what did you find?" Marge asked in a matter-of-fact tone.

"Well, I ... er... No offence, but I think I should wait and tell the Assistant Director himself."

"Good boy."

"What?"

"Just testing. Can't have you talking to just anyone."

215

"Right" Joel said a little taken aback.

"I mean you don't really know that I'm Marge, do you?"

"We spoke on the phone."

"But you didn't recognise my voice."

"I did, once you told me who you were."

"So naïve. You haven't been here long have you?"

"Six months."

"What does it say over the door."

"*Eyes and ears of the nation.*"

"What does that mean?"

"Er, well, it means we…"

"It means, trust no-one."

"I thought that was the FBI. You know the X-Files."

"Where do you think they got the idea."

They had now reached the double doors. They went through, up the stairs and along a glazed gallery overlooking the floor from which they had just come. Turning left they walked through more doors and were in a plushly carpeted area with soft chairs, a water dispenser and gentle music playing in the background. Marge led Joel to the door at the far end, knocked once and opened it without waiting, ushering Joel through.

The Assistant Director, sitting behind his desk, looked up as Joel entered, nodded to Marge who shut the door, gently padding across the room and through the other door to her own office, closing it behind her with a gentle click.

"Sit, sit."

"Thank you sir."

"So?"

"Mike sent me the results of his search. A dozen doses went missing in Brazil."

"When?"

"About two months ago."

"And we find out now?"

"We only found out 'cos we looked, sir. It was categorised as office shrinkage, along with paper clips and pens."

"That's ridiculous. Unforgivable. Incompetent."

"Sir."

"But not my main concern at the moment. Any idea where they went? Who took them?"

"Not yet. There were no external visitors, so it looks like an inside job. Maybe someone with their own personal agenda?"

"Or plausible deniability."

"Sir?"

"Deep cover or black ops. No audit trail. Anything goes wrong, we know nothing about it, who-ever investigates."

"In which case we won't get anywhere either?"

"We'll have to see about that. What's the paper?" he nodded at the sheet of paper in Joel's hand.

"The report that Mike sent me."

Joel leaned forward and slid the paper across the desk.

"Okay, thanks. Leave it with me for now."

"Yes sir."

Hocke started reading the paper, after a few seconds he looked up.

"You can go home Joel."

"Yes sir. Thank you sir."

Joel stood up and while he was deciding which way to leave, Marge opened her door and beckoned him out. As the door shut behind him, he turned to her.

"How did you know? Were you listening?"

"No!" she sounded offended. "He buzzed me when you were dismissed."

"Oh. Sorry."

"I should think so."

217

"You did tell me not to trust anyone," he smiled as she cuffed him round the ear.

"Eyes and ears," she muttered to herself as he walked away.

THURSDAY

Vatican

When Costanza walked into Cardinal Bianchi's office in the Apostolic Palace, he was talking on the phone. Waving her in and towards the chair opposite him, he was clearly trying to end the conversation.

"Si si. Certo. Anche a Lei. Ciao."

He put the phone back on its cradle and breathed a deep sigh of relief.

"Costanza, always a pleasure to see you. Can I offer you a drink?"

"No thank you Eminence. I fear today may not be such a pleasure though. What I have to tell you may be hard to hear and difficult to believe."

"Maybe I should get a drink then?" his soft eyes smiled as he sat back in his chair.

"Perhaps." Costanza smiled back, as usual the Cardinal was able to put her at her ease almost instantly whatever the circumstances.

"I think I shall be brave and remain sober. Tell me what I don't want to hear."

"On the contrary, you want to know. You asked me to look into Cardinal Bramante's death."

"Yes indeed. You have reached some conclusions?"

"We have. Or rather I have. Peter White, whom you called from England to help is more sceptical."

"I see he told you why he happened to be here."

"Yes your Eminence. I hope that you didn't call him to help me because you were not confident I could cope."

"No of course not Costanza. I have every confidence in you. I always have. But I wasn't sure who else we could trust to work with you. I already knew of Peter as I make it my business to know about everyone in the Swiss Guard, such an unusual character stands out in the files. When you started here I noticed from your file that you had a close friendship with him. I knew that he could not possibly be involved in Giuseppe's death. I knew that I could trust him; he is, after all, a Commander in the Guard. But most of all I knew that you would be able to trust him."

"How can he be in the Swiss Guard? He's not Swiss. I thought that's a pre-requisite."

"It is. But an exception was made for him. He was very helpful to the Guard some years ago, when security was overhauled. As a reward they would have made him a Knight of the Sovereign Military Order of Malta but he wasn't keen to join their ranks, apparently he said he wasn't happy to be labelled Military and didn't like the company. I must admit I would be inclined to agree! When they suggested an honorary Commander of the Swiss Guard he agreed, even though it was a title neither he nor we could ever publicly acknowledge. I'm told he said he liked the rank of Commander, even made a joke about James Bond."

"That sounds like Peter."

"He's been back to help the Guard a couple of times, but never on anything like this. You said he disagrees with your conclusion?"

"Not really. He just wanted to get more evidence before coming to you. But I think it is too important to wait any longer."

"Okay. Start with your conclusion and then tell me how you got there."

"I believe Cardinal Bramante was killed because he was about to chair the new investigation into P2 and the IOR. There are political forces at work that are protecting the previous members of P2. They are orchestrated by an organisation called the New American Century, the NAC, and they have the help of CIA agents. They have a campaign of eliminating the most likely candidates for the Papal Throne so that their own puppet can be elected.

When they are ready they will eliminate the Holy Father himself to force a Conclave. I don't know how imminent that is, maybe soon, maybe next year, but it won't be long. Once they have their own Pope in place who knows what damage they will do to the Church."

"Do you have any evidence for this theory?"

"Of course. You know that Cardinal Bramante was declared to be in full health only the day before his heart attack. We know that the CIA has a poison that induces heart attacks and vanishes without a trace in a matter of minutes. You already know that in the last few weeks there have been a number of other unexpected heart attacks such as Cardinal Figueras and Archbishop O'Leary. The website that you found linking them includes Cardinal Pescosolido and the Holy Father as targets. That would leave Cardinal Thomas as the most likely Papal candidate. He was also the last person to see Cardinal Bramante before he died. We know Cardinal Thomas gave him an apple which he ate in the gardens. Not much later he was dead."

"Costanza, I know all this. What other evidence have you got?"

"This weekend there was a secret meeting of the Bilderberg Group in Capri. They are …"

"Yes I know what they are. We have had some run-ins with them before."

"The NAC have assumed a controlling interest. A British journalist was covering the meeting and he was found dead of a heart attack, even though he had been fit and healthy. He had been investigating the NAC and had predicted that there would be conflict with Cardinal Bramante. Last night I read an underground news report that is circulating on the internet quoting a leak from the Bilderberg meeting where the death of the Cardinal was discussed and the NAC members were congratulated on their handling."

"How reliable a source is it?"

"That's debatable. It's on the internet so it could be completely fabricated. But it appeared almost simultaneously on a number of different and unrelated underground news sites, with different slants and language used. So I think there's more than one source. Which gives it more credibility."

"Still. It's a big step from there to accuse Cardinal Thomas."

"I know. But if we don't do something we may lose at least one more Cardinal and the Holy Father himself. And then it will be too late. We won't be able to do anything until after the Conclave and if Thomas is elected he'll squash our investigation."

"What do you expect me to do now?"

"Your Eminence. Perhaps if you talk to Cardinal Thomas, he will realise that we know what is happening and will make sure that all the other Cardinals will know too. Then he will have no hope of election and will give up."

"As simple as that?"

"I hope."

"Isn't that a bit optimistic. We've already seen how ruthless these people are. What if they eliminate those of us who suspect what is going on. At the moment that's just you, Peter and me. Have you told anyone else?"

"No."

"Maybe you should. Meanwhile I will think about what I should do. I will pray for guidance. Any more concrete evidence that you and Peter can find will help."

"Will you talk to Cardinal Thomas?"

"I will consider it. But first, can you go through everything again for me while I make some notes. I especially want to understand more about that website."

"Of course."

Costanza spent another fifty minutes explaining everything to the Cardinal.

Rome

Anna stood on the dry ground next to a ruined stone wall. Ahead of her she could see more ruins, low stone walls outlining the rooms of what had obviously once been an impressive villa. The so-called House of Livia had been home to Agrippina, one of Anna's heroines. Beyond were trees and more ruins on the Palatine hill leading down towards the valley in which the Imperial Forum had been built. She looked around, keen to imprint as much of this experience as possible in her memory. To the right she could see a relatively modern building – a medieval church; beneath which, out of sight from her current vantage point, she knew was the incredible Flavian amphitheatre that had so impressed the Victorians with its size that they had called it the Colosseum. To the left she could see some makeshift corrugated iron covers, underneath which were the original iron-age settlements - the first people to live here, before Romulus killed Remus, not long after Aeneas fled from Troy. She turned and looked at the ruins of the magnificent palace behind her, beyond which was the Circus Maximus, the greatest stadium the world had ever seen – but now, she had thought, a rather disappointing, sunken, oval field. Thousands of years of inhabitation on this spot. Now here she was, in Agrippina's house, at the centre of what had been for years the extent of the known world (at least to Western eyes). More than anywhere else, here she felt she belonged. Here was the place that had been calling to her throughout her life.

She could relate to Agrippina. The powerful woman behind multiple thrones. Agrippina hadn't been averse to dealing ruthlessly with people who got in her way. Nor had she been shy to exact revenge. Anna could relate to that too. Revenge was what was driving her now. Although she had always hoped to come and stand in this place one day, it was revenge that had made it happen. Revenge, and before that, tragedy.

She had loved Dave since childhood and they had been dating since ninth grade. When they were 19 he had proposed, but both sets of parents had insisted they wait until they had finished their education and established careers. The next six years had seemed to go by so slowly. After studying history and economics she had joined her father in his realty business and had been the rising star. Meanwhile, Dave had studied modern languages, becoming fluent in Italian, Spanish and Portuguese. He had taught her Italian in preparation for the inevitable trip to Rome. After college Dave was recruited by an export company, specialising in South America. Anna had previously met some of the people in the company, including Manny, when they had bought houses from her for relocated staff – she had been impressed that they cared so much about their employees, so when Dave said he had been approached to work there she urged him to take the job, even though it might mean he'd be away in Brazil, Chile or Argentina from time to time. Soon they were ready to tie the knot and they got married in a fairytale wedding with their honeymoon at Disneyland "the happiest place on Earth". Only later did she discover that Dave was actually working for the CIA and the sales she had arranged with Manny had been for safe houses. She was concerned at first, but he had told her that his was a desk job, with no dangerous assignments. Like her, Dave was a rising star in his chosen career and when he was offered a very senior position based in the US embassy in Brazil, they both decided that it was an opportunity they shouldn't miss. Her father was reluctant to let his star realtor, and only daughter, slip away from the business, but she eventually persuaded him. After all, it wouldn't be forever, just a couple of years, she had reassured him.

So she had found herself in Sao Paolo, with a husband who was a cultural attaché, and no particular rôle for herself apart from lunching with the other embassy wives. Being uninterested in modern politics, and unimpressable by any civilisation outside the ancient Mediterranean, she found very little with which to occupy herself. Unable to speak the local language she was becoming uncharacteristically dependent on Dave and others from the Embassy, so she threw herself into a language course, making remarkable progress. Suddenly the opportunities opened up for her. Even minor activities such as shopping for food became an enjoyable outing once she could go to a market and haggle like a local. She settled in to this existence and was busy preparing for the carnival when her world imploded.

The American Cardinal Thomas had come to Sao Paolo as a Papal Envoy to talk to Cardinal Figueras about the work he was doing and the political stance he was taking. Liberation theology was no longer popular among many of the senior US clergy. Cardinal Thomas was accompanied by a swarm of Vatican apparatchiks. The local Agency staff were instructed to protect him during his stay. Dave, as the only one locally who could speak Italian, was liaison with the Church. When the Cardinals met in the crowded square in front of the basilica, Dave was there to see that all went well. Though he did not anticipate any trouble and in spite of his concerns that it ruined the hang of his suit, he had eventually been persuaded to wear a bullet-proof vest. While the Cardinals were shaking hands, a gunman burst out of the nearby crowd and through the disinterested police line. He stopped to take aim and in that instant Dave spotted him and rushed towards him to block his line of fire. As Dave collided with him, the gun went off and the bullet smashed through Dave's face and fragmented in his brain. Doctors later assured Anna that he would have died instantly, like that was supposed to be a comfort. The gunman was wrestled to the ground by the police and disarmed. He had been trying to kill Cardinal Figueras.

Anna had been distraught at first. Her life suddenly had no meaning. All her future plans had revolved around her relationship with Dave. For years she had stopped thinking about 'I' and only about 'We'. Rejecting the insincere attention of the Embassy wives, she spent two weeks looking for her future in gin bottles. Suicidal, the alcohol luckily restricted her ability to seriously harm herself. Soon, and with a touch of grim humour, she realised that gin wasn't the tonic she needed. She sobered up and thought things through more clearly. She decided that killing herself would achieve nothing. But what should she do? Return to her old life? No! She had had no life without Dave. Start a new life? A new life! What was the point of a new life without the one person in it that had ever made her truly feel alive. She should probably go home to Baltimore; go back to work for her father. She couldn't change the past; she couldn't undo the damage; she couldn't bring Dave back to life; killing herself wouldn't get her any closer to Dave. But she also couldn't bear to continue with any sort of normal life knowing that the people responsible for Dave's death were being allowed to get away with this injustice. The gunman had been arrested and yet would probably only serve a few years in prison. The Cardinals were still alive. Dave was gone. It was all the wrong way round. Before returning to a lonely existence with her parents she was determined that she would redress the balance. The bullet that killed Dave had been meant for Figueras; he should have died instead. He should die anyway. He would die. She would see to it. The only reason Dave had been in the path of the gunman was because Thomas had come to Brazil and Dave had to protect him. Why should he still be alive. It was his fault that Dave had been shot. He should die too. But above all it was the Agency that had ordered Dave to risk his life to protect these men. They had made him wear the bullet proof vest. They must have known that there would be an attack. They put him into the line of fire. He was supposed to have a safe desk job.

She knew what she must do. Dave had occasionally talked about some of the more exotic weapons that the Agency used in its attempts at political manipulation around the world. Apart from commonplace blackmail and threats against governments on every continent, they also had subtle poisons. Once, when she had been in his office at the Embassy, he had shown her where they were kept. Poison appealed to her and so, when she went to the embassy to retrieve Dave's personal effects, judiciously timed tears drove away otherwise vigilant security guards who never saw her pocketing the capsules of liquid death. Now armed, she coolly and calmly planned her revenge with the detached precision she had admired in Agrippina. The Cardinals would die along with Manny whom she believed had recruited Dave into the Agency. But before she could act, Cardinal Thomas had flown back to Rome. She would have to deal with Figueras first, pursue Thomas and then find Manny.

So now here she was in Rome. When she had first discovered that Manny was here too, she was sure that fate was intervening to help her. But, although she had been wrong about Manny, there was no mistake about Thomas' guilt and she was determined to make sure he paid. She had failed once but she wouldn't fail again. She shook herself out of her reverie and, looking back across the Circus Maximus, she focussed on the characteristic plane trees on the horizon. She was glad she had come here, although she would rather have shared the experience with Dave. Now her campaign was almost at an end she would soon be leaving Rome and returning to the bleak future ahead of her. But first she had to deal with Cardinal John Thomas. Tomorrow, she thought, tomorrow.

She picked up the bag which had been lying at her feet and walked briskly across the dry, dusty paths that criss-crossed the hill, heading back down towards the Forum. Tomorrow.

Once again, Anna sat before the mirror in her hotel room. Gazing into her own eyes she saw a different person. Helen Wates was needed one more time. She would have to see Thomas tomorrow. After their last meeting he would not be expecting to see her again, but she had learnt years ago never to burn her bridges; he would have no reason to refuse to see her. However, the apple having failed to reach its intended target last time, she would need a more direct and reliable way of delivering the coup de grace. The others had been easy. Coffee, tea. But she realised that she knew very little about the Cardinal's likes or dislikes, habits or fears. She should have done more research. Dave would have researched a subject very thoroughly, he was always careful to know who he was dealing with, even though, of course, he had never assassinated anyone. She was becoming careless. Taking too much for granted. Too confident. She would need to find the way to the Cardinal's heart.

Vatican

Cardinal Bianchi smiled as he knocked on the door of Cardinal Thomas' office.

"John. Can I have a word with you please?"

"Of course Angelo, come in, sit down."

"Do you mind if I close the door?"

"No, of course not. What can I do for you?"

Bianchi settled himself in the chair and then looked Thomas straight in the eyes.

"I have been given some rather unsettling information, that I wish to discuss with you."

"Concerning?"

"Concerning you, John."

"Me? Fire away, I'm intrigued."

"It has been determined that there are people who are trying to usurp the position of Holy Father. They are eliminating the most likely candidates to be the next incumbent and then they will eliminate the Holy Father himself."

"What has this to do with me?"

"You are the one they wish to see elected."

"Me? Ha! Is this some kind of joke? April fool's day was months ago Angelo."

"No. I'm not laughing?"

"Well you should be. It's ludicrous. Whoever has been spinning you this story is obviously intent on damaging the credibility of one or other of us."

"There is evidence that has been shared with me and various other people."

"Do I get to see any of this evidence?"

"Not at the moment. I thought it fair to tell you immediately so you could consider your response."

"My response? My response is don't be so stupid. Any so-called evidence must have been concocted."

"The evidence is all a matter of public record John."

"Who is supposed to be behind this plot?"

"American neo-conservatives, CIA, maybe others too."

"Maybe? I thought this was all a matter of public record?"

"The deaths of Cardinals Figueras and Bramante were certainly quite public."

"What? But Giuseppe had a heart attack. Figueras too if I recall correctly."

"Apparently so."

"Angelo this is just too ridiculous for words. If you've got some evidence against anyone I suggest you check it. If it's against me I suggest you check it again. Because it must be false. Come back when you're ready to apologise."

Thomas stood up and walked to the door, opened it and waited in silence for his visitor to leave.

Rome

As Maria-Grazia left Sandro's studio, a large man in a dark suit and sunglasses was about to press the buzzer. He caught the door as it shut behind her, stopping it from locking, and pushed it open again. Oblivious, she walked away, past two more men apparently fascinated by the window of the boutique next door. This had been a good session, Sandro had really managed to bring out the look she wanted for her portfolio pictures. She was sure that these photos would get her the modelling work she craved.

The large man held the door open as he waited for his two associates to sidle over from the boutique. The three of them quietly climbed the stairs up to the studio. Sandro was nowhere to be seen, but a small red light was shining above a door on the far side of the room. Striding over to the door, Short gently tried the handle but the door was locked.

"We'll wait for him to come out of the darkroom," said the third man, leaning back against the plain whitewashed wall.

They stood waiting for a few minutes and were finally rewarded by the sound of the lock disengaging on the other side as the red light was extinguished. The door opened and Sandro emerged looking at a large black and white photo of Maria-Grazia as he walked. So engrossed in the photo that he failed to notice the three men behind him, Sandro ambled across the studio to his desk. Grabbing an arm each, Small and Large suddenly seized Sandro, the photo flying out of his hand and fluttering to the floor.

"Che fai?" yelled Sandro.

"Sorry don't speak Eyetalian" said Small.

"What are you doing? Who are you?" Sandro was struggling, trying to escape from the two men.

"Who we are is unimportant. We want something and we think you can help us get it." The soft voice came from behind him, not from either of the men holding his arms.

"What?" as Sandro spoke he tried to turn to see who was talking, but two gloved hands grabbed his ears and held his head facing forward.

"A manuscript. It's very important to us."

"I don't have any manuscripts. I'm a photographer not a publisher." Sandro struggled again to no avail.

"But you can help us get what we want."

"How? I have no idea what you're talking about."

"I'm talking about leverage. We can't get to your wife directly but we can use you."

"My wife? What do you want with Costanza? This has got nothing to do with her."

"Oh but it has. It has everything to do with her. You're just a pawn, unimportant and dispensable, worth sacrificing to protect the Queen."

"Queen? What Queen? What do you want with Costanza?"

"Actually she's leverage too. We need to use the Queen to get at the King."

"Who's the King?" Sandro was confused now, if these Americans had come for Tim's manuscript what did they want with Costanza? The files had been sent to him. Costanza had never even met Tim, so why would anyone think that she had them?

"Elvis," muttered the large man holding Sandro's left arm.

"What?" asked Sandro and Small simultaneously.

"Elvis is the King. Oh, ignore me," Large grinned, "I'm not here to talk. I don't do the talking. I hurt people. That's what I do. That's why I'm here." He grinned again.

Ignoring the large man as instructed, Sandro again tried to turn his head, but was again restrained.

"All this chess talk is confusing me. What do you want and why?"

"We want your wife to get us inside the Vatican."

"She's just a programmer in the accounts department, she doesn't have access to any of the money or treasures. There's no point in trying to threaten her, she can't help you steal anything."

"We're not after money. Well, not directly. We want to get into the Library."

"What library?"

"You know what library, the Vatican Library."

"What's that got to do with Costanza? I told you she works in accounts. She's got no special access to any library. Anyway I thought the Vatican library was open to the public, you just need to make an appointment."

"Don't be stupid, and don't assume that we are either. We know she works in the Library. We know there's a lot more than the public sees. The secret archives, that's where we want to go."

"But I've told you, she's an accounts programmer. If you think she's a librarian, you really are stupid."

"Don't call me stupid," hissed Small through gritted teeth, "it really annoys me."

"Don't BE stupid then, " Sandro started to say but was stopped by a jab to his kidney from Small, "aaargh."

"Now gentlemen, please desist. At least for now. Let's take Sandro here for a ride. Get him downstairs, I'll call Luca."

As Sandro was manhandled down the stairs he heard the quiet man behind him open a mobile phone and press a couple of buttons.

"Luca. Now please."

By the time they had reached the door at the bottom

of the stairs, a black Fiat was pulling up outside. Small loosened his grip on Sandro to open the door, giving him the opportunity to wrench his arm free and spin round to try to pull away from Large as well. But a well aimed elbow in the small of his back disabled Sandro again and he found himself being half carried, half dragged through the door and across the pavement to the waiting car. Bundled in the back before he had a chance to think straight, he had no opportunity to try and shout for help. It would have done no good as there was nobody else in the street to come to his aid. With Small on his right and Large on his left, he was tightly sandwiched in the back seat of the small car. The third man got into the front seat and as he shut his door the driver accelerated away from the kerb. Sandro still could not see his interrogator's face. While they drove, Small took a large handkerchief out of his pocket and tied it as a blindfold around Sandro's head. From the twists and turns of the car, and the few noises filtering through the closed windows, Sandro guessed they were going towards the centre of the city. Suddenly they stopped. He heard one of the car doors open, he guessed it was the front passenger door, and felt the small car rock on its springs as someone got out. Through the open door he heard footsteps on stone steps, distant traffic, but little else. Then a whistle and he felt the two men either side of him open their doors. After a second or two of relief at no longer being squashed, Sandro was dragged out of the left door and both men bundled him quickly down some steps (he counted 27) and through a doorway into a room. He heard a large, obviously heavy, metal door shut behind him and the scraping of locks at it was secured. Again he was roughly dragged across the floor, a wooden chair being kicked out of the way, up a step and thrown onto a sofa. His head bounced off a bolster and he kept as still as possible, frightened, confused and worried for Costanza.

"Now what?" asked Sandro.

"We wait."

"For what?"

"For your lovely wife to miss you."

Sandro heard the other two men talking quietly across the room.

"We're hungry," said one. It sounded to Sandro like the Elvis fan.

"There's a pizza place across the road. I'll go and get take-out."

"Get enough for all of us, even him," the quiet man said, "we're going to be here a while."

As the locks scraped open on the metal door, Sandro felt a rumbling beneath the floor for a few seconds. A metro train.

As a photographer he was able to count time very accurately, a skill quickly developed in a darkroom. By the time the door scraped open again, Sandro had heard the metro twice more and within an hour he had worked out the relative timing of the trains in each direction. As a regular traveller on Linea B he knew that he must be near Termini on the Colosseum side. Thank God Rome's metro network was so small and reliably regular.

Years of having to work in the blackout of a darkroom along with his photographer's ability to visualise meant that, despite the blindfold, he had built up a picture in his mind of the room in which he was being held. The different floor levels and narrowness of the room made it unlikely that this was purpose built as an apartment. He was fairly sure that he was in the ground floor of an older building, maybe converted from a storage area – the acoustics of a vaulted stone ceiling were readily recognisable. The man who had brought the pizzas back had also bought ice cream from a gelateria "on the way". All in all, Sandro was pretty sure he could guess where he was being held. He had worked in this area many times. The steps outside down which he had been dragged from the car, had been his choice of location for many shoots as they were never very busy.

"I need to use the toilet." Sandro said in what he hoped sounded like a desperate tone.

"Take him." The quiet man said.

Sandro was dragged up from the sofa and pushed across the room. He heard a door being opened and a light switch click, and was pushed into a small bathroom.

"Can I take off the blindfold please. It will be a bit difficult otherwise."

"Okay," said the quiet man "let him take it off, but make sure it's on again before he comes back out."

Sandro reached up to slip off the blindfold as the door shut behind him. He turned, slid the lock across, turned back and sat down on the toilet cover as his eyes became re-accustomed to the light. There were no windows, but to his right was a walk-in shower, and in the far corner of the shower cubicle was an air vent through which he could see daylight. He stood up, quietly slid back the shower door and gingerly stepped inside. Although not tall he could still see through the vent, it didn't open into an alley or roadway but into a storage vault next door, which was full of rubbish – it seemed unlikely that anyone would be there to hear him if he called for help. But what he could see confirmed that he was in one of the old storage buildings. He was now convinced that he knew exactly where he was. Sighing, he stepped back out of the shower and looked around the rest of the bathroom. There was nothing useful in the small cupboard in the corner, and apart from toilet tissue and a hand towel there was apparently nothing else in the room. But in the small bin under the sink he noticed a broken safety pin. Bending down he fished it out and was about to put it in his pocket when he had an idea. He took the blindfold from the hook on the door where he had hung it, and made a hole in it with the point of the pin where his left eye would be. Putting the pin in his pocket, he reached over, pressed the button in the wall to flush the toilet and then washed his hands in the sink. Standing in front of the door he pulled the blindfold back over his eyes and adjusted it until he could see through the pinhole. He shut his eyes, leant forward, undid the lock and turned the handle. The door flew open and he could feel someone standing in front of him. Resisting the urge to open his eyes, fearful of reacting and giving away his new-found ability to see at least partially, he waited until he was guided out of the room and towards the sofa. Once lying down again he carefully opened his eyes and found he could just make out the three men sitting around a table between him and the metal door. To the right of them was a small kitchen. In his part of the room there was a staircase leading up next to the bathroom door, presumably to a bedroom.

"What time is it?" he asked.

"Time for you to keep quiet," snapped the large man.

"About three," said the quiet man, "but don't worry, we're not going anywhere soon."

"What are you waiting for?"

"I told you. We're waiting for the delightful Costanza to miss you. That won't happen until you don't come home tonight. Then she'll start worrying and will be more receptive to our conditions."

"She won't worry. I often don't come home. Night shoots, sudden location shoots too far away to get home. She's used to it."

"It must be tough staying away from your wife. At

least you have beautiful models to keep you company."

"What? I've never been unfaithful to Costanza. I love her. And she loves me."

"We're counting on it. She better love you enough to betray her bosses."

"I told you, you've got it all wrong. She has nothing to do with a library, or secret archives or whatever it is you want. She's an accounts programmer. Boring stuff with numbers, databases of invoices and things like that."

"You seem to know a lot about it. As if you've learnt your story well."

"What! Don't be ridiculous. She comes home at night and tells me about her day. Just like I tell her about mine. She knows who I've been shooting and why. I know about her accounts and invoices. It's what interests her, so I pay attention."

"Oh how sweet. Well, we don't believe you. We know she's a big shot in the Library and we know she can get us what we want."

"Which is what?"

"A manuscript. A very old manuscript. Two thousand years old to be precise. Very important too, to them and to us. That's what we want."

"But I've told you she won't be able to help. Something like that is bound to be heavily protected. How would an accounts programmer be able to get to it?"

"An accounts programmer wouldn't, but she will."

"I've told you…"

"Shut up now. Or my friend here will shut you up," the quiet man looked at Large who grinned.

Sandro decided to bide his time. At least he knew where he was. He would need to find a way of letting someone else know, someone who could help him.

New York, USA

Oblivious to the fact that her every move was being scrutinised by the NSA, Rebecca stepped out of the elevator and walked confidently into the room. She stopped and blinked. She had never realised how much smoke a room full of social workers could generate in less than half an hour. Most of them worked in environments where they were not allowed to smoke, so they had set to with gusto when they found that today's conference was not in a smoke-free room. She shook hands with some of the members she had met recently in union meetings in Boston, they had decided to come down to New York to this conference to help generate ideas for positive action. Everybody was concerned about the impact the federal government's budget cuts were having on national welfare programs, and even more concerned about the knock-on effect they were having on city funding for social workers and other welfare staff. Many of the union's members were focused purely on keeping their own jobs, but some were prepared to spend their own time and effort to try and safeguard the people in their care. Rebecca was proud of every person in the room and felt honoured to know them. She was even more honoured that they all considered her their erstwhile spokesperson and leader. None of the elected union leadership had been interested in attending.

She slowly made her way to the long table at one end of the room, where she was warmly welcomed by Matthew and Dione Wardell who had organised the meeting here in New York. After checking a few administrative details Dione rang a small hand-bell. The room quickly settled to a silent and expectant hush.

"If you could all take your seats we can start now Rebecca is here."

The silence was demolished by the squeak and squeal

241

of fifty chairs being dragged around, the creak of fifty chairs being sat upon, and the clink of fifty coffee cups being deposited under fifty seats.

"I think everybody here knows Rebecca Bedford so I don't need to waste any time in introductions." So saying Dione sat down and turned to Rebecca.

Rebecca stood up and looked at the fifty faces in front of her. She smiled, but then her face took on a thoughtful frown.

"You all know why we're here. The government has let our people down. The cities have let our people down. Our so-called leaders have let our people down. We mustn't let them down too. We have to stand firm. We have to take action. We must show them what is right, even at great cost to ourselves. Today we can take the first step together and show New York and the rest of the country that we mean business."

She bent down to pick up her handbag, to get her notes detailing the budget cuts and their impact on the lower social strata of New York's citizens.

At that moment, convinced that Rebecca was reaching for some remote detonation device to show New York that she meant business, ten NSA agents dressed in black cat-suits and balaclavas burst into the room brandishing automatic weapons and screaming "FREEZE!". Unsurprisingly there was instant panic and the last thing that anyone did was freeze. Most dived for the floor, some stood and tried to run.

Rebecca picked up her handbag and Adam, so desperate not to be too late that he didn't wait for any real evidence of her intent, aimed his weapon at her and pulled the trigger. Twenty bullets tore through Rebecca's body, shattering her right arm, shredding her lungs and throwing her backwards in a series of staccato jerks as if she was being controlled by an epileptic puppeteer. Adam's

242

gunfire unnerved Laurie who fired at a man running to the other side of the room. As if the shooting were contagious, within seconds all the agents were firing wildly into the crowd of people cowering on the floor. Soon Adam and Laurie had stopped and they called out to their team to ceasefire.

Slowly Adam stood up and started picking his way towards Rebecca's prone form. He found her mangled body wrapped around a chair, the handbag still clutched in one hand. Prising it out of her dead grip he gingerly looked inside to see what she had been reaching for. There was no weapon, no remote detonation device, only a sheet of paper which he withdrew and unfolded.

"Well?" asked Laurie.

Adam read and reread the paper and then sank down onto the chair, dislodging Rebecca's leg which had become caught in it and causing her body to slump to the ground with a sickeningly wet thud.

"Well?" Laurie repeated. "Does it detail their plans?"

Adam looked up at her.

"Yeah," he whispered, "it does. She wanted to shame the city into increasing the budgets for welfare and homeless programs. She was hoping to persuade as many social workers as possible to give up their wages for one day next week."

"What?"

"Don't you see? The reason they kept to their cover as social workers so well, is that they really were social workers."

"And we've killed them all?" Laurie was looking a little pale.

"Looks that way," said Adam, "Oops."

"Oops? Is that all you have to say? We kill nearly sixty innocent people and you say oops?"

"Shhh!" Adam was looking around him nervously.

"Bad intel. Not our fault. Anyway, there's no-one to say what happened here but you and me. We can always bend the facts a little. Damage limitation. As far as the others are concerned they've taken out a bunch of terrorists, only we know they were just social workers." He started to look less nervous.

"They are all dead aren't they?" he asked. "We can't afford any witnesses."

"What?" Laurie was staring at Adam.

"If there is no-one left to say what happened we can make up what we like. We can turn this to our advantage; say we've foiled a massive plot to attack New York City. Who would know any different?"

"Actually, they were anarchists anyway," he added.

"How d'you figure that?" she asked.

"Well they were plotting to take action against City Hall. They were conspiring against the federal government."

"And that makes them anarchists?"

"At the very least. Yup, that's our story. But we've got to be consistent on this Laurie. Or we're finished. Okay?"

Laurie was shocked at first, but the more she thought about it the more she had to agree with Adam. If they admitted they had slaughtered a room full of innocents they would lose their jobs and probably face manslaughter charges. At the very least there would be hours of paperwork to complete. However, if they were to identify the dead as an active terrorist group caught in the very act of initiating an attack, they would be able to walk away while the clean-up squad came in and prepared the scene for the police to deal with. No paperwork, no charges, possibly even promotion. What's more she'd definitely get to uncle Mo's birthday party this evening.

"Okay," she finally answered.

"This one's still alive," came a shout from the other end of the room.

Adam stood up and went over to the agent who had found the survivor.

"Which one?"

He pointed to a young black woman lying on the floor. She was breathing, but almost imperceptibly. Adam swung his gun around, pointed it at the woman and pulled the trigger.

"I don't think so," he said as he walked back to Laurie.

Later that evening, while at uncle Mo's party, Laurie heard her father listening to the news on the radio in the kitchen.

" ...a group of Christian fundamentalists who had been planning a terrorist strike against St Patrick's Cathedral here in New York. The mayor's office has said that thanks to a coordinated effort between the NYPD and federal agents, using intelligence information gathered by the security services, the plot was foiled, but the terrorists had all committed suicide rather than be arrested. A spokesman for the White House has praised the operation and confirmed that this outstanding success was a result of the new and unprecedented co-operation between agencies to protect homeland security, a co-operation instigated by the current administration."

"You know Laurie," her dad began, "these fundamentalists are all up to no good. It's always us Moslems who get tarred with that brush and sometimes you wonder if they don't just make up stories like that to give Islam a bad name. So in a weird way I'm glad that for once it was Christians up to no good."

Laurie smiled weakly.

"Yes Dad."

Vatican

Costanza answered the ringing phone on her desk.

"Pronto."

"Costanza?"

"Yes, who is it?"

"It's Camilla Cicchinelli. How are you?"

"Fine thank you. How are you?"

"I'm well. Is Sandro okay?"

"As far as I know, why?"

"I had a shoot arranged with him at the studio but the door's locked and there's no response to the buzzer. I tried ringing his cell phone but there's no answer. I tried calling your home but there's just your machine there. I thought maybe he was ill and couldn't work today. I'm sorry to bother you at work, I know you don't like to be disturbed there."

"No don't worry, it's fine. This isn't the busy part of the month for the accounts. I'm afraid I don't know where Sandro is. He went out at the normal time today, I think he was having a session with a new model first thing this morning, portfolio shots. I remember he said he would be seeing you this afternoon. I don't know what's happened. Listen, accept my apologies on his behalf. Whatever has happened must be important and unexpected for him not to let you know in advance like this. I have a key for the studio, I haven't had my lunch break yet so I'll go over there now and see if I can track him down."

"Okay Costanza. I hope he's okay."

"I'm sure everything's fine. I'll get him to ring you to apologise himself when I find him. Thanks for calling. Ciao." She hoped she had kept her voice calm enough not to worry Camilla.

Langley, Virginia, USA

"Sir."

"Yes Marge?"

"It's five before eleven."

"Thanks Marge."

"Do you need me to get you anything for your meeting with the Director?"

"No. Thanks."

Just as she was shutting the door, Hocke called out to her.

"Marge."

"Yes sir."

"I've put a few things in this burn bag. You'd better take it and keep it safe. If anything happens, burn it, don't open it. You know the drill."

"Yes sir. Is there a problem sir?" she walked back into the room towards the desk.

"I hope not. But just in case…" his voice trailed off, as he forced a smile.

Standing up he handed her a large sealed envelope, took the hanger from the coat stand behind his desk, removed his jacket and slowly put it on. Straightening his tie as he walked, he started towards the door.

"Hold on," Marge said, walking towards him. She reached out and picked some fluff from his shoulder.

"Okay, you can go now," she smiled.

"Thanks Marge."

Five minutes later he was standing outside the Director's office. The PA's intercom buzzed.

"You can go in now, sir," she said.

"Thanks."

As he opened the door, a voice from inside began.

"John. Come in. You didn't tell me what was so urgent. I'm intrigued. Sit down. What's the problem?"

"Okay, I'll get straight to the point. Some TA21 has gone missing from a field office."

"TA21? That's …?"

"Agency developed Termination Accelerant. Causes a heart attack. Leaves no trace. Of course we've always denied it exists."

"But now some is missing?"

"Yes. Twelve doses."

"Carelessness?"

"Looks like it was deliberately removed. But no-one external had access. It must have been one of our people. So before we look any harder I wanted to check whether there might be a, shall we say, good reason why it might have gone missing."

"You're thinking black ops?"

"Seems like a possibility."

"Why? A minor weapons theft. Hardly enough to arouse suspicion."

"Exactly!"

"Okay. What else haven't you told me?"

"There have already been some fatalities. Unexpected heart attacks, no obvious medical cause. Too clean. It looks entirely consistent with TA21. Given that the first was local to the office where it went missing …"

"Where?"

"Sao Paolo, Brazil."

"The others?"

"Boston, England, Italy."

"What's the link?"

"Two Catholic Cardinals, an Archbishop, a Rabbi."

"A religious campaign?"

"Maybe. But now the latest is a journalist. The others were also all linked by a website."

"What?"

"A website that's a front for a contract hit squad. At

248

first we assumed they were ex-agents turned mercenary, from a defunct agency in Eastern Europe. But with the TA21 going AWOL it's starting to look like it might be some of our own people."

"Rogue?"

"Or worse."

"You think the Agency is doing this?"

"It had occurred to me."

"Well if we are, I don't know anything about it."

"You wouldn't, would you? But if it is a black op, you're the only one who can stop it."

"Okay John. Give me everything you've got. Files, dates, names, whatever. I'll start making some waves and see what surfaces. If it comes to it I'll go to POTUS."

"Yes sir."

"And John."

"Sir?"

"Thanks for bringing this to me."

"Yes sir."

John Hocke stood up and walked back out through the door.

Rome

Costanza arrived home after a fruitless trip to Sandro's studio. There was no sign of him and no messages on the answer-phone. She sat down on the sofa.

Under normal circumstances she wouldn't be in the least bit concerned if Sandro wasn't home on time. She knew that some shoots overran and at times they stayed late on location to get 'the right light'. Sunsets were a bit of an obsession for Sandro and he would often spend an hour just watching the light change from second to second. He had shot hundreds of rolls of film at sunset. But these weren't normal circumstances. He usually phoned Costanza to let her know what he was doing and he would never have left Camilla standing at the door to the studio with no explanation. He always made sure he had his cell phone with him, even if he wasn't always careful about keeping the battery charged. So finding his phone on the desk at the studio had worried her. Where could he be?

Sitting in the quiet apartment she started to imagine various scenarios. She was sure that the NAC men from Capri who had killed Tim Shah must have tracked down his emails to Sandro's account and had now come looking for Sandro. What would they do? If they had found him would they threaten him into telling them what he did with the emails? Would they hurt him? Or kill him? Surely they would want to ensure that they had erased any copies of the emails before they got rid of witnesses?

She jumped up and ran into the bedroom, scrabbling around in the bottom of the laundry basket to lift the base. The disc was still underneath. She breathed a sigh of relief, put the dirty clothes back in place and returned to the sofa.

She wasn't sure what to do now. If Sandro was just out somewhere he would eventually come home and she would feel foolish but relieved. If he had been captured by the NAC, he would never tell them about the disc in case they came to the apartment and tried to hurt her. He would probably say that he had deleted Tim's emails as he wasn't at all interested in politics. Hopefully they would believe him and let him go. The alternative didn't bear thinking about. But if they had tracked the emails to Sandro that must mean they had got access to Tim's email account. Had Sandro replied? Had he promised to look after the files? She had never thought to ask him. If he had, then his captors would not believe that he would have deleted them. If they had checked the computer at his studio they would have discovered that he didn't pick up his email from there, so they would come to the apartment anyway. But surely they would have come to the apartment first, during the day when it was empty, yet there was no sign that anyone had been here. Maybe she was worrying unnecessarily. Sandro was probably busy somewhere. He'd be home soon and she could relax.

After a while she decided that there was no point in sitting on the sofa fretting. She was sure Sandro was okay. The best thing to do would be to freshen up ready to welcome him home. She went into the bedroom, undressed and was just taking her dressing gown from the hook on the back of the door when the phone rang. She ran to pick it up.

"Sandro?"

"Si bella." There was a pause.

"They say I must talk in English only."

"Who?"

"I don't know who they are. They want you to get something for them. I don't understand what is happening. I don't know what they'll do to me. Pray to my patron Saint Prassede and her sister, that between them they will find me. I ..." Sandro's voice was abruptly interrupted as the phone was obviously snatched away from him.

"No-one's going to find him unless you co-operate." A quiet but hard American voice replaced Sandro's on the line.

"Who are you?" Costanza asked in as calm a voice as she could manage, desperate not to betray the fear she felt for Sandro.

"That's irrelevant. We want something from the Vatican Library Secret Archives. You will help us get it."

"I'm just an accounts programmer. I write programs to pay salaries and bills. I have nothing to do with the Library. I can't get you into it. I ..."

"Your husband, who is, incidentally, lying blindfolded on the floor in front of us, said the same thing. But I don't believe either of you. We know you work in the Library. You will help us get the manuscript."

"Manuscript? What manuscript?"

"That's better. Co-operate and Sandro here won't be hurt. Any more."

"How do you know what you want is in the Library? If it's supposed to be a secret archive then surely no-one knows what's in it."

"There's no point in playing dumb. As I said we know you work in the Library, you know all about the secret archive. We want the Codex Albustensis."

Costanza suppressed her surprise.

"I told you I can't get anything from the Library. I have no idea what this Codex is or where it might be."

"Well you better find out or you'll never see your husband again. At least not alive."

"But how can I get something if I don't know what or where it is?"

"Think of a way. Either you get it. Or get me into the secret archives and I'll find it. But no tricks. No police.

252

My people here will still be keeping hold of your husband until we have the manuscript and have left the country."

"I don't know what to do. I'll have to think about it. Work it out."

"You have 24 hours. We'll call again this time tomorrow night. I'm sure it will be easier to get in to the Vatican unnoticed at the weekend."

"You must be joking. Even in the summer it's swarming with people at the weekend."

"Precisely, so no-one will notice one more visitor. Till tomorrow."

"Please can I talk to Sandro again?"

"Tomorrow. If you are being co-operative. Until then remember this."

As Costanza listened she could hear the sound of Sandro being kicked and moaning with pain. She put her hand to her mouth as the phone line went dead. She sank onto the bed feeling bewildered. This surely had nothing to do with the NAC and Tim Shah's story. Who were these people? Why did they want this legendary manuscript. It would be priceless but couldn't be sold on the open market if stolen. It would be of interest to historians or theologians, none of whom would resort to these measures to see it. Even the most ardent collector would surely baulk at such tactics. The only people who could possibly have such a keen interest, enough to murder and steal for it, would be those religious fundamentalists jealous of the Church's power and determined to destroy it. What should she do? Call the police to tell them about Sandro's kidnapping? Call the Vigilanza to warn them about an intended breach of Library security? Call Cardinal Bianchi with her suspicions? She needed to think this through. She couldn't afford to do anything that would hurt Sandro, but there was no way that she could get them the manuscript. She would call Peter and ask his advice.

Still sitting on the bed, she pressed the redial button on the phone and scrolled down to the number of Peter's hotel. While she waited for it to connect she recalled the awful sound of Sandro's pain.

"Hotel Hassler."

"Signor White per favore."

"Certo signorina."

There was a click on the line and then another ringing tone. After a few seconds it was answered.

"Pronto."

"Peter?"

"Yes. Costanza? Are you alright?"

"No. Yes. I don't know. I need to talk to you. Sandro is missing. I had a phone call..." as she spoke she heard a click on the line and stopped.

"Costanza? You said you had a call about Sandro?"

"Yes. Look I don't think we should talk on the phone. Can you come over here. Straight away?"

"Of course. It'll take me a few minutes to get dressed. I'll get the hotel to arrange a taxi for me. I'll be there as soon as I can."

" Dressed? Oh sorry, I didn't realise it was that late."

"It isn't. I've had a luxurious soak in the bath and was just about to get dressed anyway before going for a spot of fresh air on the Pincio. Don't worry. I'll see you soon."

"Thanks Peter."

She pressed the on-hook button on the phone and dropped it beside her on the bed. She stood up and walked out of the bedroom into the lounge, sat down on the sofa and looked at the clock.

"Please be as quick as you can Peter," she thought out loud.

For the next forty-five minutes she sat on the sofa,

staring at the clock, remembering Sandro's yelp of pain, and listening out for the traffic outside. Whenever she heard a car stop she would leap up and look out of the window to see if it was Peter.

Langley, Virginia, USA

Despite what Hocke had told him, Joel was determined to continue his investigation. If there was going to be any credit for busting open this hit squad, Joel was darn sure he'd be getting at least some of it. 'Trust no-one' Marge had said. Everyone here was out to improve their own career prospects with scant regard for anybody else. To get on in this place you had to be ruthless. But most of all you had to be noticed. Joel would make sure he was noticed.

As he was collecting more details about the deaths of the cardinals, archbishop, rabbi and journalist, Joel had become more convinced than ever that they were connected. He discovered that other agencies had already been making enquiries and that the investigation into O'Leary's death in Boston had been managed by the NSA and fronted by the FBI – unusual for a supposedly straightforward heart attack victim.

Finally he felt the pieces of the jigsaw were starting to fall into place. The last one arrived on his screen in the form of the SIS report into Rabbi Cohen's death. Joel had been building a database of common factors between all of the deaths, into which he entered the pertinent details as he scanned this latest report. When he had finished he clicked the Correlate button and was surprised by one of the entries in the list that appeared. Apart from the common parameters he already knew, it suggested that there was a reference in every case to a tall blonde female. Without bothering to cross-check, he deduced that the hit man was in fact a hit woman; a tall, blonde hit woman. Checking the data from Sao Paolo, however, he was disappointed to find that none of the visitors to the office, over the crucial period between inventories of the TA21, fitted the description. In fact only one female visitor appeared in the list, the widow of an agent collecting his personal effects. Looking in the personnel file of the dead agent he found that she was brunette and only five foot eight. Hardly tall, he thought, and not blonde, so he rejected her as a possible suspect. Unwilling, however, to give up on the tall blonde theory, he decided that an accomplice must have taken the TA21 for her.

He knew that the Vatican had made another attempt to elicit help from CNC this week and had again been rebuffed. Convinced, now, of the appearance, if not the identity, of the assassin he decided to warn the Vatican. However, nowhere on the official transcripts or the call logs was any contact number provided and there was no-one still around who would know. Aware of the time difference he concluded that the most expeditious route would be via the Agency office in the Rome embassy. Looking up the number in his directory, he dialled and reached a voicemail system.

"Hi. My name is Joel Schitzenberger from CIC/AG. I have been investigating a series of murders that were brought to our attention by a Vatican Intelligence Agent. I only know her first name, Costanza. Can you contact Vatican Intelligence and inform them that while we are not yet able to identify the assassin, we have a description of 'tall, blonde, female, late twenties or early thirties'. Tell them I hope it helps. When I get anything more I will let them know. Thanks."

Feeling that at last he had achieved something worthwhile in this investigation, Joel composed an email to the Assistant Director outlining his conclusions. As he was about to send it he decided to copy it to Mike Probey. Then he clicked Send. Now he would definitely be noticed.

Mike Probey had already left for the day. That evening on

his way home the brakes on his SUV mysteriously failed and he crashed into the back of a tanker. He didn't survive to read Joel's email.

Joel left Langley about seven o'clock in the evening and was never seen again.

Rome

Before I even had a chance to ring the bell, Costanza's door flew open and she leapt at me. Almost suffocating in her hug I could feel her sobbing on my shoulder.

"Let's go inside." I suggested.

She nodded and, loosening her hold on me, she whispered "I'm so worried for him."

"I know." As I spoke I gently guided her back through the doorway into the apartment, pushing the door shut behind me with my foot.

She was still clinging to me, but now I could see her face. Rivers of tears had carved channels through the soft down of her cheeks. This usually serene, gracious and exquisitely beautiful woman was utterly devastated, and yet, typically, completely oblivious of her appearance. I gently wiped the tears away from her eyes and gazed into those deep, brown windows of her soul.

"Don't worry, I'm sure we can sort this out. Sit down and tell me exactly what's happened."

A little nod, a deep breath and she looked back at me.

"Thank you Peter."

She untangled her arms from me, grabbed my right hand in her left, turned and walked me to the sofa. As I followed her I noticed that she was wearing a dressing gown and pink slippers. These were probably the least elegant clothes I had ever seen her wearing, and with her tear-streaked face and tousled hair she was the most unkempt, yet she had never looked lovelier – mind you I have always been attracted to vulnerable women. The dressing gown was wrapped tight around her and accentuated the shape of her hips. As she walked the shimmering effect of the satin of her gown, combined with the undulations of her buttocks, had a very disturbing effect on me. This was a woman I loved like a niece, almost a daughter, I shouldn't be noticing how sexy she was.

She sat down on the sofa and let go of my hand. As I sat down next to her I couldn't help seeing that, although her gown was tight below the belt, it was loose above with gaping folds. I quickly looked her in the eyes.

"Shouldn't you get dressed?"

She looked down as if she hadn't realised that she was wearing so little.

"Oh. I was about to have a shower when they called. I've just been sitting here since I spoke to you."

She put a hand to her face and wiped a tear from her cheek, then pulled her hand away and looked at it.

"Goodness, what do I look like. I'm sorry Peter. You must be shocked to see me like this."

"Shocked? No. Concerned. Tell you what, you go and have your shower, get dressed. I'll make us a drink. Then we can talk about what to do next."

"No, we must talk now. There's no time to waste. Sandro is in danger."

"You'll think clearer if you're feeling fresh. And I'll think a lot clearer when you're wearing more clothes."

My eyes involuntarily flicked down to the gaping gown. Costanza's eyes followed mine and she gasped.

"Oh!" She clasped her hand to her breast, flattening the gown. "I'm sorry."

She stood up.

"You're right, I'll have a quick shower, if only to wash my face. And I promise to put on less revealing clothes."

She looked at me and smiled. Then, turning to go to the bathroom, she walked away.

"What do you want to drink? Hot or cold? Alcoholic or non-alcoholic?" I called after her as I watched those shimmering hips disappear across the floor.

"Surprise me" she said as she closed the bathroom door.

I stood up and went to the kitchen. Looking in the drinks cupboard I remembered the baby and realised that her options would have to be non-alcoholic. We needed to think straight, so strong coffee was called for. I unscrewed the top half of the espresso pot and filled the base with water. In the freezer compartment of the fridge I found some ground coffee and packed it into the filter. Re-assembling the pot I put it on the hob and switched the ring on. While I was waiting for the sounds and smells of the coffee I found two espresso cups and saucers in a cupboard. I put them on the work surface and went back to the sofa to wait. As I sat there I could hear the water running through the pipes to the bathroom. Then it stopped. The smell of the coffee was wafting its way out of the kitchen and when I stood up to check on it the bathroom door opened. In a cloud of steam, Costanza walked out with a towel wrapped around her head, her dressing gown now carefully fastened and the pink slippers on her feet.

"Coffee smells nice," she said, "pour it out, I'll be dressed in two minutes."

As instructed I went into the kitchen, took the pot off the hob and poured out two generous cupfuls of espresso. I carried them carefully to the dining table and sat down. Moments later, Costanza appeared, looking as lovely as ever, pulling a dark jumper down over the top of her jeans. She glided over to the table, pulled out a chair and sat down opposite me. Picking up her cup, she closed her eyes and breathed in the essence of the coffee. Taking a sip she opened her eyes again.

"You were right. I feel a lot better now."

"Good."

"While I was having my shower I was thinking and I want to say 'Thank you'."

"For what?"

"For being you."

"Me? Well I guess it comes naturally," I smiled back, "but what do you mean?"

"You could have said nothing before about my gown. You could have just enjoyed the view. You could have... Would you have enjoyed the view?"

"That's an unfair question. If I say yes, you'll be offended. If I say no, you'll be offended. Either way you'll be offended. So I won't answer the question." I held up my hands in submission.

"You don't really need to answer the question," she said, "either way I wouldn't have been offended you know, perhaps a little embarrassed, but no more than I already was..."

"You? How embarrassed do you think I am?"

"You could have taken advantage of me, but you didn't. I trust you and I love you. Not in the same way as Sandro of course. You've loved me for years too, I know. It's never been a problem and I don't want it to be one now. My hormones are all over the place at the moment because of the baby, so I'm behaving erratically."

She leant over to give me a kiss on the forehead.

"To be honest, Peter, I don't know what I might have done if you had been less of a gentleman."

"Curses. Missed my chance." I said, smiling and twirling imaginary moustaches.

"And I know you don't mean that," she smiled again.

"Anyway, now you can tell me what's going on."

"You already know about the emails from Tim Shah who died on Capri. They were his notes for an article he was writing about the NAC, and he sent them to Sandro for safe-keeping."

"Yup, you already told me that."

"This afternoon a model was due for a shoot at Sandro's studio. But she couldn't get in because the door was locked and there was no answer when she buzzed. So she rang me to see if I knew where Sandro was."

"Why did she ring you?"

"She'd tried his mobile and got no answer. She's been working with Sandro for years, she's more like a friend now. We often go out for meals together, the four of us."

"Four?"

"She's married."

"I went to the studio with my key." She continued. "He wasn't there, but his mobile phone was on the desk. He always takes it with him, so that was a bit odd. Otherwise everything was normal, except a print lying on the floor which had obviously still been wet when it fell."

"Any signs of a break-in or a struggle?"

"No, nothing."

"So I came home and waited. I checked to see if Sandro's disc was still where I had put it."

"I thought you had taken it away?"

"I had, but once I'd spoken to Sandro about it we put it back where he'd hidden it. Well actually, we made a new disc, encrypting the files using a better password, and hid that. I destroyed the original disc. We have very powerful shredders in the office."

"Was the disc still there?"

"Yes. There was no sign anyone had been here. I waited. I was very worried, Peter. If they had no qualms about killing a high-profile journalist, they wouldn't think twice about hurting my Sandro. Anyway, after a while I decided I was being silly – I wanted to believe that I was just over-emotional because of the baby. So I thought I'd have a quick shower. I got undressed and was putting on my gown when the phone rang. It was Sandro, but before he could say very much there was another man talking. An American. He said that they would hurt Sandro if I didn't co-operate. He said they wanted me to get them into the Vatican Library, the secret archives. I told him I didn't have access and he said that Sandro had already told them that but they didn't believe him either. I asked what he wanted and that's when it became very strange. He said he wanted a manuscript. I assumed he must mean Tim Shah's article, but couldn't understand why he would think it was in the Library. Then he told me he wanted the Codex Albustensis. I said I couldn't get it for him and he said in that case I would never see Sandro again. He said I should get it or find a way to get him into the secret archives so he can take what he wants. Or else."

"Then what?"

"Then he hung up. Peter it's very strange. I sat there for a minute completely confused. What does any of this have to do with the Tim Shah e-mails. I didn't know what to do for the best. There's only one person I can trust, so I called you. I've been sitting here thinking about everything until you arrived. I've been going around in circles in my mind trying to understand what's happening. But making me have the shower was a good idea, because it also cleared my head and I'm starting to see what's going on. I think."

She took a large slug from her espresso, clunked it back down into the saucer so hard I was worried it would break, and looked at me.

"Before you enlighten me, can I ask a few questions?" I asked.

"Of course."

"No-one else knows you work at the Library?"

"No, everyone thinks I'm a boring accounts programmer. Apart from Sandro. But he would never tell anyone. They said he had confirmed my cover story, so they hadn't found out from him."

"They already knew before they kidnapped him."

"I'm sure of it."

"There's nothing to link Tim Shah's article with the Library, or you. So it can't be anything to do with that."

"That's the conclusion I've reached too."

"Their target must be the Library itself and they're just using Sandro to get to you."

"Agreed."

"What was this Codex Albicocca you mentioned?"

Costanza smiled. It was good to see.

"Not apricot. Codex Albustensis."

"Whatever. Can you get it, give it to them. Is it valuable?"

"That's the thing, Peter. It would be priceless. It would be of great interest to many people around the world. Even if we had it in the Library I certainly wouldn't be able to give it to them."

"If? You mean it's not in the Library? Where is it then?"

"Nowhere."

"What?"

"It doesn't exist. It was a fiction created by a bored 16th century teenager."

"So why are these people looking for it?"

"No-one outside the Library knows for certain that it doesn't exist."

"But you do?"

"Of course. There was a young girl, well-educated, rich and bored, growing up in a castle in Austria. Her father was a Count and she was destined to be married off to the son of another Count. So she knew she would eventually become a Countess with her own household to run. But meanwhile she was very bored. She loved to read and had read the Bible many times. Her cousin was a monk and copies of many manuscripts and books were made in the library of his monastery. He took her there and, with nothing else to occupy her time, she read her way through many volumes. She had heard various versions of the Holy Grail legend, like everyone, and she was spellbound by the histories of the Crusades. She became fascinated with the idea of a mysterious treasure brought back from the Holy Land by the returning knights. One day when she was reading one of St. Paul's Epistles, she asked her cousin why, when there had been such bitterness between St. Paul and the Apostles in Jerusalem, eventually both Peter and Paul had gone to Rome and become the leaders of the Church. He told her that Paul had persuaded Peter and James to support his view that Jesus' message was for all people, not just Jews. No-one knew how he had convinced them, the accepted view was that they were inspired by the Holy Spirit to understand the truth. She said it would have been interesting to know what had been said at the meeting between Paul, Peter and James. Then she started to fantasise about it. She was somewhat ahead of her times and had never liked Paul's views on women, so she decided Paul would not have been above using underhand tactics. What if he had somehow blackmailed Peter and James? If Paul knew something about them that would destroy their control on the fledgling church in Jerusalem, they would have had no choice but to support him. She further embellished the fantasy. To safeguard his position, Paul had a record kept of the meeting, including the details of what he knew, making Peter and James put their marks to it. That document was hidden to keep it safe, but then lost for centuries until it was found by the Crusaders when they captured Jerusalem. They couldn't read it because it was written in Aramaic, but they recognised that it had the seal of Simon Peter. They brought it back to Europe. She decided that after many years of languishing in a casket in a castle somewhere, the manuscript would have come into the possession of a scholar, her cousin for example, who was able to translate it and knew what it really was. She span the story to her cousin and now, she told him, he was in possession of this manuscript. He must vow to protect it. If the contents became known they would be ammunition for the protestants who would like to see the power of St. Peter's successors diminished. Laughing, the monk vowed to protect this imaginary document, he would even deny its very existence if put to the test. When she went back to her rooms that night she decided to write the story in her journal. But with one crucial omission. She failed to record that it was a fantasy of her own invention. She wrote it as fact and identified her cousin, the monk Albustensis, as the keeper of the manuscript. Over a few weeks she gradually added to the story in her journal, documenting imaginary events in which her cousin had been called on to protect the manuscript from falling into unscrupulous hands. Soon she had become so engrossed in the fantasy that maybe she even forgot it was all her own invention. Within a few months she was married to her promised Count and taken to his castle on the other side of the empire, where, sadly, she died in childbirth the following spring. Albustensis had all but forgotten her story and his part in it. However, it seems that after her death the Count had read through her journal and recounted the tale of his wife's cousin and the mysterious manuscript to various of his friends. The story gradually spread and, over the years, reports began to reach the monastery that scholars were keen to read the manuscript that, it was alleged, Albustensis was still hiding there. Some even came in person to request access to the document. Eventually a request came from Rome that the Holy Father wanted the manuscript brought to him for his own study. Albustensis tried in vain to convince everyone that there was no manuscript – his cousin's journal had, of course, predicted that he would deny it even existed. In despair, Albustensis came to Rome to see Pope Gregory XIII. He told him what his cousin had written and assured him that there had never been any manuscript. The Pope heard his private confession. Although we have no idea what was said in that confession, Albustensis was allowed to leave Rome and Pope Gregory never again asked for the manuscript. The Library records show that the whole thing was a childish fantasy penned by a bored countess. Soon it was forgotten."

"So if it was forgotten why are these people looking for it?"

"Unfortunately, the countess' journals were recently put up as lots in a Viennese auction room. No-one had bothered to read them before offering them for sale. They went for a small sum to an American academic who then actually read them. When he got to the story of St. Paul's blackmail he was overjoyed because he was an anti-religious bigot who saw the opportunity to cause trouble. So without bothering to do any corroborative research he published the story as she wrote it. There had been a few references elsewhere that had caused comments over the years, but nothing significant and certainly not to this level of detail. His publication immediately caused various groups to start to actively search for evidence of the manuscript. It was decided in the Library that the best position for us to take was to continue with dignified silence. Just as 400 years ago, the lack of any concrete evidence would soon lead most researchers to abandon the hunt. Any denial from us would have merely fanned the flames."

"And?"

"That was three months ago. There are various chat

rooms on the internet where it is discussed. The most popular theories, of course, are that Albustensis hid it somewhere; either in the monastery in Austria, which still exists today and currently has a big problem with unwanted visitors; or wherever he went when he left the monastery. He retreated into the Swiss Alps to a little church where he died years later. I don't know if anyone has actually tracked down the church yet. As far as we were aware no-one knew he had come to Rome to see the Pope, but if these people do, then presumably they have assumed that he left the manuscript here."

"So the people that have Sandro are…?"

"Well I don't think they're historians!"

"Enemies of the Church?"

"Yes and hence likely to do anything, sacrifice anyone, especially if they think that in some perverted way they are doing God's work. Peter, I think I'm even more worried about Sandro than when I thought it was the NAC."

"It still might be."

"What?"

"Two pronged attack. Classic approach. On one front try to defeat from within by taking over the leadership. Meanwhile, on the other front, pursue anything that will discredit and destroy the authority of the existing leader."

"So this might all be related to the murders."

"We need to talk to Cardinal Bianchi. What time does he arrive in the mornings?"

"He's usually around before seven o'clock. He says an early Mass in one of the side chapels before the basilica is opened to the public. But he won't see anyone before eight thirty."

"Okay, why don't you phone and leave him a voicemail that we need to see him first thing. We'll get there for eight thirty and see what he can suggest.

Meanwhile, I'll go and get some sleep."

I stood up to leave.

"You can't go. I need you to stay here. I don't want to be alone tonight."

"Costanza. Cara. What can I do here? You need some sleep. I need some sleep."

"Fine, we'll sleep together."

"What?"

"No that came out wrong. I'm tired and my English starts to suffer when I'm tired. I meant we can both sleep here. But I'm too worried to sleep. I need you here. I won't be able to cope alone tonight."

"Okay. But I'm older than you and I need my sleep. So don't take it personally if I nod off."

"Thank you Peter. Come to the sofa, we'll see if there's anything on the TV worth watching." She stood up.

"If I know Italian TV, at this time of night it'll be soft porn or astrologers." I laughed.

"Which do you want?"

"Not the astrologers."

Costanza looked at me askance as we walked towards the sofa.

"Nor the soft porn."

She picked up the remote and switched the TV on. As the screen flickered into life there was an advert for religious statues and paintings of the most popular patron saints.

"That reminds me. When I spoke to Sandro he said something very strange. He said I should pray to his patron Saint Prassede and her sister, that between them they would find him."

"So?"

"St Prassede isn't one of his patron saints. It only just struck me that he was talking rubbish."

"Why would he say that unless he was trying to tell you something. What exactly did he say?"

" I told you, 'pray to my patron Saint Prassede and her sister, that between them they will find me.' It means nothing."

"Sandro isn't stupid, he wouldn't say something like that for no reason."

"He'd been held captive for a few hours, maybe even hurt. Perhaps he wasn't thinking straight."

"I don't buy that. Come on, think. What can it mean?"

"I don't know."

"Who was Saint Prassede? I've never heard of her."

"She saved the remains of martyrs from the Romans. Her house is now a church near Santa Maria Maggiore. Interesting mosaics on the ceilings. I went there with Sandro a while ago."

"Okay. Who's her sister?"

"I have no idea."

"Do you have a book of saints?"

"Over there on the bottom shelf."

I walked over to the bookshelves and bent down to retrieve the book of saints. I flicked through until I found Santa Prassede. Her sister was Santa Pudenziana. I bent back down and picked up the telephone directory for central Rome, S-Z. I quickly found it.

"Here we go, the church of Santa Pudenziana, Via Urbana."

I carried the phone book to the table and turned to the map section.

"Do you have a pencil?" I asked Costanza.

She opened a drawer and produced a slim grey pencil which she handed to me. I marked a small cross at the location of the Church of Santa Pudenziana.

"Near Santa Maria Maggiore."

I found Santa Prassede and marked its location with a cross too. Laying the pencil down as a line connecting the two marks I looked expectantly at Costanza.

"Well? Does this area mean anything to you?"

"I've been there of course. Wait. Sandro knows that area well, he often shoots near there. There are some steps, a wide set of stone steps that he likes to use."

She looked closely at the map and then stabbed at it with her finger, right next to the pencil that was lying there.

"Here. Via di Quattro Cantoni."

"So do you think he was telling us that he's being held somewhere around there?"

"He must be. Come on let's go."

"Where?"

"There." She pointed at the map.

"And do what exactly? It's late. It's dark. If we turn up outside they'll see us, hear us, long before we find them. It may force their hand. We can't do anything now."

"But I'm not going to sit around doing nothing. Not if we know where he is."

"Look there's no point in us going blundering in. We need professionals to do this. Experts."

I thought for a few seconds.

"Did you leave the message for Bianchi?" I asked.

"No not yet."

"Do you have a number where you can get hold of him in emergencies?"

"I have his housekeeper's number. But she won't be happy."

"Call her, get him on the phone and arrange for us to see him as soon as possible."

While Costanza tried to get through to the Cardinal, I made some calls of my own.

FRIDAY

Vatican

We walked into the Cardinal's office from a corridor dimly lit by night lights. The office was bright by contrast, but still subdued by normal standards. The gentle uplights lit the beautiful frescoes on the ceilings, with Raphaelesque angels gazing down at us with hands outstretched offering their supernatural help. Cardinal Bianchi was already sitting behind the desk. He stood up.

"Costanza, cara. And Signor White, it is good to meet you at last. I have heard a lot about you."

"Oh dear. I'm sure none of it was true, your Eminence. And only venial, nothing mortal."

He laughed and held out his hand to shake mine.

"Yes, as I heard, always ready with a joke. I hope you haven't dragged me from a warm bed in the middle of the night for a joke."

"Of course not your Eminence. This is deadly serious." Costanza replied.

"Yes I'm sure it is. I trust you implicitly Costanza, and I know you trust Signor White. Otherwise I wouldn't be here."

"Please call me Peter, your Eminence."

"Of course, and you must stop calling me Eminence. My name is Angelo. I have been telling Costanza this for years, but she still insists on formality. Perhaps you could help persuade her by example."

"I don't know your Eminence, she's never done anything I've suggested." I grinned as Costanza dug me in the ribs with her elbow.

"In that case, at least call me Father. I'm still a priest, even when I wear the scarlet."

"Okay Father, of course." I said, nodding, and looked at Costanza who nodded.

"Oh alright then, Father," she smiled.

"Good. Now sit down both of you and tell me what is

so urgent."

We pulled the two chairs up in front of his desk and sat down, as he made a steeple with his fingers and watched us intently. I looked at Costanza and inclined my head slightly.

"Oh, okay. I'll start. Err ..." she was temporarily and uncharacteristically lost for words.

"Sandro has been kidnapped." I blurted out in an attempt to fill the silence.

"What!" said the Cardinal sitting up with his eyebrows raised and involuntarily disentangling his fingers.

"Yes," said Costanza, "I don't know who they are, but some men have taken Sandro and want me to get them into the Secret Archives."

"Why you?"

"I don't know. They seemed to know I am connected to the Library, even though Sandro and I both followed the cover story. But it's what they want that is most disturbing."

"What?"

"The Codex Albustensis."

The Cardinal laughed before he had a chance to control himself and looked at Costanza.

"Sorry, I know this is no laughing matter. But really. That's what they're after?"

"That's what they asked for."

"So this is nothing to do with our discussion yesterday?"

"I don't know. Peter thinks they could be related."

"Really? How?"

"The NAC could be funding both activities, if either succeeds they are closer to achieving their goal."

"Which is?"

"Nothing short of world domination. They need to remove any form of organised opposition, and the most dangerous form of opposition from their perspective would be morally inspired rather than political or nationalistic. The Church is a threat."

"I think you might be right about that, but could they really be behind this foolish attempt to steal a non-existent book?"

"We have no clues about who may have kidnapped Sandro, although we may have an idea where he is being held. I spoke to him briefly and he made some comments that seemed odd at the time, but later Peter and I realised that he was trying to guide us to his location."

"Where?"

"Near Santa Maria Maggiore."

"Well done. And I may be able to give you some help in identifying these people."

"Really! How?"

"We have surveillance photos of the people who were following you, Peter. They were intercepted when they tried to abduct you. It's a reasonable assumption that it is also them who have abducted Sandro."

"Me? No-one has tried to abduct me."

"I'm afraid they have, but your guardian angels managed to divert them before you were even aware of it."

"Guardian angels? What are you talking about?"

"Since you arrived here in Rome there have been a team of my best people assigned to keep watch over you. I call them my guardian angels. See, I can make jokes too." His eyes twinkled as he spoke. He was obviously proud of his guardian angels.

"But I had no idea."

"Actually you did. On Sunday you told the Guards that you thought you were being followed. I'm afraid that the first team were not up to scratch, so they were replaced by my two best men. You have been under their watchful protection ever since."

I looked at Costanza and raised my eyebrows.

"Did you know about this?"

"No," she said, shaking her head, "I've never even heard of these guardian angels."

"But," the Cardinal interrupted, "nonetheless, you too have been protected by them over the last few days. In fact your angel has been my best. She always prefers to work alone. However, I'm sorry to say that I never considered that Sandro might be a target."

"When did they try to kidnap me?" I asked.

"Wednesday afternoon. You left the Vatican and walked to Piazza del Risorgimento. Just as you arrived there they tried to isolate you from the crowd."

"I wasn't even aware of it."

"Of course not. My people moved in, turned the tables and isolated them instead. They were forced to get on a tram going back over the river. You carried on oblivious."

"I certainly did."

"Did you say you have photos of them?" Costanza asked.

"Yes. One of our team took surveillance pictures before and during the incident. I'll get them retrieved and the Guard will ensure that the Vigilanza and Rome police are briefed straight away."

"They said that I shouldn't involve the police if I want to see Sandro again."

"Of course, kidnappers always say that. But we have an idea where they are, thanks to Sandro, so we can get a suitably covert operation mounted to find them and move in before they are expecting it. When are they getting in touch with you again?"

"They said I had twenty four hours, that was about nine o'clock this evening."

"That gives us all day to look for them. I'll get it organised now."

"Thank you, your Em…" Costanza started to say, but when she saw the Cardinal's stern look she said "Father. What shall we do now?"

"Wait here while we get the pictures, just in case you recognise them. They may have been hanging around before. Then I suggest you go home and get some sleep. Leave this to the professionals. You've got a different puzzle to crack."

"Okay" I said and looked at Costanza, who nodded.

Rome

After his brief conversation with Costanza, Sandro had been pushed onto the floor. He had been unable to hear what else was being said to his wife, but at one point he was, apparently gratuitously, kicked in the side. He could still feel the pain from the blow, and wasn't very proud of the yelp he had let out involuntarily. He just hoped that Costanza hadn't heard, although he suspected it had been entirely for her benefit. After a while he had been picked up and put back on the sofa where, despite the pain, the worry about Costanza and the fear of what might happen, he had fallen asleep.

This morning he awoke to find one of the men guarding him, sitting in a chair at the table reading a magazine. The others were nowhere to be seen, even allowing for the limitations of the pinhole in his blindfold. He assumed they must be in beds upstairs. He kept as still and quiet as he could to take the opportunity to look around the room. He couldn't see anything that would be helpful in any escape bid, so he very ostentatiously yawned and stretched his arms and then tried to sit up. Within seconds his guard was standing in front of him.

"I wouldn't try going anywhere if I was you."

The voice sounded like the Elvis fan. Peering slyly through his pinhole he was now able to associate a face with that voice.

"I need the toilet." Once again he tried to sound desperate.

"Okay, hang on, I'll help you up."

He felt two strong hands on his arms and was lifted almost bodily off the sofa. His head was spinning when he was put down again and led forwards to the bathroom door.

"Remember no funny stuff."

"I remember."

279

He was propelled through the doorway and heard the clunk of the door closing behind him. Taking off the blindfold he bent down and splashed cold water from the basin onto his face. Once again he looked around the bathroom for anything that could help effect his escape. Once again he was frustrated to find nothing. He dried his face, put the blindfold back on, adjusting it so he could once more see through the pinhole. When he was ready he opened the door and walked through straight into the Elvis fan.

"Hey look where you're going."

"How can I? I'm wearing a blindfold."

"Oh yeah. Okay. Well. Anyway. Go and sit down and shut up."

"I need help to find the sofa again."

"What? Oh, straight ahead about three steps and then stop."

"Need more toilet paper in there," Sandro said as he carefully took three steps with his eyes closed and felt in front of him for the sofa.

"Damn. We'll send Benny out to get some, soon as he wakes up."

Cheltenham

Tony's phone rang. He'd been away from his desk for a few minutes so he deftly wiped both the earpiece and mouthpiece clean as he picked up the handset.

"Hello, Tony Hey, Crypto."

"Tony, it's Katie Cannon."

Tony's heart sank, he'd heard nothing from her all week so she had probably been busy trying to get him fired, or at least demoted. Still, he had his dignity, he would remain civil.

"Hello Ms Cannon,' he said as coldly as possible.

"Look, Tony. I want to apologise for Monday."

"What?" he nearly dropped the phone in shock.

"I was fed up, it had been a long weekend and then you were being all secret squirrel…"

"I don't think I…"

"Let me finish. You were being all secret squirrel and that's MY job," she gave a nervous laugh, "so I was rude and took it out on you. And you were right, I should have picked up the deadbet reference and I should have been up to date on reading the reports you guys send up here. So, all in all, I wanted to say sorry."

"Oh. Okay, apology accepted."

"I spoke to our esteemed colleagues at Langley. They knew about deadbet."

"Of course."

"They said they are monitoring the website. There have been a few recent successful bets, but there's no way of telling if they've all been by the same person. They said they hoped to have a lead to follow soon, but they didn't say what and they didn't mention the tracking software you told me they'd embedded in electronic money."

"You didn't let on that we hacked it, did you?"

"Well…"

Tony groaned.

"No! Of course not. They may be colleagues in some sense but they are also foreigners."

"and the competition" muttered Tony.

"Precisely. Actually, while we're on that subject maybe you can explain something to me."

"Okay."

"How did you hack the money software. I've been checking things out on the deadbet website and elsewhere on the internet and that electronic money system claims to be perfectly secure."

Tony laughed.

"Nothing's perfectly secure. Least of all their system. When they released their early versions, based on some PhD work at a minor US college, they were very slapdash. We think the NSA hacked into their development system and put in a backdoor for the CIA, or they may have had someone actually working in the development team. Anyway, after a while, they started to take security more seriously and the public versions became much better protected, with digital signatures and SHA-1 checksums, so when…"

"SHA-1 checksums?"

"Sorry. When you create a file, whether it's transaction data, email, or a piece of software, you can digitally sign it by calculating a checksum and encrypting it. The checksum is effectively a number that is supposed to be unique and is calculated from the contents of the file. It's a bit like adding up the values of all the bytes of data in the file, but more complex and involving some fancy maths. If the contents changes, even by just one bit of data, then the calculated checksum would be different. So when you receive the file you can re-calculate the checksum from the contents that you've received and check it against the one that was encrypted into the signature. If it's the same then the file has been untouched and you can trust it, if it's different then the file has been tampered with so you don't trust it. That's how you can download software across an insecure network like the internet and still be sure that you're not installing virus-ridden code. It's also the way that credit card transactions are protected."

"Okay, I think I understand."

"Right. So when we got interested in the electronic money software we found that the CIA hack was already in it, inside the file that had been checksummed."

"They changed the checksum?"

"No. They changed the file before it was signed. That's how we know they either hacked the development system or had inside help. It was too late for us to do the same, we had to change the version that was on the public servers for people to download. So we changed the program, put in our hack bypassing the CIA's, then put it back on the servers."

"But I thought you said that the checksum would be different if the file was altered."

"Yeah. Well everyone uses a standard algorithm to calculate checksums."

"Huh?"

"It's like a recipe for a piece of software. It defines what you have to do. Then you can write your own program but as long as you follow the standard recipe, the algorithm, you know the result will conform and hence it will work with everyone else's programs that implement the same algorithm. The checksum uses an algorithm called SHA-1. A few months ago we discovered a flaw in SHA-1."

"A bug?"

"Not really. A bug is when a program does something wrong. What we found was that there was a way in which you could fool the algorithm into coming up with the same checksum for two different files, which can theoretically happen but is supposed to be very rare, like once in the lifetime of the universe. We could make it happen to order. But crucially we could do it for two versions of the same file that only had minor differences. So we could alter the money program and then tweak it so that the checksum came out the same as the original."

"So you can change anything that's been signed. Does that mean my credit card transactions are no longer safe?"

"Not quite. Transactions and emails are very short. The technique we developed only works for very large amounts of data where you can hide a few additional bits without anyone noticing."

"Does anyone else know about this?"

"We thought it might come in handy so we haven't told other agencies. But I'm sure someone else will find the same flaw too and then make it public. When that happens everyone will start using a different algorithm and we'll be back to square one. The NSA may already have worked it out, but they'd keep quiet too. They always do."

"This has happened before?"

"Of course. Neither we nor the NSA tell anyone about the weaknesses we find in widely used security algorithms. Eventually someone in academia finds it independently and there's a flurry of activity to replace the algorithm. Then it all starts again. We spend a lot of our time here looking for flaws in the signing and encryption algorithms used in commercial products."

"I never realised."

"Yeah. The only difference is that we're doing it for national security, while the NSA have a wider remit to protect the US national interest which seems to include industrial espionage and sabotage. See, we do other things than surf the web looking at dodgy websites."

"Talking of which, let's get back to deadbet."

"Oh yeah."

"If I understood you correctly on Monday, when your stake gets cashed, you'll get some data to track down where it is?"

"That's right. And if the Americans have put some bets in, we should get the data from theirs too."

"One thing puzzles me though," said Katie.

"What?"

"The CIA said that no-one won the stakes on Rabbi Cohen. There were no bets sufficiently close to be deemed accurate enough to win, so all the stakes have gone into the website organiser's funds."

"So?"

"So, either our killer cocked-up, or..."

"...he didn't kill Rabbi Cohen."

"Exactly. Why do you say he?" Katie asked. "It could just as easily be a woman."

"Statistically more probable that it's a man. Why? Do you suspect a woman?"

"No. It's just that the only anomaly at Leeds Castle was one of the catering staff. She went missing after lunch. So we spent a couple of days looking for a tall blonde woman."

"I thought you told that nice Italian lady that nothing unusual happened?"

"I did. She's the competition too, you know. Can't tell any of them too much. Anyway, catering staff skiving off for the afternoon to avoid the washing up is hardly unusual."

"Is that what she did?"

"Yes. Sort of. She was having a surreptitious snog with her boyfriend in the Castle grounds when she got spooked by a Police helicopter that buzzed them. She decided to go home rather than back in to do her stint at the washing up. She left by a little-used service road that wasn't being properly monitored. When she turned up for work on Monday they docked her pay, but that was all. No-one thought it important to tell us what had happened, so we spent a day trying to find her when she was in the Castle kitchen all along. Eventually we found her there, asked her a few questions. No harm done."

"So she's not even a suspect?"

"No. But I would have assumed the killer is a man too, until I'd spent some time looking for this woman and realised that there's no reason to make that assumption."

"Not every tall blonde is a homicidal maniac."

"And not every killer is a maniac."

"True," said Tony, "so what now?"

"We can't do anything else until you get some data back from one of the bets. Then we decide whether we have the jurisdiction to follow it up or pass it over to the competition."

"Okay. I'll let you know when I get any data."

"Incidentally, who did you bet on?"

"I thought I'd hedge my bets, literally, and go for two victims – one destined for heaven and one for the other place. So I bet on both John Paul and George Bush."

"John Paul and George. What about Ringo?"

"What?"

"Never mind. Hang on, one to heaven, one to hell? Which is which?"

"Ah that depends on your point of view I guess. We'll never know."

"Hmm. Let me know when you hear something."

"Will do."

"Bye Tony."

"Bye Ms Cannon."

"Call me Katie."

"Oh. Okay. Bye Katie."

Vatican

Late in the morning, Helen walked into Cardinal Thomas' office. He looked up to see the tall blonde standing there, more composed than when he had last seen her. He half rose from his chair.

"I thought you were going back to the States?" he said.

"Yeah, this evening," she said, "but I wanted to come back and say thank you first".

"My dear, I did nothing."

"You listened."

"Anyone would."

"No-one else has." She closed the door behind her and slid into the chair opposite him.

"I wanted to give you something," she began again.

"There's really no need." He sat down.

"Oh I insist. But I didn't know what you like. Alcohol, chocolates. All a matter of taste and the risk of having to share with others." She smiled.

"As I said, there's no need."

"Do you like chocolate?" she asked.

"Yes."

"European chocolate? Or Hershey bars?"

"I like Italian chocolate, especially Perugina. But you're right, nothing beats a Hershey bar."

"I knew I could rely on good old American chocolate." She smiled again with an almost discernible twinkle in her eye.

Reaching into her bag she produced a bar and handed it to the cardinal with a flourish.

"First in favour and flavour" he grinned.

"It's so difficult to get here I'm sure you haven't had any for a while. But don't waste it by giving any to your staff. They can't appreciate it like Americans do. Sin a little!"

"Thank you, you really shouldn't have. But where did

you get it?"

"I have friends at the embassy. They get food parcels flown over in the diplomatic bag with the essentials of civilised life that you can't get here. Like proper chocolate and jell-o."

"Jell-o?"

"Yeah."

"I remember my mother making jell-o for tea. Strawberry."

"If I'd known I would have brought some along. I'll tell my friend at the embassy to send it over."

"Thank you. Here you must have some of this chocolate." He started to open the wrapper.

"No!" she said, more sharply than she'd intended "I'd love to, but I have so few clothes with me, I can't afford for them to stop fitting and chocolate goes straight to my hips." She stood up.

"You enjoy it for me," she smiled, "Goodbye." She turned and walked to the door.

"God speed," he said, watching her leave.

He looked down at the unwrapped bar of chocolate in his hands.

"Should I?" he asked himself. "Fat, sugar, God knows what chemicals. All the things the doctors warn me are bad for my health. Still what harm can one little bar do?"

"Thank you Lord for this thy gift which I will gratefully receive." So saying, he broke off a piece of the chocolate and smiled beatifically as it melted in his mouth. He put the rest down on his desk. "I'll make it last" he thought.

Anna walked down the grand staircase, past the Swiss Guard and into the colonnade. Turning right she continued across the piazza, past the nice clean-cut young men performing the security and clothing decency checks and up onto the atrium in front of the Holy Door of St Peter's. She stopped, looked around at the crowds and smiled to herself. Then walking to the main door she entered the church. She dipped her fingers in the enormous marble stoup and, crossing herself, walked slowly towards the grotto in front of the tomb of St. Peter. Even unbelievers were impressed by this huge church. For many Catholics it was a spiritual home, the core of their religion, almost more relevant than the Holy Land; far more pilgrims came to St. Peter's than ever ventured to Jerusalem.

Anna stopped at the railings and looked down to the small grille at the back of the grotto.

"Forgive me," she whispered.

After a moment she walked around the edge of the grotto, avoiding the many pilgrims who were standing or kneeling there in silent prayer oblivious to all the tourists around them busily taking photographs or gazing up at the dome. She walked to the pews set out in front of the high altar and sat on the end of the back row.

"Easy," she thought, "so easy."

"Too easy?" she frowned but then shrugged lightly and turned her attention to the alabaster window image of the Holy Spirit as a dove, which dominated the wall in front of her.

Finding out that the Cardinal had a sweet tooth and a, largely unfulfilled, predilection for Hershey bars had been child's play. When Anna had phoned his office yesterday, his ever so efficient secretary had been only too eager to suggest what might make a suitable gift from a grateful penitent. Her friends at the embassy had been equally helpful and had raided their own tuck box when she said she had a craving for some proper American chocolate. This time the damn Cardinal wouldn't give it away to someone else. Even if he shared some he should still eat enough to reach critical mass and have the desired heart attack.

The pews in front of her were filling up, as the midday Mass was due to start. She remained in her seat.

Rome

By eight o'clock in the morning, the Vigilanza and Rome police had co-ordinated with SISDe who had established a team of undercover agents at various points in the precincts of Santa Maria Maggiore and around the surrounding streets. As cafés and bars opened they each had a visitor, ensconced at the table with the best all-round view, nursing a drink and a newspaper. In the nearby supermarket, a young man sat chatting to the cashier. At the gelateria another man was propping up the counter all morning making small talk with the young girl who was working there today. As the morning wore on, the two pizzerie started to unfurl their awnings and tablecloths appeared, transforming the dull veneer tables into a crisp clean environment for the enjoyment of food. Cutlery, glasses and breadsticks soon sprouted on the tables. No sooner were they ready to encourage the passing tourists to sit down to eat, than one of the agents was sitting at an end table in each pizzeria, sipping a glass of water and eyeing the menu cautiously while maintaining a hawk-like lookout. Lunch time came and went along with the tourists.

Just before the supermarket was due to close for the siesta, a short man walked in. As he picked up a basket and made his way towards the hygiene section, the agent talking to the cashier took a handheld radio out of his pocket and started speaking quietly into it. Putting his radio away, he walked around to the other side of the checkout, picked up a pack of gum and waited to pay for it. Soon the short man reappeared with a packet of toilet tissue and some chocolate biscuits in his basket and stood behind the young man, awaiting his turn.

"Hello," the young man said, glancing at the new arrival.

"Hello," grunted the short man.

"English?" he asked.

"American."

"Ah. Not in a hotel?" he nodded down at the contents of the basket.

"Apartment."

"You like Rome, yes?"

"S'alright. But I wish I was at home."

"Yes, so do we." He smiled enigmatically at the short man, picked up his change and gum, stuffed them in his pocket and sauntered over to the exit.

"Bye."

As he left the supermarket he caught sight of two of his colleagues walking as a couple down the street towards him. He ambled towards them, stopped, nodded and leant against the railings in front of the building opposite the supermarket. He slowly took the gum from his pocket, opened the packet and placed a lozenge in his mouth. Meanwhile he was carefully watching the supermarket exit to see which way the small American would leave. When the door opened, the man came out and, turning to his right, walked along the road just ahead of the strolling couple. He reached the steps a few seconds before them, slowly walked down and crossed over to the large metal door in the building on the left. He was knocking on the door as the couple reached the bottom of the steps. They continued past, apparently oblivious, as he disappeared inside. Once around the corner and out of sight they unlocked arms and took out their radios. Confirming the location of the door through which they had seen the man go, they waited for clarification of the next move. Standing there, they saw one of the other men from the Swiss Guard's surveillance photos crossing the street towards them in front of the gelateria. They couldn't tell if he had noticed them talking on the radio, but realised that they couldn't let him return to the building if there was even a slight chance that he now knew that it was being watched. Surreptitiously sending hand signals to the agent in the gelateria, they decided to take immediate action. Walking together to cross the street directly opposite their new target, they separated as if to walk either side of him and as they passed deftly grabbed his arms, sending his two pizzas flying, and frogmarched him backwards across the road. Coming up behind him, a third agent jabbed the barrel of a pistol in his back putting a hand around his head and covering his mouth. Within seconds, after being searched and relieved of his cell phone, he had been bundled away into the back of a police Fiat that was parked out of sight down the hill behind the shops.

"You can't treat me like this, I'm an American," he protested once he was able to speak again.

"This is how we treat yankee scum like you. You better answer our questions or you'll soon be an ex-american."

His interrogators were two carabinieri sitting in the front of the car, separated from him by a bullet proof screen. There were no handles on the inside of the doors and nothing suitable for him to use as a weapon or a tool to attempt to open the doors or windows. He banged the glass partition with his fist and then started to try and smash the glass in the door.

"Bullet proof," offered the swarthy man in the driving seat, sitting proudly resplendent in his neatly pressed blue uniform.

"How many people are in the apartment, yankee?" asked the other Carabinieri while smoothing his hair in the vanity mirror.

"I don't have to answer your questions. I want to see the US Consul. I want a lawyer."

"The US Consulate is closed for lunch and they never

reopen on a Friday afternoon. They all go away for the weekend. Anyway I think they've already disowned you. No lawyer is going to come out at this time of day and miss his siesta. We need answers now. So you better start talking."

"And what if I don't?"

"The compartment where you're sitting is not only bullet proof, it's air-tight. No leaks. Nothing can get out, nothing can get in. That's why we're talking to you through an intercom. We control the locks on the door from in here. We also control the air conditioning. It gets very hot when we switch the air conditioning off. Specially at this time of day. Luckily for us, we can keep it set to ideal conditions here in the front, even if the air supply to your compartment is completely switched off."

"You can't do this. I know my rights."

"You don't have any rights, yankee. You gave up all rights when you chose to become a terrorist."

"What?"

"We know all about your plot to break in to the Vatican and destroy the Church. Kill the Pope and replace him with a yankee. What were you going to use? An anti-matter bomb in Peter's tomb? Haha! Typical yankee. You think we're all stupid here in Italy?"

"I'm no terrorist."

"You deny you want to destroy the one true Church?"

"It's no church, it's Satan's brothel. The antichrist and the scarlet whore of Babylon together."

"So, you admit it then. Now tell us how many are in the apartment."

"I'm telling you nothing."

"Okay. Do you hear that hissing noise?"

"Yes."

"That's the air supply to your compartment."

The officer in the driver's seat reached forward to the

dashboard and flicked a small switch.

"Still hear it?"

"No."

"Good. Make yourself comfortable. We are."

"You can't do this to me."

"We can do whatever we need. Giudice Petrone signed a warrant at seven o'clock this morning allowing us to do anything at all to defeat your group and extract the hostage. He removed all of your rights using the anti-terrorism law. He confirmed, with the ministry of the interior, that, as terrorists, you have no rights to any special treatment as foreigners. And, of course, the ministry of the interior confirmed with the American Ambassador that you would be treated under Italian terrorism laws. America has washed its hands of you. You're stateless. You don't exist. We can do what we want and nobody cares. Enjoy our beautiful Roman sunshine."

There was a click as the intercom switch flicked off and a small red light in the corner of the passenger compartment was extinguished.

"But this is inhumane. You can't do this. I thought the Vatican valued life?"

There was no answer. He could see the two officers sitting the other side of the glass barrier, looking cool and unperturbed. He was already beginning to feel hot and short of breath. It was just psychological, he couldn't actually be succumbing to the heat after only a few seconds. He banged on the glass partition again. The red light came on.

"Are you ready to talk now?"

"You can't do this. I thought the Vatican valued life?"

"You're not in the Vatican, yankee. This is Roma. We do value life, but not that of terrorist scum like you. Now, how many in the apartment?"

"Go to hell."

"You'll get there first."

The red light went out again. Within two minutes the air was feeling thicker and he was finding it even more difficult to breath.

"They can't just sit there and watch me die," he thought.

The red light came on.

"Anything to say?"

"No."

"Okay. We're going for our lunch now. We'll be back in two hours, see you then. Well, we'll see you, but you won't see us of course. Ten minutes at the most is what I give you in this heat. Goodbye."

A click and the light went out. The two officers opened their doors and slowly got out of the car. They removed their hats from the purpose-built hooks behind the seats and carefully straightened them on their heads, checking each other and acknowledging that they looked just right. One door and then the other were slammed shut. The shorter of the two men walked around the front of the car to join his colleague. They both turned and waved goodbye. As they were about to turn back and walk away they noticed their prisoner frantically nodding and banging on the window. The driver opened the door, reached in and flicked the intercom switch.

"A last request?"

"Okay I'll tell you what you want, just let me breathe." By now his voice was strained and his breathing was short and fast. He was obviously hyperventilating.

"How many in the apartment?"

"There are three of us."

"Including the hostage?"

"No."

"So there are now two left inside with the hostage?"

"Yes."

"Are you sure?"

"Yes."

"Where is the hostage?"

"Inside."

"Upstairs, downstairs? Front, back?"

"Downstairs, back." His breathing was getting more rasping.

"Please give me air," he gasped.

There was a click and suddenly a hissing noise filled his ears. Almost immediately he could feel cool fresh air being pumped into his small prison. He fell back onto the seat, lay on his back as much as he could and breathed deeply. His head was swimming and when he closed his eyes he seemed to see a firework display.

"What condition is the hostage in?"

"Better than me. We aren't this inhuman."

"Is anyone armed?"

"No."

"Sure?"

"Yes."

There was another click and the red light went out. He felt the car shake as the door was slammed shut, but he didn't even bother to open his eyes, he was too desperate to make sure he was breathing as deeply as he could.

"I'll radio in," said the shorter officer as he pulled the microphone from his epaulette.

Minutes later, once everyone was up to date with the situation inside the apartment, SISDe agents and Carabinieri officers took positions on the wall either side of the metal door. They sidled nearer. When they were close enough to reach, one of the agents knocked on the door in the same way that he had heard the short man knock when returning from the supermarket. After a few seconds there came the scraping sound of locks being undone and the door opened slightly.

"Martie?" a voice asked from inside.

"No!" yelled a Carabinieri as he kicked the door wide open while others jumped into position behind him with their weapons trained through the opening. He lobbed a tear gas grenade through the doorway and dropped to the floor.

A small explosion was followed by billowing clouds and, within seconds, by two men staggering through the doorway into the street and the clutches of the waiting police.

The Carabinieri officer on the floor reached behind him for a gasmask, pulled it over his face and got to his feet. He slowly walked into the cloud-filled apartment. Making his way carefully between the kitchen and table, avoiding tripping over the step, he found the sofas at the back of the room under the stairs. Lying prone on one was Sandro's body, blindfold still in place. His hands had been tied behind his back and his feet were bound together. Pulling the blindfold off, the officer could see that Sandro's eyes were streaming. He picked him up and carried him out of the room as fast as possible. Outside on the pavement, Sandro's feet were unbound and the ropes around his hands were cut. His eyes were bright red and he was coughing. The other two men were dragged off to another police car and driven away at speed into the depths of the Italian justice system.

Vatican

Despite his best intentions, Cardinal Thomas had not resisted the allure of his favourite chocolate for very long. Only a few minutes after the first piece, he had succumbed to two more in quick succession. Within half an hour most of the bar had gone. He had never been very good at abstinence, and chocolate had often been his downfall, especially during Lent.

"Oh well," he thought "gluttony might be a sin, but one bar of chocolate is hardly going to be deadly."

Two hours later, as he was finishing his morning's paperwork ready to go for lunch, he suddenly felt a crushing pain in his chest. Unable to breathe, it was as if the very life was being squeezed out of him. His left hand started to tingle and the arm fell uselessly onto the desk. So short of breath he was unable to call for help, he was too weak to reach the phone. He lurched forward across his desk, lashing out in a terminal paroxysm with his right hand and sending files and a glass of water crashing to the floor. In his dying moments he realised that his face had smashed into the remains of the Hershey bar, smearing melted chocolate across his cheek. The last thing he saw as his eyes closed for the final time was the torn edge of the chocolate wrapper.

The crash of the glass had echoed through the door and along the corridor. His secretary was already at lunch, but a monsignor in a nearby office had heard the noise. After trying two other offices looking for the source, he had walked into the Cardinal's room and stopped in shock. Regaining his composure he ran forward and lifted the Cardinal's wrist to feel for a pulse. There was none. He picked up the phone handset and dialled the medical centre.

I was with Costanza in Cardinal Bianchi's delightful office

when we heard about Cardinal Thomas. We were both shocked, Costanza perhaps more so than me. It seemed that he too had been killed in the same way as the others, yet another healthy middle-aged man having an unexpected heart attack. It could not have been a coincidence. So much for our belief that the motivation behind these killings was to ensure that he would be the next Pope. But before we could even consider the full implications, we received much happier news. Sandro had been found and rescued from his captors, who had all been arrested by the Italian police. Costanza was intrigued to find that the Italian Secret Service, SISDe, had co-operated with the Vigilanza, the Carabinieri and the Rome Police.

"Well done, your Eminence…"

"Father."

"Well done, Father. You managed to get them all to work together."

"No my dear, I don't believe that I can be thanked for that. I asked the Guard and the Vigilanza to persuade the Rome Police to help. But apparently when they contacted them there was already a plan in place, a Judge had already signed warrants and approved the handling of the case as counter-terrorism and SISDe had already been involved. I understand that the Italian Minister of the Interior was informed and he warned the Americans that some of their nationals were to be picked up and held on charges of conspiracy to perform terrorist acts."

"But how did they already know if you didn't organise it. We were the only three who knew what was happening."

"I'm afraid that I am to blame." I said.

"Blame? Hardly. But how?" Costanza asked.

"While you were busy disturbing his Eminence's housekeeper, I was disturbing a cousin of mine. A distant cousin, it must be said, but one who I have actually met a few times. He's a Judge here in Rome. After apologising for calling him so late I briefly explained what was happening. I may have laid it on a bit thick in places, but he understood the gravity of the situation. His fiancée was one of those killed by the US air force plane in Trento in 1998. He has always resented the fact that the pilot wasn't prosecuted, so he is no fan of Americans and it didn't take very much to persuade him that there's a US backed plot to rig the next Conclave, or worse. I told him they were trying to get into the Vatican to destroy the Church, I suspect his imagination filled in a few extra details – helped no doubt by fabulist fiction about hi-tech bombs and secret societies bent on destroying the throne of St Peter. He said he would arrange warrants and talk to the Minister of the Interior who is a personal friend."

"That's incredible." Costanza leant forward and kissed me on the cheek. "Thank you."

"Truly remarkable my son. I'm so glad you came to Rome!" the Cardinal added.

"There is one thing I haven't told you though."

"What?" they both said in unison.

"I might have intimated that there would be a personal audience in it for him."

"A Papal audience?" asked Costanza, laughing.

"Yes. Is that a possibility?"

"I'm sure we can arrange it," said the Cardinal, "but first you should go and meet Sandro. He's being brought here in an ambulance. They're taking him to Martha's Hospice. Go and see him and we can decide what to do next, tomorrow."

"You're taking the death of another Cardinal very calmly." I said.

"There's nothing I can do about it now. Your theory seems to have been proved wrong, at least in terms of motivation if not execution. We need to consider the facts and look for more evidence. We can start again tomorrow. For now be thankful for today's victories."

Just then his phone rang. As he answered it he waved us away.

"Si? CIA? Okay. Una donna bionda. Grazie," he was saying as we walked out of his office.

The quickest route to Martha's Hospice was out into the Piazza and across in front of the Basilica. Costanza and I were walking briskly, hoping to get there in time to greet Sandro as he arrived.

Inside the Basilica, Helen was still sitting in the pew. Mass had finished almost an hour before, but she had been deep in thought. She finally stood up and slowly walked back down the length of the church, reading the markings on the floor comparing the length of the building to other great cathedrals around the world. As she passed the inscription for Cologne cathedral she moved over beside one of the immense columns supporting the ceiling. A small confessional was open with a sign hanging outside saying 'Deutsch'. She entered, pulled the curtain shut behind her and knelt down.

"Ja?" said a soft voice from behind the grille.

Helen said nothing.

"Beginnen Sie," said the voice.

"I'm sorry, wrong language." Helen said.

As she stood up she pulled her wig off and dropped it on the floor of the confessional, kicking it into the corner underneath the kneeler. She opened the curtain.

Anna stepped out of the confessional, ran her fingers through her hair and shook her head lightly. She walked away towards the main door, past the vast holy water stoups and out, through the portico and into the blazing sunshine in the Piazza. She walked down the steps and crossed in front of the two Swiss Guards protecting the archway. As she did so she stumbled on a cobblestone and bumped into a couple who were walking towards the Guards.

"Excuse me," she said.

As Costanza and I reached the Arch of the Bells a young American woman stumbled into us.

"Excuse me," she said.

"No harm done." I replied.

"I tripped on these darn cobbles."

"Are you alright? If you've twisted your ankle there's a first aid station just over here." Costanza looked concerned.

"I can help you get there if you want." I added.

"No I think I'm fine. Thank you. I have to go catch a plane now. Goodbye."

"Goodbye."

We went towards the archway and were saluted through by the Guards.

"Another damson in distress," Costanza whispered to me.

"I've been meaning to tell you." I said, "It's damsel. A damson is a kind of fruit."

"I knew that." She laughed, it was good to see her laughing again.

Epilogue

No more senior figures in the Church died of unexpected heart attacks. No-one else on the deadbet.net list died. Three months later the website was closed down after pressure on the ISP from various law enforcement agencies. No-one, as far as I know, has been identified as organising the site or winning any of the bets. The electronic money system has been withdrawn after the developers found that their code had been hacked. Somewhere, in a prison in Italy, three American terrorists are still protesting their innocence; one claims he was framed by angels. Meanwhile, the oldest Library in the world continues to safeguard our Souls.

Afterword

I have written the account of these events from my own diary. Obviously, descriptions of actions taken by others and conversations occurring when I was not present have been based on official transcripts, other participants' notes that have been made available to me†, and a degree of poetic licence to interpolate from the resulting events. This account is based on real events. Only the facts have been changed to protect the innocent. Since these events occurred, both Yasser Arafat and His Holiness Pope John Paul II have died (neither from unexpected heart attacks!) and the new Pontiff is not American.

Peter White, Kent, April 2005

---

† For which I'm very grateful. I can't thank the participants by name or their real identities would be revealed, but they know who they are. So thank you Costanza, Sandro, Peppino (RIP), Carlo, Simon, AD Hocke, Mark, John Paul, JC, Nobby, Phil the Greek, Eddie Calzone and 'Fingers' Pantalone.

Acknowledgement

I feel a great debt towards those who have supported and encouraged me during the creation of this book. I must especially thank Karin, Sue, Ninian, Ben, Alexander and Stephania for reading it and providing useful comments and feedback. They have helped to spot the inevitable errors which I have endeavoured to correct; but any that are left are entirely my own responsibility. Thanks also to Sue and Stephen Dean for permission to quote from Cardinal Figueras' favourite hymn.

The production and publication of Library of the Soul has been an interesting learning experience, and I am grateful to the various people who have helped during the process, not least the wonderful staff at Alnpete Press who now feel just like family!

I must thank those who have inspired the characters and situations in this story, albeit unknowingly and unwittingly. Some of you will recognise your influence, others may just have to wonder. Thanks especially for inside information on US intelligence agencies to John and Steven.

Last, but most certainly not least, I must thank Alison for support, encouragement, proof reading, lessons in grammar and history, a sturdy shoulder to cry on, and the endless supply of coffee, biscuits and TLC. Without you I would not only never have finished this book but I would never have picked up a pen again (okay, that's obviously a metaphor as I actually typed this straight into my iBook, but you get my point).

Simon Buck

Alnpete is an exciting, innovative new independent publisher.
Watch out for the next two Peter White mysteries from Simon Buck:

Crypto da Vinci
a Peter White mystery

A simple birthday present, an old book. The *Works of Virgil* translated by John Dryden, 1730 edition. Peter White already has a copy, yet he becomes fascinated when he notices that all the illustrations have been replaced with subtly altered versions. Examining the differences he uncovers a secret text written by Leonardo da Vinci describing a highly effective cryptographic technique. Intrigued, not only by the text itself, but by why it had been hidden in this book, Peter pursues its provenance and finds himself drawn into two different worlds through two very different manuscripts both protected by this code.

One, described in a diary penned by Leonardo himself, charts the genius' descent into despair and disillusionment as he strives to fulfil a commission from a powerful cardinal, all the while struggling with spiritual and philosophical challenges to his beliefs.

The other, a lost Jacobite manifesto from the '45 Rising, presents a confession from Queen Anne revealing a scandal that undermines the Act of Settlement and hence the very legitimacy of the British Monarchy, even today.

Coming Summer 2006 ISBN 0-9552206-2-9

Iscariot
a Peter White mystery

In 33AD Judas Iscariot betrayed Jesus for thirty pieces of silver. In 2005AD those same silver coins still exert their malign influence over the weak and treacherous.

Raffaella, one of the Vatican's secret Guardian Angels, enlists Peter White to help her investigate a cult group who are apparently looking for the coins. Do they really believe these ancient coins have supernatural power? Why are they searching the 12th century octagonal Castel del Monte? Is the sudden arrival of an American TV evangelist just a coincidence? How exactly are the local mafia involved? What is the significance of the raunchy mermaid? Raffaella and Peter must race against the clock and answer these questions in order to stop impending disaster on the rapidly approaching saint's day of St. Michael.

Coming Spring 2007 ISBN 0-9552206-4-5

Alnpete is an exciting, innovative new independent publisher.
Watch out for these forthcoming titles:

Devoted Sisters
Alison Buck

Elderly sisters Lizzie and May live quiet, ordered lives in the house in which they were born; their self-imposed seclusion and the unchanging predictability of their lives shielding them from the changing world beyond.

But the day comes when this protective isolation is broken; the world outside forces its way in. A stranger appears, unsettling them, bringing with him the threat of danger, upheaval and violence.

Fearful and alone, with all semblance of comforting routine wrenched from them, Lizzie and May are driven to desperation. Dark memories emerge from their buried past as the sisters gradually slip from reason into their own confused realities, within which even their former carefully regulated world seems only a distant memory.

Coming Spring 2006 ISBN 0-9552206-1-0

Abiding Evil
Alison Buck

A sleeping menace is roused deep in the darkness of the forest. For decades it grows, biding its time, reaching out to tug at the ordinary lives of those living beyond the shadow of the trees.

Their children begin to disappear.

Unaware and unsuspecting of the danger, a group of families, friends for many years, journey to a newly opened hotel. It stands alone in a clearing a mile or more within the forest boundary.

For some this will be their last reunion.

Coming Autumn 2006 ISBN 0-9552206-3-7

Visit the Alnpete Press website www.alnpetepress.co.uk
for the latest information on our titles, authors and events

Simon Buck has been a consultant for many years to blue chip companies including banks, retailers and telecom service providers. He has been widely published in the fields of Internet security, electronic commerce and data communications. This, his first published novel, is one of a series of Peter White mysteries. He was born and brought up in Kent by an Italian mother and English father. He still lives in a village in the Garden of England and has a wife, two teenagers and an Apple Macintosh habit to support.